"I now pronounce that they be man and wife."

Constance's gazed snapped to the earl. She hadn't even been listening to that final declaration and now she was married. Just as well she didn't attend to omens, because surely...

The worry evaporated in the warmth of the gaze Lord Spenford—*her husband*—turned on her.

A half smile on his lips, he reached for her veil, lifted it.

His brilliant blue eyes scanned her face.

Constance smiled shyly.

His mouth straightened into a line that could only be described as grim.

"My—my lord?" Constance's voice faltered as she absorbed his expression.

He looked appalled.

ABBY GAINES

wrote her first romance novel as a teenager, only to have it promptly rejected. A flirtation with a science fiction novel never really got off the ground, so Abby put aside her writing ambitions as she went to college, then began her working life at IBM. When she and her husband had their first baby, Abby worked from home as a freelance business journalist…and soon after that the urge to write romance resurfaced. It was another five long years before Abby sold her first novel to Harlequin Superromance in 2006.

Abby lives with her husband and children—and a labradoodle and a cat—in a house with enough stairs to keep her semifit and a sun-filled office with a sea view that provides inspiration for the funny, tender romances she loves to write. Visit her at www.abbygaines.com.

The Earl's Mistaken Bride

ABBY GAINES

Love Inspired

Recycling programs
for this product may
not exist in your area.

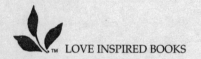 LOVE INSPIRED BOOKS

ISBN-13: 978-0-373-82897-5

THE EARL'S MISTAKEN BRIDE

www.LoveInspiredBooks.com

Printed in U.S.A.

For the Lord takes pleasure in His people; He will
beautify the humble with salvation.
—*Psalms* 149:4

For Mary Griffiths, neighbor extraordinaire.
Thank you for your enthusiasm, your treasure trove
of Regency books...and all those cups of tea!

Thanks also to Dr. Gerald Young
of Auckland for the use of his name.

Chapter One

April 1816
Piper's Mead, Hampshire, England

"I wish to marry one of your daughters."

Marcus Brookstone, Earl of Spenford, was certain his position and wealth more than compensated for the urgent, somewhat irregular nature of the request. Every father in England would be honored to hear those words from him.

"I gathered as much from the message you sent." Reverend Adrian Somerton removed his spectacles. "How *is* your dear mother?"

Marcus spread his fingers on the arms of the rosewood chair and forced himself to appear at ease. The reverend's study was a fine enough room, but smaller than Marcus was used to. Whether it was the room, or the awkward nature of his mission, he felt hemmed in. Trapped.

He turned his neck slightly within the starched collar of his shirt, seeking relief from the constriction. He couldn't bear to discuss his mother's fragile condition, even with her parson. More particularly, he couldn't bear any delay.

But the Earl of Spenford always behaved in a manner befitting his position.

"The dowager's health is somewhat worse," he informed the reverend stiffly. "I hope my marriage will be a source of strength for her."

"Indeed." Reverend Somerton's smile managed to convey both understanding and a shared grief.

A churchman's trick, Marcus supposed, but a good one. He wondered if the reverend had positioned the leather-topped oak desk precisely so the fall of April afternoon sunlight through the study window should bathe him in its glow, making him look as reverent as his title suggested.

Sitting in relative dimness, Marcus recalled assorted sins of which he probably ought to repent. He quelled the instinct to squirm in his seat. He was here for his mother's sake, and the reverend's affection for his patroness, the Dowager Countess of Spenford, was both genuine and reciprocated, which was why Marcus expected full cooperation.

A series of framed embroideries hung on the wall behind the rector. The colorful words were Bible verses, Marcus guessed, though they were too distant to read. The kind of needlecraft with which genteel country ladies occupied their time. There were five of these works of art, each presumably the handiwork of one of the reverend's five daughters. One of them Marcus's future bride.

"Am I to understand," Reverend Somerton inquired gently as he polished his spectacles with a handkerchief, "your primary aim in seeking a wife is your mother's peace of mind?"

Marcus bristled, unaccustomed to having his actions questioned by men far more important than the rector of a quiet parish in Hampshire. But this particular parson was not only the man whose sermons he'd sat through as a child, he would soon be Marcus's father-in-law.

"I have always planned to marry, of course," he said. "The age of thirty seemed reasonable. I'm now twenty-nine. I won't deny my mother's illness has spurred me to action, but only to bring forward an inevitable event."

He didn't mean *inevitable* to sound quite so distasteful.

The rector gave him a quick, assessing glance. "I fear my daughters," he said, "lovely though they are, may lack the sophistication to which you are accustomed."

"I have had ample opportunity to—" *take my pick* "—engage the interest of a young lady in London, but this has not occurred." Rather, though Marcus might have engaged their interest, they had not engaged his.

Reverend Somerton and his wife would prove more pleasant relatives than some of the grasping parents he'd encountered in the city, he mused. The rector was of excellent birth, even if he'd forsaken his noble connections to "serve the Lord," as Marcus's mama put it. Two of the Somerton daughters were beauties—in the absence of fortune or title, the world would expect Marcus to settle for nothing less. His father would have insisted upon a bride worthy of the Earl of Spenford. Marcus insisted upon it, too.

"I am still at a loss to understand why you alighted on the idea of one of my daughters." The rector's manner remained pleasant as ever, but his persistence was beginning to grate on Marcus's taut nerves.

"It is my mother's desire—and mine—that I should find a Christian bride." He schooled impatience out of his voice. "I have known your daughters at least as long as any other young lady of my acquaintance, and I hold them in the highest regard."

No need to mention the bargain he'd struck with God on the subject. He wasn't sure how reverends felt about mere mortals bargaining with the Deity.

Marcus Brookstone, Earl of Spenford, would bargain with whomever he chose.

He pressed into the arms of the chair, ready to leave if the reverend didn't come to heel. "Sir, I regret to inform you this is a matter of some haste. While I would like nothing better than a courtship of normal duration—" an untruth, since he could think of nothing more tedious than courting a country miss "—upon securing your consent I must return to London immediately. I'm not happy to have left Mama even for the journey down here—her physician has said she may have only a week...."

Mortifyingly, his voice cracked. Somerton made a hum of concern.

With the ease of long practice, Marcus set sentiment aside and pursued that slight advantage. "The marriage would take place as soon as a special license can be obtained," he said, his words thankfully steady.

Today was Monday. He could have the license by Thursday evening and return here Friday morning. In normal circumstances, Marcus would avoid the unsavory implications of such a hasty wedding, but his mother's failing health ensured no gossip would attach to his actions.

"I would wish the marriage to take place here." Reverend Somerton settled his spectacles back on his nose. "To perform my daughters' wedding services is a long-cherished ambition."

At last, some indication the man would consent! Marcus had expected this condition, had reconciled himself to it on the journey down.

"Of course," he said magnanimously. "All I ask is that my bride and I leave for London in time for me to present the new countess to my mother that evening."

Somerton pressed his thumb to the distinctive cleft in his chin.

"Which of my daughters do you have in mind?" he asked. "Serena, my oldest, isn't here. She is governess to the Granville family in Leicestershire."

Marcus frowned. That would have to cease. The Earl of Spenford couldn't have a sister in any form of employment.

He'd left London struggling to remember any of the Somerton girls' names—five was a ludicrous number of daughters for any family—despite having encountered them many times previously. Not only in church, where they filled the front left-hand pew in the company of their mother, but also at dinners and receptions held at the homes of nearby gentry. Including Palfont, the estate bequeathed to Marcus's mother, which would return to her family coffers upon her death.

She will not die. I have agreed it with God.

He'd had nightmarish visions of taking tea with all five Somerton sisters, inspecting them as if they were horseflesh before making his choice.

Thankfully, circumstance had spared him that.

"Miss Constance Somerton..." he suggested.

"Constance," the rector said, delighted. "Why, that is excellent news." All of a sudden he seemed more kindly disposed toward Marcus's request.

Marcus could guess why. He'd encountered Miss Constance Somerton a short while ago in the village, when he'd climbed down from his curricle at the Goose & Gander, not wishing to be forced to prevail upon the rector for refreshment.

Having eaten, and about to leave the inn, he'd heard a female cry out. In the stable yard, he'd found the prettiest girl he'd ever seen, trying to sidestep around a young man of clearly amorous intentions.

"May I be of assistance, miss?" he'd inquired of the girl.

"Yes, *please,* sir." She turned a relieved face toward him. Then recognized him. Alarm flashed across her features, putting a pretty pink in her cheeks as she curtsied. "I believe, my lord, Mr. Farnham was just leaving."

Bellingham, the squire's son, Marcus recalled, stammered

an apology to the girl before scuttling away like a beetle. Marcus took a step after him.

"He meant no harm, my lord," the girl said quickly. "I'm certain he regrets presuming on our friendship."

Marcus decided to let the youth go; doubtless he'd learned his lesson. "That is gracious of you, Miss…?"

She blushed deeper. "I—I'm Constance Somerton, my lord."

Marcus started. "How remarkable. I'm on my way to visit your father."

"Indeed, my lord?" She'd recovered her composure and spoke with a demureness belied by the dimple dancing in her left cheek.

"Allow me to drive you home in my curricle."

She cast a longing look toward the fine pair of gray horses an ostler was walking up and down. "My lord, Papa would not be pleased to discover me abroad in the village. It's best if I walk home."

"But that will take at least an hour," he protested.

"My sisters and I walk it all the time."

Perhaps that explained her slender figure. In which case, how could Marcus complain?

"Very well." He executed a bow of a depth he would usually reserve for an equal in the peerage, and was rewarded with an appreciative twinkle in her near-violet eyes. "Your servant, Miss Somerton."

Her beauty and lively nature were more than he'd dared expect. She would command the admiration of Society…he just hoped she was of marriageable age.

"My lord…" She hesitated as she curtsied. Her eyes widened in an unspoken plea.

He guessed what she wished to ask, and appreciated her delicacy in not framing the question outright. Yes, with a little guidance, Miss Constance Somerton could be the ideal bride.

"No benefit will be served by my mentioning to your father that I met you here," he assured her.

"Thank you," she breathed. Her hand touched his arm ever so briefly.

Now Marcus returned Reverend Somerton's smile with understanding. Constance Somerton's liveliness was doubtless a source of concern to her parents—he suspected the average parson's daughter was far more docile. Not to mention her appeal to the local young men. Her parents would be delighted to have her safely off their hands.

"I believe I don't speak out of turn when I assure you Constance holds you in the highest esteem," Somerton said.

"I'm happy to hear it." Marcus wondered why the man felt obliged to say such a thing—naturally all the Somerton girls would appreciate his position. He remembered there was still one potential obstacle. "Er, how old is the young lady?"

He would have put her at seventeen, better than sixteen, which would have been impossible, but still arguably too young. Though in a year or two the maturity gap between them would narrow....

"She turned twenty last month," Somerton said. "She is my second daughter."

Twenty? Marcus was surprised, but pleased. Though no one would dare accuse him to his face of robbing the nursery, he hated to be the subject of gossip. His father had spent years schooling him to be worthy of his title—he would not let it fall into disrepute again.

"Unfortunately, Constance is sitting with a sick friend this afternoon," Somerton said. "I could send for her...."

"That won't be necessary." Knowing full well Constance wasn't at a friend's sickbed, Marcus had no desire to land her in trouble. "I must return to London—in addition to the wedding license and to reassuring my mother, there are marriage settlement documents to be drawn up. I propose an allowance of—"

Reverend Somerton held up a hand. "My lord, your family has never been anything but generous to mine. I trust you to create a settlement that will be fair to my daughter and her offspring."

Marcus would do exactly that. His position demanded it. But still, such naïveté seemed irresponsible. "Sir, your trusting nature does you credit, but you might be wiser—"

"Naturally, I will read the settlement document thoroughly before I sign it." The reverend smiled kindly. "If it's not fair, I won't sign it and the marriage will not take place."

Not so naive after all. He knew Marcus wouldn't risk that. The settlement wouldn't be fair; it would be more than fair.

"Of course," Marcus said stiffly. He gathered his riding gloves and stood.

"One more thing." The reverend did not rise, a surprising breach of courtesy, yet his holy calling made it impossible for Marcus to take offence. Or to take his leave. "You do not love my daughter."

Just when Marcus thought the awkwardness past!

He had the uncomfortable sensation his face had reddened. "I cannot love what I do not know."

"An excellent reply, my lord." Somerton's smile bordered on indulgent. "For to know Constance is to love her."

It was the comment of a hopelessly doting father. The kind of father Marcus had never had. He found himself touched by the rector's paternal loyalty.

"Sir, you know enough of my family's history to understand that a—an infatuation is the last reason I would marry," he said. "But it is my hope a strong and natural affection will develop in my marriage." He would not use the word *love,* as the parson had. Love was what a chambermaid might feel for a groom. Love had almost destroyed the Spenford earldom in the past; it would not be given the chance to do so again.

Affection seemed a proper objective for his marriage.

"I know your mother to be a lady of great faith," Somerton said. "Do you share her faith, my lord?"

Marcus tensed, but he said lightly, "Indeed I should, sir, having listened to your sermons for so many years. However, I believe a man's faith to be his own business."

"And God's," Reverend Somerton added with a slight smile. Not before time, he rose to his feet. He came around his desk, stepping out of the sunshine that made him look so dashed holy. "You are right, my lord. It's not for me to judge a man in his faith. However, I wouldn't like any of my daughters to marry an unbeliever."

"Then I'm happy to assure you, you need not fear," Marcus said. This was the worst interview of his life—he thanked heaven a man must only be interrogated by his father-in-law once. An irritating urge to prove himself worthy of Somerton's paternal devotion, the kind of urge he should have outgrown, made him add, "It may comfort you to know I prayed before the outset of this journey."

Perhaps not a conventional prayer of the kind a reverend might favor…but Marcus had spoken to God, had he not?

"Thank you, it does indeed comfort me." The reverend moved to open the study door. This awkward encounter was finished.

"I wish you Godspeed." Reverend Somerton shook Marcus's hand. "I will discuss your offer with Constance this evening. If she does not wish to accept, I will send word immediately."

Living in a house filled with women must have addled Somerton's brain. The parson's daughter—*any* parson's daughter—would be honored to marry the Earl of Spenford.

Marcus didn't waste time pointing that out. He'd come here for a wife; he'd found one. Nothing else mattered.

The curricle pulled out of the rectory gate right in front of Constance, so close that one more step would take her smack into the side of a very large gray horse.

She gave a yelp of surprise, and the driver, who'd been looking to his left for traffic, somehow heard her over the clatter of hooves and the rattle of bridles. He immediately reined in the horses, coming to a stop.

"My apologies," he called.

Lord Spenford! It had been an age since she'd seen him. Why was he here? She wanted to call out an assurance that no apology was needed, though in fact it was: he should have been looking. But as usual, the sight of him reduced her vocabulary to a few nonsense words and made her feel as if it had been days since her last meal. She steadied herself by reaching a hand to the brick wall that ran along the front of the rectory grounds.

Lord Spenford jumped down, still holding the reins of his grays. "Are you all right?"

His voice was exactly as Constance remembered—deep, beautifully modulated. It sent a delightful shiver through her.

He glanced behind him at the rectory. "Miss Somerton? You've had a shock. Should I drive you inside?"

Such consideration! Such— She realized that by now he must be wondering if she'd been struck mute since the last time they met. "I'm quite well," she said. "Thank you, Lord Spenford."

It sounded as if she was thanking him for almost running her over.

"I was going too fast," he said ruefully. "In a hurry to get back to London. No excuse for such poor driving."

"Don't think about it," she said. "I know you must be worried about your—about the dowager countess."

He gave her a surprised look, then his face closed over. "Indeed," he said briefly. "If you truly are unhurt, Miss Somerton, I will resume my journey." He sprang back up onto the curricle. About to drive off, he checked the horses. "We will meet again soon," he said, and smiled.

Then he was gone, and all that was left to show he'd been there was a cloud of dust and what Constance knew must be a sappy expression on her face at the memory of that smile.

"He wishes to marry me?" Constance sat stunned on the sofa in the rear drawing room, closed off from the front room except when the family had company. "*Me?* Not Isabel or Amanda?"

It was the answer to a prayer she'd never dared utter. A dream come true, an absurd fantasy…now about to become reality?

"He can't have meant *me,*" she said faintly. Hoping against hope that he had. "I saw him outside. He didn't say a word." *He almost killed me!* Although, he *had* said, *We will meet again soon.* How could she have guessed he meant *in church, at our wedding?*

"Nor should he, before your father spoke to you," her mother said. "Besides, Lord Spenford was in a hurry to return to town…but he definitely wanted you, my dear." Her mother patted her knee, as she smiled at her father, occupying one of the Hepplewhite chairs he frequently condemned as too spindly. "Didn't he, Adrian?"

"So he did," her father confirmed. "Mind you, Constance, I'm not telling you the earl's in love with you."

"Of course he's not," she said quickly. "His sort doesn't marry for love." *Unlike my sort.* She frowned, still struggling to believe this marvelous proposal. "Why me?"

"His mother must have recommended you," Margaret Somerton suggested. "Her ladyship was always fond of you."

"That must be it," Constance agreed. "It's been more than a year since I last spoke to Lord Spenford. He has certainly not been enchanted by my conversation."

It went without saying he hadn't been enchanted by her physical charms: she had none.

"His lordship's desire to marry now is largely to please his mother," Adrian inserted.

Constance nodded. She did not find that odd, quite the opposite. Marcus Brookstone, Earl of Spenford, might be rumored to enjoy every pleasure of the ton, but he loved his mama dearly, always had, and Constance admired him for that.

Among other attributes.

As if he read her thoughts, her father prompted, "I was correct in assuming, my dear, that you would welcome this proposal?"

Constance felt pink in her cheeks. Her long infatuation with Lord Spenford hadn't gone unnoticed by her family. "Yes, Papa," she murmured. Slightly defensive, she added, "I know him to be a good man."

Her father thumbed the cleft in his chin. "My dear, his reputation is not spotless."

"None of us is perfect," Constance pointed out.

"True," her father agreed.

"Constance, you don't find him a little *proud?*" her mother asked.

"Margaret!" The reverend shifted on his chair, which wobbled, causing him to mutter ominously.

"Much as I admire your reluctance to condemn people, Adrian," Margaret Somerton said, "Spenford is widely regarded as a proud man. I preferred him before he became the heir."

"Mama, he was just a boy," Constance protested. "The man is always different from the boy."

Marcus had been born the second son of the previous Earl of Spenford. Stephen, his older brother by six years, had been by all accounts the perfect heir. Until he died in a hunting accident when Marcus was fifteen.

"A *delightful* boy," Margaret corrected her. "Until his father, who by the by was also a proud man, took him in hand."

"I don't find Lord Spenford at all proud." The event that had informed Constance's opinion would seem trivial to her parents. But three years ago she'd realized Marcus Brookstone was a man worthy of her deepest feelings.

"All I'm saying is, you're not obliged to accept this offer," her mother said. "Your father's future may be uncertain, but we are confident God will supply."

Constance didn't know how, even with their faith, her parents could remain so calm. Her father's insistence on taking the Word out to the laborers in the fields, or wherever they might be, had landed him in trouble with his bishop. He'd been accused of Methodism, of creating a schism in the parish. It was monstrously unfair, when her father held unity and inclusiveness within the church as one of his dearest tenets. There was a risk the bishop might remove him from the parish; her parents would lose their home and livelihood.

"I don't expect any of you girls to marry if you don't wish it," the rector confirmed. "St. Paul himself said it's better not to marry if one can be content in the single life, and while my heirs will never be wealthy, you will live in modest comfort. But blessed as I have been in my own marriage—" he reached across to squeeze his wife's hand, almost oversetting his chair "—it wouldn't surprise me if God's providence should include loving husbands for at least some of my daughters."

Constance's youngest sister, Charity, vowed frequently to live with Mama and Papa the rest of her days. But in truth, Constance had expected to be the spinster of the family.

With four sisters prettier than she, she was used to going unnoticed by all, with the exception of her parents. And perhaps of older people, like the dowager countess, who seemed to find her plainness soothing.

Though the local young men were scrupulously polite in greeting her, in asking her to dance after they had danced with her sisters, no marriageable man had ever, as far as she was aware, seen *her*. Looked past her sisters, past all other young ladies, and chosen *her*.

Marcus Brookstone had.

Her mother said dubiously. "I hope the earl will know how lucky he is to win you, Constance."

"How blessed he is, my sweet," her husband corrected her. Though in many ways the most tolerant of men, he didn't allow luck to be given credit for divine Providence.

Constance took a deep breath. "Papa, I believe God has given me this opportunity, and I wish to accept his lordship's proposal. I am certain we can make each other happy."

Chapter Two

Had he changed his mind?

Five minutes past eleven o'clock on Constance's wedding day and no sign of a bridegroom for the ceremony that should have started on the hour.

Standing in the churchyard, trying to appear nonchalant while her body vacillated between chills and extreme heat, Constance was conscious of all eyes upon her. Most discomfiting.

She could almost feel sorry for Isabel and Amanda, the two of her sisters acclaimed as beauties. To be stared at so intently... Constance shivered in the spring sunshine.

"Cold, my love?" Isabel asked. Instilled with the supreme confidence that came with beauty, she wouldn't understand Constance's petrified state.

Constance shook her head. "Thank goodness you added this veil to my bonnet," she said to Amanda. "At least I don't have to meet the eyes of everyone wondering if the earl plans to make an appearance."

"Veils are all the rage in London and Paris," Amanda said, oddly defensive.

Constance patted her arm. "I trust your knowledge of the fashions, dearest, for you know I have none." She considered taking back the reticule and small posy of flowers Amanda was holding for her, but there was too much chance her nervous fingers would shred them.

"It looks very becoming on you," Amanda said. She'd used the same French lace for the veil as Constance's mother had for the elegant trim she'd added to Constance's best blue muslin dress. Without compunction, Margaret Somerton had cut into a beautiful tablecloth that had been a gift from her own mother.

The trim made a fine feature on an otherwise simple dress, drawing attention away from Constance's face, and down to her figure. The veil, anchored to her bonnet with a cream-colored satin ribbon and reaching to her chin, achieved the same end. Constance dared not ask where Amanda had obtained the ribbon. Her sister managed to fancy all her clothes with furbelows that Constance suspected were gifts from young men.

"You realize, Amanda, as Countess of Spenford I will be in a position to offer you a London Season," Constance said. "Perhaps next year..." So long as they weren't in mourning for the dowager, of course. Amanda had yearned for a London Season for as long as she'd known such a thing existed.

Amanda merely squeezed Constance's hand. Maybe she still had the headache she'd complained of earlier when she'd begged to be excused from the ceremony. Constance had in turn begged her to attend. It was bad enough to be getting married lacking one sister's presence—there hadn't been time to send word to Serena in Leicestershire and have her travel home to Piper's Mead.

Now, that seemed a good thing. Serena might have had a wasted trip.

The villagers were growing restless, despite the valiant attempts of Reverend Somerton and his wife to engage them in conversation. While most of the men were working, a good number of the women thronged the churchyard, eager to witness the most prestigious wedding in the village for at least a generation. A couple of lads had taken advantage of the festive atmosphere to station themselves on the churchyard wall, normally forbidden territory. They nudged and jostled each other, enjoying the risk of an imminent fall.

"Maybe his lordship had an accident," Mrs. Penney, the baker's wife, suggested. "Could be overturned in a ditch on the London road."

"Or footpads," said Mrs. Tucker, from the Goose & Gander. "They'll kill a man soon as look at him, these days."

"No!" Constance said sharply.

"Sorry, love," Mrs. Tucker said. "Don't you worry, his lordship won't let you down. He's like his father in that respect. A stickler for his duty."

Even as she spoke, Mrs. Tucker glanced at Isabel, confusion written on the older woman's broad face. She was doubtless wondering why any earl would choose Constance over Isabel, whose fair beauty had been a source of village pride since she'd been in the cradle.

"You look lovely, Constance." The assurance came from Charity, who, although just turned fifteen, displayed an unusual sensibility for other people's feelings.

Constance smiled her thanks, though her sister probably couldn't see through the veil.

Constance had never wished for beauty…at least, not since she'd accepted, years ago, that she would always be the most ordinary of the Somerton girls. Not that her face sent small children screaming for their mothers, or anything like that. She'd spent enough hours in her youth searching the mirror for signs of beauty to know her brown eyes were warm, her eyebrows nicely shaped. Those features ensured she was acceptable. And she'd inherited her mother's excellent figure, for which she was truly grateful.

It was just…on this day, when she was about to marry one of the most handsome men in all England, she would have given much to be pretty.

"God sees the heart," Charity reminded her, still reading Constance's thoughts. "Perhaps He has revealed your gentle heart to the earl."

"Perhaps," Constance said doubtfully. She hoped the Lord hadn't revealed her besottedness to Lord Spenford—the poor man would be mortified to know his bride cherished such romantic notions for a near stranger.

She could only hope it was indeed her gentle spirit, whether revealed through divine guidance or through the dowager, that had caused the earl to settle on her.

One of the urchins perched on the churchyard wall shouted, "He's coming! And he's got a bang-up rig, too."

His mother boxed his ears for referring to Lord Spenford as "he" rather than "his lordship" and for daring to express an opinion on the earl's conveyance. The women set to straightening their dresses, adjusting their bonnets in a panicked flurry that reminded Constance of the Bible parable about the foolish virgins readying themselves for the bridegroom.

Constance stayed still. No minimal adjustment would elevate her to sudden beauty.

"Mama," Amanda said, "I think I'm going to faint."

A stir of interest ran through the crowd at her words, dividing attention between her and the churchyard gates.

"Oh, gracious." Margaret Somerton was visibly torn.

"Stay there, Mama," Amanda told her. "I'll sit in the side chapel until I feel better. Excuse me, Constance."

"Of course, love. I should have let you rest at home."

Amanda did look wan. There was no sign of the dimple in her left cheek that had inspired several young men to attempt poetry, with woeful results. As she handed over Constance's reticule and posy, she asked with a strange urgency. "Connie, this is what you wish, isn't it? To marry Spenford?"

It wasn't like Amanda to show such care for others; Constance blinked away unexpected tears. "It's what I wish more than anything," she confirmed. Hoping it was true.

Almost before she finished speaking, Amanda was hurrying into the church. And Constance's attention was drawn to the fine curricle pulling up behind the dowager's coach, sent earlier from Palfont to convey the Somerton women to the church.

Constance didn't recognize the gentleman driving the curricle, nor did she notice the groom on the back. She had eyes only for her betrothed, sitting alongside the driver.

Poor Lord Spenford would be exhausted, having traveled so far the past few days. *Marcus, I must learn to call him Marcus.*

But the moment the curricle stopped, he jumped down with an energy that made a mockery of her concern.

His dark hair lifted in the breeze as he strode toward her father. The crowd melted back in a flurry of curtsies and, from the boys, removal of caps.

"Sir, forgive me." He shook her father's hand. "We encountered an overturned post chaise on the road out of Farnham and stopped to render assistance."

An impeccable reason for tardiness. Constance wouldn't wish to marry a man who failed to render assistance.

Her father inquired of the injured passengers, declared his intent to pray for them.

"May I introduce you to the Marquis of Severn, who will stand with me as groomsman," Marcus said.

His friend, the same impressive height as the earl, but to Constance's eye not as handsome, exchanged bows with the reverend. Reverend Somerton introduced his wife to the Marquis…goodness, would the formalities never end?

Then, suddenly, they were finished, and her father was beckoning to Constance.

Isabel gave her the slightest of shoves; Constance made her way on trembling legs.

She dropped a tiny curtsy, afraid if she sank too low she would never rise again. To nurse a girlish dream was one thing; to live the reality quite another. *I can't go through with this.*

The earl took her hands in his, an intimacy she hadn't expected. His fingertips curled beneath hers, warm through the fabric of her best gloves, anchoring her.

"My dear Constance." His smile held kindness, chagrin and an uncertainty that somehow boosted her confidence. "How fortunate I am that your nature aligns with your name, and you have waited for such a tardy wretch. Will you do me the honor of accompanying me into the church?"

Her gaze darted over his shoulder to the worn stone building she loved as well as her own home. She would enter the church a parson's daughter; she would leave it a countess. A wife. *His* wife.

The earl's grip tightened. Her doubts lifted like mist warmed by the sun, to drift away on the breeze.

"I will," she said.

He brought her left hand to his lips, and through her glove pressed a kiss to her knuckles. Warmth flooded her, traveled directly to her legs where it had a bizarre weakening effect. Constance locked her knees, put all her energy into holding her ground.

"Come," Spenford said, "let us be married."

"I, Marcus Albert Edward Spencer Brookstone, Earl of Spenford, Baron Brookstone, take thee, Constance Anne Somerton…"

Constance calmed her nerves by focusing on the string of names. And reflected she would be more pleased if he were mere Marcus Brookstone.

Her father recited the next portion of the vows in the dear, measured tone that had guided her life. "To have and to hold...to love and to cherish..."

He spoke clearly, rather than loudly, but the words rang to the rafters above the heads of the enthralled congregation.

"To have and to hold...to love and to cherish," the earl repeated firmly.

Constance let out a breath of relief. He had sworn to love her. Not today, or tomorrow, necessarily, but he would try, and when he succeeded it would be—

"Till death us do part..."

Yes. That.

She made the same vow, her voice shaking, adding the bride's promise *to obey.*

Behind her, she heard a small sob. *Mama.* Pragmatic Margaret Somerton had surprised her daughters, and herself, with several bouts of sniffling over the past few days. Her mood had been unimproved by her husband's assurance she was not losing a daughter, but gaining a son.

Constance slid a sidelong glance at her mother's new "son." At several inches taller than she, at least six feet, his height was potentially intimidating.

"Do you have the ring?" her father asked.

The earl—Marcus—turned to his groomsman. Constance had forgotten his name... Severn, that was it, the Marquis of Severn.

Severn handed over a circlet of gold. After a moment's pause, Constance realized everyone was waiting for her.

She fumbled to free her left hand—*the one he had kissed*—from her glove. Marcus took her bare fingers, and for the first time they were flesh to flesh. About to be made one.

"With this ring, I thee wed," he repeated after her father.

Another few moments, and the gold band slid down her finger. Making her his.

Constance's mind shied away from the thought.

"Those whom God hath joined together, let no man put asunder," her father intoned.

The next phrases washed over her, until she heard, "I now pronounce that they be man and wife."

Constance's gazed snapped to the earl. She hadn't even been listening to that final declaration and now she was married. Just as well she didn't attend to omens, because surely…

The worry evaporated in the warmth of the gaze Lord Spenford—her husband!—turned on her.

A half smile on his lips, he reached for her veil, lifted it.

His brilliant blue eyes scanned her face.

Constance smiled shyly.

Marcus's mouth straightened into a line that could only be described as grim.

"My—my lord?" Words died away as Constance absorbed his expression.

He looked appalled.

Chapter Three

"Who the blazes are you?" Marcus snapped the moment they attained the privacy of the carriage.

The girl—the woman—his *wife*, blast it!—shrank back against the seat, her bonnet with that veil, that—that *instrument of deception*, askew.

"You know who I am." Her voice quivered as she rubbed her elbow where he'd gripped it to escort her from the church. "I am Constance…."

She stopped. As if she had been going to say *Constance Somerton*, but that was no longer true, because now she was—

She could *not* be Lady Spenford.

Outside, the villagers cheered and shouted good wishes as the coach pulled away, headed for the rectory, for the wedding breakfast.

Thoughts and images whirled in Marcus's head, blurred by fatigue. Could some artifice—cosmetics, perhaps?—have made her look so different last Monday? Her voice was slightly altered, but in the church he'd attributed that to nerves.

"Remove your bonnet," he ordered.

She clutched it to her head. So much for that promise she'd made not five minutes ago to *obey*.

He leaned forward; she gasped as his fingers closed around the ribbon beneath her chin. Then she froze as he worked the knot, careful not to touch her.

He lifted the bonnet from her head, tossed it to the floor of the coach. Which elicited another gasp.

"Your bonnet is the least of your worries, madam," he said roughly. His gaze raked her face. Not at all the same. Brown eyes, not violet-blue, a perfectly ordinary nose in place of the charming version he'd seen on Monday. Thinner lips, a chin that might be described by someone in an uncharitable mood as pointy.

Marcus was in a very uncharitable mood.

In place of ink-black curls, this girl's hair was a drab brown, drawn up in a knot, with a few tendrils curling around her nape.

"What is this trick?" he growled. "You must have planned it before I even arrived in Piper's Mead. I swear, if your holier-than-thou father played a part in this—"

"You will not say a word against my father," she blurted.

And now she dared issue orders to him!

Well, that wouldn't last, nor would this marriage. He'd been duped into marrying this plain-faced fraudster, and fraud was grounds for annulment. There'd been the case of Baron Waring, some years ago…Marcus couldn't remember the details, but the woman involved had misrepresented herself, and the bishop declared an annulment.

The girl, Constance, or whatever her name was, picked up her bonnet. As she settled it on her lap, it slipped through her trembling fingers and fell to the floor again.

Instinctive courtesy had Marcus reaching to retrieve it at the same moment she did. His fingers brushed hers, and she flinched.

"I would like an annulment," she announced.

Marcus jerked backward, the unfortunate bonnet once again hitting the floor. He hoped the infernal thing was damaged beyond repair.

"*You* want an annulment?" He'd heard of women hatching preposterous schemes to entrap a titled husband, but he'd never heard of a scheme that included a request for an annulment.

She tilted that chin—definitely pointy—at him. "On—on grounds of insanity."

"You admit to a weakened mind?" So much the better!

She blinked and her brown eyes widened. "Sir, *you* are the insane one."

Marcus's mouth opened and closed, and he had the uncomfortable sensation that he looked like one of the carp in the Japanese pond at Chalmers, the main Spenford estate.

He suspected such an expression did not convey complete, calm rationality.

She knotted her fingers in her lap, which seemed to firm her voice. "I have heard married ladies talk of an illness that gentlemen can acquire as a result of—of dissolute living." Her cheeks flamed. "It drives them mad."

"You accuse me of dissolute living?" he said dangerously.

Her gaze dropped, then rose again. "Papa warned me your reputation is…not quite spotless."

Marcus felt himself reddening. Outrageous! What kind of man was Somerton to talk to his daughters in that way?

She didn't realize how perilously she trod, for she continued. "It occurs to me that perhaps you chose a bride from Piper's Mead because…"

She didn't finish. She didn't need to. Her implication was clear: because no lady of sense in London would have him.

"I am pleased to inform you my health is perfect," he snapped.

"Which implies you are *deliberately* accusing me and my father of dishonesty," she warned.

"I apologize," he said, teeth gritted, aware that *she* hadn't apologized for her suggestion that he lived an improper life. But he had to admit, she seemed as baffled by the situation as he was. Surely a parson's daughter could not have cooked up this wild scheme. He breathed out through his nose, calming himself. "May we start this conversation again, in an attempt to untangle this confusion?"

"I suppose so," she said dubiously.

As the coach swung into the lane that ended at the rectory, Marcus grasped the strap overhead. "What is your name?"

Her guarded expression suggested she still harbored suspicions he was a half-wit. "My name is—was Constance Anne Somerton."

Marcus tipped his head back against the seat. "I met Constance Somerton in Piper's Mead on Monday, and believe me, she looked nothing like you."

She frowned, putting a little furrow in the middle of her forehead. "That's not possible."

"I suspect she was younger than you—" this woman looked all of her twenty years "—with dark, curly hair and eyes an unusual blue. She called herself Miss Constance Somerton."

His bride pressed her fingers to her mouth, and he remembered how they had felt, fine and slender, in his grasp.

"Amanda," she moaned.

He pounced. "Is that your name? Amanda?"

She didn't quite roll her eyes, but only, he sensed, through heroic self-restraint. "*I* am Constance. Amanda is my sister. She is of somewhat…mischievous temperament."

"You call passing herself off as you *mischievous?*" he barked. "I asked your father if I could marry her!"

She closed her eyes. "Of course," she murmured. "It wasn't me you wanted at all."

He had thought that perfectly obvious from the moment he'd lifted her veil.

"How could I have been so stupid?" She sounded *broken*.

Marcus felt a twinge of concern. But he was virtually a stranger to her; she had no reason for heartbreak. This was likely part of her act. "Certainly one of us has been stupid," he said bitterly.

To his horror, tears sprang to her eyes. Marcus averted his gaze as he offered her his white linen handkerchief.

But she held up her hand, palm out in refusal. "I want nothing from you."

For the barest moment, her dignity impressed him…then he remembered, she'd already duped him once.

"Of course you don't," he said. "You can buy all the handkerchiefs you want, thanks to the generous settlement documents your father signed on your behalf this morning."

Those tears clung to her lashes, held there by force of will, it seemed, not spilling onto her pale cheeks. Marcus stared at the ceiling of the carriage as she fumbled in her reticule, presumably for a handkerchief of her own.

Instead of a scrap of fabric, she pulled out a folded sheet of paper. "What's this?"

"I hardly think I would know," he said coldly.

She opened the note. "It's Amanda's hand."

At the mention of her "mischievous" sister, Marcus plucked the paper from her fingers. "Allow me to read it to you."

It wasn't a request.

The opening words of the missive, written in a girlish hand, jumped out at him.

Forgive me!

Foreboding filled him as he began to read aloud.

"'Forgive me! Constance, darling, I have done something very Dreadful, and you will think me Wicked. On Monday, I encountered Lord Spenford in the Village....'"

His mouth tightened and his voice lowered as he read the shocking account. Afraid of discovery by her father, who had warned that if he heard of Amanda talking inappropriately to any more young men, she would be sent to Miss Petersham's Seminary—an institution one of Marcus's cousins attended, it was renowned for its austere discipline—she had supplied Constance's name in lieu of her own. The moment she heard Marcus had offered for Constance she knew his mistake.

"'*Constance, dear, I could not marry a man so old!*'" he read, before he realized where the text was going.

Constance muffled an exclamation, darting an involuntary look at him.

So old? He was in his prime!

Marcus read on.

"'I do not wish to be a wife without ever having a Season in London. I wish to dance the waltz with handsome young men, to have them pay me compliments....'"

He'd seen enough. "The girl's a fool," he said, as he handed the letter back.

Constance bristled in her sister's defense. "You didn't think her foolish when you flirted with her in the village on Monday. With a sixteen-year-old girl barely out of the nursery."

"I did no such thing," he retorted. "Your sister was engaged in heated discussion with the squire's son. I offered my assistance."

"And when you asked her name, despite having met her on at least twenty occasions, you did not notice her lie." She sniffed and, thankfully, blinked away those tears that were starting to wear on his conscience. "My father taught me it's common courtesy to remember the names of those I meet."

Was she setting her manners above his?

"There are five of you, madam," he said bitingly. Yet he found he could not meet her gaze, which annoyed him still further.

She pushed the note back into her reticule. "Amanda, you fool," she murmured, seemingly forgetting she had just castigated Marcus for saying the same. Then she swallowed and that pointy chin went up in the air again.

Marcus braced himself.

"I apologize for suggesting you were insane," she said, with a graciousness that in a true countess might have been convincing.

Marcus was not convinced. As the coach approached the rectory, he observed the garden had been decorated—bunting strung through the trees.

The wedding feast. Though there would be a private meal indoors, the entire village had doubtless been invited to the public celebration outside.

He'd never felt less like celebrating in his life.

A curricle passed the coach with less than an inch to spare: Severn, tooling his grays like the expert horseman he was. His closest friend had commiserated over the need for Marcus to marry a parson's daughter, but he had understood entirely.

It would be hard to understand how Marcus had come to marry the wrong girl.

Even harder to explain to the reverend. Impossible to imagine the story wouldn't spread around the village and thence to London. That Marcus, Earl of Spenford, wouldn't end up looking a fool.

The carriage turned in through the rectory gates.

"Home!" Constance clasped her hands together, her eyes shining as she peered out.

"Might I remind you," Marcus said sourly, "this is no longer your home."

She recoiled. "But…you cannot mean to stay married to me? Not after Amanda's trick."

He took grim satisfaction from her shock. "I don't know if your sister's letter is true, or whether it's part of some elaborate deception. Either way, your family has made a fool of me, and that's something I cannot forgive."

The carriage jolted over a bump in the driveway; she clutched the door handle.

Marcus pinched the bridge of his nose as he brought himself back to what really mattered. "But my mother is deathly ill. She awaits tidings of my nuptials. I will not disappoint her. We'll attend the wedding breakfast for a minimum time, then leave for London as planned."

Constance swallowed. "You mean…an annulment later?"

It irritated him that she asked with such hope. *He* was the one entitled to hope this was all a nightmare from which he would awaken.

"Since I am not insane," he said coldly, "and since you are indeed, or were, Miss Constance Somerton and not a fraudster—" *and since I have no stomach for telling the world I was duped by a sixteen-year-old chit* "—there will be no annulment."

Chapter Four

The hours spent on the drive to London were the longest of Constance's life. The coach was comfortable beyond her experience…but she experienced it alone.

Marcus rode with the groom, which she felt certain must provoke speculation in that servant's mind. What bridegroom didn't want to spend the hours after his wedding with his new wife?

A bridegroom who'd married the wrong bride.

The man who had so warmly reassured Constance at the church, apologizing for his tardiness, kissing her fingers, had believed he was talking to Amanda.

His shock was understandable, as was his sense of being deceived. Any man who believed himself to be marrying one woman would be…*disappointed* to find himself bound to another. But Constance was innocent in the matter, as he would surely realize. Sooner or later.

Through the coach window, she eyed his square-set shoulders. He was doubtless thinking on it right now. He was not an unreasonable man.

He is a proud man.

Her mother's warning came back to her.

Who was Constance to accuse him of excessive pride,

when her own pride was smarting? Nor could she condemn his anger, when she was furious with her sister.

They reached a particularly rough patch of road, and Constance braced herself in her corner. It was obvious that due to the dowager countess's precarious health they were traveling as fast as possible, and no coach could be so comfortable as to remove all discomfort.

By the time they stopped at an inn outside Esher to change horses and to dine, Constance felt as if she might throw up.

The innkeeper's welcome was hampered by his heavy head cold and accompanying cough, but he ushered them into his best parlor, where the earl asked what she desired to eat.

"Just a little bread," she said. "Thank you."

His mouth compressed, but she wasn't about to explain the combination of exhaustion and nausea that precluded anything more substantial. At least he no longer radiated hostility…although that could be for the benefit of the landlord. She took it as a good sign that he ordered a hearty meal, even though he looked as tired as she felt.

"How much longer is the journey?" she asked, to break the silence left in the wake of the innkeeper's departure.

"Less than two hours. Mama will be trying to stay awake in the hope of seeing me. Us."

His mother. The reason for their wedding. The reason he was mistakenly wed to Constance.

"She will be pleased?" Constance asked tentatively.

His lips flattened. "Yes."

"My lord—" She broke off. "What should I call you?"

"Most people call me Spenford," he said. "My mother and my cousin Lucinda call me Marcus."

Not much help. She'd heard that ton couples didn't necessarily address their spouses by their Christian name.

"You may call me Constance if you wish," she prompted.

He looked baffled.

She pressed on. "It's not my fault, sir, that you married the wrong wife."

"So you claim."

She ignored that aspersion on her honesty. "My father says—"

"Is your father to be quoted in our every conversation?" he asked.

Her cheeks warmed. "He is the wisest man I know."

"Nevertheless, I don't wish to hear his views."

She clenched her jaw. "Here is *my* view, then," she said. "You're angry, I understand that. I'm angry, too."

His chin jerked back. "*You* are angry! What have I done—"

"At my sister," she snapped. "I'm so angry with Amanda I could—I could slap her." She realized her voice had risen, her chest was heaving. And her husband was eyeing her quizzically.

"You don't look the slapping sort," he said, surprisingly mild. "Have you ever slapped anyone before?"

"Er, no," she admitted. "But if Amanda were here right now I would do it." Her sister had wisely not shown her face at the wedding breakfast.

He raised one eyebrow, which even in her ire she could see was a handsome trick. "I don't believe you," he taunted.

She puffed out an irritated breath, ready to defend her violent tendencies…and suddenly deflated. He was right. "I don't suppose you would ever hit a woman?" she asked morosely.

"Of course not!"

She sighed. "There's not much point wishing Amanda here then, is there."

One side of his mouth twitched in what might almost have been a smile, except there was nothing to smile about. "*I* certainly don't wish she were here," he said.

For an instant, there was something like camaraderie between them.

Then the landlord entered with their food. He and the maid began to set out dishes. As she sat in the chair the man held out for her, Constance noticed his nose was reddened from his illness. The maid seemed similarly afflicted, making heroic efforts to avoid sniffling.

"You are not well, either of you," Constance said with concern. "The earl and I can serve ourselves. Please don't worry."

The maid dropped a relieved curtsy, but Marcus said, "Your carving skills will be appreciated, landlord."

Both man and maid stayed several minutes to serve the meal.

Constance had been biting her tongue, but the moment they left, she said, "That was unnecessary. They were both clearly in need of rest."

"So am I," he said. "So are you. They should do the job they are paid to do." He cut into his rib of beef. "I thought parsons' daughters were supposed to be the forgiving type."

It took her a moment to realize he was referring to Amanda again.

"Parsons' daughters aren't perfect," Constance said.

He nodded his acceptance of her flaw. But he was right; she would need to forgive Amanda—the little wretch had even asked it of her in that note. *I will forgive her. One day.*

She nibbled on her bread…and realized her husband had set down his silverware.

"What is it?" she asked, conscious that her blue muslin was rumpled and she'd paid no attention to her hair since he'd torn the bonnet from her head.

"Is this some kind of parsonage austerity diet?" He indicated her bread. "Because I don't think I can sit opposite you eating dry bread every night—"

"I am travel sick," she said.

He stood, and moved swiftly to her. "You should have said. Do you have a fever?" His hand moved uncertainly at his side, as if he was considering touching it to her forehead.

For one moment, she craved the comfort of that touch.

"Just a little nausea," she said. "The bread settles my stomach."

It was odd to be talking of her physical ailment to a man other than her father. Yet she welcomed the concern that creased his brow.

"You have a strange view of parsonage life," she observed, as he returned to his seat, "if you think we eat dry bread."

"I don't number many daughters of the clergy among my acquaintance." He resumed eating.

Constance took a sip of water, and licked her lips. "Do you plan to tell anyone what happened today? About the… mistake?"

He didn't look up. "I have no desire to be the subject of gossip."

"Nor do I." She'd been overlooked her whole life; to come to the world's attention in the worst possible way would be too cruel.

Now he did meet her gaze. He wiped his mouth with a napkin, drawing her attention to the lips that had kissed her hand. "No one anticipates an emotional attachment between us," he said. "Mutual respect is what they expect to see. What they should see."

It sounded cold to Constance, when she thought of her parents' loving marriage. But much better than humiliation.

"I am most willing to show respect to you," she said.

He gave a little jolt, as if he'd taken that for granted. "And I you," he replied.

It seemed they had reached a kind of truce.

It also seemed he didn't feel compelled to say more.

They finished their meal, and then it was back to the solitude of the coach.

It was nine o'clock when they drew up outside a fine town house in Mayfair's Berkeley Square.

By the time Constance alighted with the assistance of the groom, the front door stood open. Marcus offered his arm, then escorted her up the steps, into an entrance hall where an array of servants lined up to greet them.

"Dallow," he said to the butler, "may I present the Countess of Spenford." No affection in his tone, of course, but the respect he'd promised.

"Your ladyship." The butler bowed low to Constance. Her own family had servants—a cook, two maids, a manservant and an occasional gardener. But none so grand as this personage.

Dallow introduced her to the rest of the servants. She managed to say a word or two to each, smiling at a young lad who barely stifled a yawn. She suspected they were all as tired as she, having been preparing the house for a new mistress.

"How is my mother?" Marcus asked the butler.

"I believe Lady Spenford is awake and anxious to see your lordship. And your ladyship."

Constance sensed Marcus was forcing himself to slow to a genteel pace as he escorted her up the imposing staircase. He knocked on the door of the dowager countess's room. It was opened by a middle-aged maidservant.

She curtsied. "My lord."

"Good evening, Powell. May I present the Countess of Spenford?"

Powell curtsied to Constance, the frankness of her appraising gaze suggesting a servant of long standing.

"Is my mother awake?" the earl asked.

"Is that you, Marcus?" a voice called.

His face lit. "She sounds stronger."

They passed through a small but charming sitting room to reach the dowager's bedroom. She sat in bed, propped against an enormous number of pillows. Her wrapper and cap were the most fetching Constance had seen.

"Oh!" Helen, Lady Spenford, pressed her hands to her cheeks. "Constance, my dear, it's really true! You married Marcus!"

"Yes, my lady." Constance approached quickly, and dropped into a curtsy.

The dowager laughed as she grasped Constance's hand. "I half thought I must have dreamed Marcus telling me on Tuesday you'd agreed to be his wife. And now here you are!"

"Mama, it's wonderful to see you looking so well." Marcus leaned down to kiss her cheek.

"I do feel better," the dowager admitted, on a note of revelation. "Your happy news must have boosted me. I've always been fond—extremely fond!—of you, Constance, and now you're my daughter."

"Thank you, ma'am." Her effusiveness was embarrassing, but Constance basked in its warmth. "Is there anything I can do for you?"

The dowager smiled. "Two things, my dear. Call me Mama, and accept my warmest welcome into our family. Marcus, I'm persuaded a wife as gentle and sweet as Constance will soon be dear to your heart."

Marcus made a noncommittal sound.

Given that he'd taken a fancy to Amanda, Constance suspected *sweet* and *gentle* sat low on his list of desirable wifely qualities. As for his heart…

The dowager patted Constance's hand. "Of course, you never had any thought of marrying my son—" Constance blushed "—so this has been very sudden. I hope you are happy?"

She'd just endured the most miserable few hours of her twenty years.

"Mother," Marcus protested, "it's late, and Constance has had a long journey."

It was the first time he'd spoken her name since the wedding. Even after all that had happened, she liked hearing it on his lips.

Foolish.

"My—Mama, I agreed to marry the earl of my own free will," she said. "We made our vows before God. So I'm certain I will be happy." She wouldn't lie and say she was happy now. But she had faith for the future.

The dowager directed a questioning glance at her son.

His hand settled on Constance's shoulder. "I share my wife's certainty," he said.

Really? He felt they could overcome this awkward beginning, too? They had no choice, of course, but still…Constance hadn't hoped for a softening this soon. She was suddenly aware of his thumb, aligned with the edge of the dress where it met her shoulder.

"That's all I could want." Helen pushed herself higher against the pillows. "I declare, I haven't felt so lively in months."

"I hope you'll be still livelier tomorrow," Marcus said fondly. "But Mr. Bird would be alarmed to see you overexerting yourself. He would worry you'll weaken your heart further."

His mother sighed. "Constance, dear, you never met such a man as my doctor for depressing one's hopes of recovery! He can be quite an old woman."

"That 'old woman' is the finest doctor in London," Marcus said.

"I know, darling, and he's so worthy." The dowager pulled

a face. "But when I think how I never used to go to bed before midnight…"

"Maybe those days will come again," Marcus said gently, "but not, I suspect, today."

"You're right. I should sleep. Constance, will you come to me tomorrow?"

"I'll spend the day with you, Mama—" she shot a glance at Marcus "—that is, if Lord Spenford doesn't have other plans."

His look, full of approval, warmed her through. "Certainly you could spend much of the day here."

"The morning only," the dowager corrected. "Constance mustn't stay cooped up in a sickroom, when she has a new home and a new husband to enjoy. Good night, my dears."

Back out in the hallway, Marcus waited until the maid, Powell, had closed his mother's door. "Thank you for offering to spend time with Mama," he said. "I appreciate your willingness to do your duty after today's…difficulties." It was an odd speech, spoken stiffly but with an underlying vulnerability that touched Constance's heart.

"Sitting with your mother will be a pleasure, not a duty," she said. "I've always been fond of her." Would he think that impertinent, a parson's daughter holding fondness for a countess?

His eyes searched her face, which she knew to be wan and drawn. This was the closest she had been to him since they'd exchanged their vows. She tried not to look at his lips, not to wonder if they would feel the same against her mouth as they had against her fingers.

"It's late. You should go to your chamber," he said.

"Yes." Bed sounded wonderful…or did it? The realization that this was her wedding night hit her. *Is he sending me to my chamber because he wants…*

Perspiration broke out on her forehead—should she pull out a handkerchief, or hope he didn't notice?

"Are you all right?" he asked, frowning.

"I don't know where, er, my chamber…"

His face cleared. "The other side of the landing. First door on the left."

"You must be tired, too," she suggested.

"I have a few letters I must read tonight. I'll retire soon."

Unfortunately, he omitted to mention which room he planned to retire to.

Chapter Five

A footman conducted Constance to the countess's bedchamber. *Her* bedchamber.

A young woman dressed in a plain dark dress was waiting. She curtsied. "Good evening, my lady. I am Miriam Bligh, your maid."

"Oh," Constance said, surprised. She'd known she would end up with such a servant, but not so soon.

"I was a senior housemaid at Chalmers—the main Spenford estate," Miriam clarified, assessing Constance's blank look, "but I'm used to acting as lady's maid for guests." She rubbed her palms down her skirt. "But if your ladyship would prefer to hire her own maid…"

Constance had no idea what she preferred. But Miriam's pleasant face and tall, angular shape were practical and oddly reassuring. "Thank you, Miriam, I'm sure you will serve. Er, I suppose I should call you Bligh." Being addressed by her surname was a sign of superior status, just as it was for a valet.

Another curtsy, this one more a bob. "Yes, my lady, though I daresay I'll answer to either. If you're ready to retire, I'll assist you in undressing."

Constance had undressed herself, unassisted but for the

occasional help of one of her sisters, for as long as she could remember. But she wouldn't argue. Papa always said one should understand something before one sought to change it.

Did the same rule apply to husbands?

As Miriam unhooked her dress, Constance surveyed the room. The rose brocade canopy over the high bed matched the elegant curtains at the window. In addition to the dressing table with its padded stool, there was a French-style writing desk with matching chair. The carpet was woven in a floral pattern of faded reds and greens. Even in the candlelight, it was clear everything was of the finest quality.

"I took the liberty of arranging your clothing in the press, my lady," Miriam said.

That wouldn't have taken long.

"And I have laid out your nightdress," the maid continued.

Constance glanced involuntarily toward the bed. The one new item in her trunk had been this nightdress of finest lawn, sewn by her mother and sisters over the past few days.

"Madame Louvier will visit tomorrow morning," the girl continued. Correctly interpreting Constance's murmur as one of ignorance, she added, "Madame is the best modiste in London."

Constance would ordinarily be delighted at the thought of new dresses. But her immediate thought was that Amanda would be even more delighted, and the recollection of her sister brought a welling of sharp anger. She clenched her hands into fists.

"My lady?" Miriam held up the nightdress.

"I—yes—" she shook her fingers loose "—thank you."

When she was attired for bed, Miriam brushed out her hair.

"My lady has thick hair," she approved.

"The color is unremarkable," Constance pointed out.

She was pleased the maid didn't lie to flatter her, merely contented herself with, "The sheen is attractive."

Certainly under Miriam's vigorous brushing it did have more sheen than usual. In her beautiful new nightdress, her hair smooth and gleaming, Constance felt more a bride than she had during the wedding ceremony. *This is my wedding night.*

"If you need me, my lady, you have only to ring." Miriam indicated the bellpull.

"The, er, the earl's chamber?" Constance asked, as she climbed onto the bed.

"Through there." Miriam indicated a doorway to Constance's left. "Good night, my lady."

Constance lay in bed, blankets pulled up to her chin, observing the shadows that flickered on the wall.

Her wedding night. She'd thought of this moment in the past few days…what bride wouldn't? Curiosity, anticipation and—thanks to her mother's scrambled words on the subject of wifely duty—some trepidation had mingled within her.

When her husband came to her, she would be a wife in deed as well as in name.

Would he come to her tonight? He had been angry. With good reason.

She didn't want him to come to her in anger.

But they had struck a moment of accord during dinner, and he'd assured his mother he intended to be happy. If his anger had cooled, if he wanted to further his intimacy with the woman he had married…

He had thought he was marrying Amanda.

But he didn't love Amanda, Constance was certain. So although he might have wished for a prettier wife, he had no sentimental attachment to her sister.

If he came, he would forge a bond intended by God to unite man and wife.

Probably, he would not come.

But perhaps he would.

If Amanda was to be believed—she knew far more about it than any young lady ought—even the highest-ranked gentlemen looked forward to their wedding night with eagerness.

Could the intimacy God had designed overcome anger?

Of course it could.

Constance pinched her cheeks in the hope of bringing some color.

It had been probably thirty minutes since she left Marcus. He must by now be in his own room. She listened, but heard nothing through the thick walls. She wondered if he'd had a new nightshirt made for the occasion, and stifled a giggle.

Would he come?

He'd said there would be no annulment. He was punctilious in the performance of his duties, or so everyone said, and this was indeed a duty.

Constance arranged her hair about her shoulders. A nice sheen, Miriam had said. Maybe she should light another candle, to allow the sheen to be displayed.

Vanity, she chided herself. What must God think of her?

Oh, dear, she hadn't prayed tonight.

Constance slipped out of bed and onto her knees. With this deep carpet, a far more comfortable experience than at home. She prayed quickly, one eye cracked open to watch the door from her husband's chamber, and finished with a request for God's forgiveness of her haste.

She felt better when she was back in bed. More peaceful.

The candle sputtered, causing a moment's alarm, then it strengthened again. Real wax, not tallow, as they used at home whenever there was no company. The smell was far more pleasant.

Smell. Her mother had given Constance a small pot of precious perfume. Surely a bridegroom would prefer a fragrant bride on his wedding night?

If he were to come.

She slipped from bed again, scurried across the room like a thief, found the perfume on the dressing table. She dabbed a little on each wrist, and behind her ears, as she had seen her mother do. She sniffed her wrist. Floral. Sweet.

Once more, she settled herself against her pillows. She would not get out of bed again. She would be at peace, ready to welcome her husband.

She wished he would come.

"Your cravat survived the day in excellent shape, my lord," Harper, Marcus's valet, observed as he removed Marcus's left boot.

"You were right, as always, Harper," Marcus said. "The Mathematical was the style for the occasion."

Harper inclined his head. "I've had enough years dressing your lordship to know what's what."

Marcus smiled as he stifled a yawn.

"A very long day," Harper said sympathetically, pulling off the other boot. "The second time this week you've driven all the way to Hampshire and back."

"I remember both occasions only too well, thank you," Marcus said.

Harper chuckled. "Miss Powell said her ladyship, the dowager countess, seems well."

"Her improvement makes the long journeys worthwhile," Marcus agreed.

His mother's renewed strength had the quality of a miracle. Proof that the Almighty had accepted the bargain Marcus offered. He was inordinately thankful, at least as far as his mother was concerned. As for the rest...no denying the day hadn't turned out as planned. One could almost think the Lord intended a joke.

Marcus sighed. He wouldn't trade his mother's health for anything…but to have married a sparrow, when his position commanded a—a swan, and in such humiliating circumstances. He wasn't yet convinced his bride was innocent in this. Surely the sister, Amanda, would have confessed to Constance—no sibling would be that "mischievous."

If she'd confessed, and if Constance had decided to take advantage of what she dared consider his lack of courtesy in failing to remember which sister was which…it wouldn't be so strange. Plain as she was, she must have had limited marriage prospects. With bitterness he'd realized at the wedding breakfast that every other Somerton sister was livelier, and prettier, and more charming than the one he'd married. Which heightened his suspicions of a plot.

It had happened before—Marcus may not read his Bible often, but he knew the story of Rachel and Leah. Jacob fell in love with the beautiful Rachel, but at the wedding, his scheming father-in-law substituted his other daughter, Leah. Marcus imagined a veil had been used on that occasion, too. He couldn't remember if the text stated as much, but he'd always assumed Leah, the older girl, to be an old maid, with no prospects of marriage.

And now, he, Marcus, Earl of Spenford, one of England's most eligible bachelors, had rescued a soon-to-be old maid.

The worst of it was, people would say he must have been mad with love for her to choose her over her sisters—the kind of vulgar display of emotion to which he would never stoop. The kind of vulgar display against which Marcus's father had issued dire warnings, that had seen his grandfather almost destroy the earldom. The day the ton saw the Earl of Spenford sick at heart, chasing after a woman, would be a marvelous day indeed!

Marcus was glad his father wasn't here to witness the debacle. The previous earl had made no secret that he doubted Marcus was worthy of the title. Marcus had spent every day of every year after his brother's death proving himself, becoming a sincere imitation of his father. By the time his father died, he had almost succeeded.

At least his mother liked his bride. Marcus felt tension leave his shoulders at the thought. Indeed, he had inadvertently chosen her favorite Somerton girl. Or someone had, he thought wryly, as he unbuttoned his shirt.

Next time he negotiated with the Almighty he would be more specific in his demands.

Harper held out a nightshirt. "Is the countess—the new countess—satisfied with her maid, my lord?"

"I presume so." Marcus took the nightshirt. "Why wouldn't she be?"

Harper brushed at a speck on Marcus's coat before he replied. "Mrs. Collins sent Miriam Bligh up from Chalmers. You know what *she's* like."

"Should that name mean something to me?" Marcus said. Harper knew better than to refer to those days before Stephen's death, when Marcus had spent much of his free time with the servants' children. Back then, Harper had been the gamekeeper's son and Marcus's friend. Back then, everything had been different.

The valet ducked his head. "I know something of the skills and demeanor required for a senior lady's maid, my lord." He deftly removed any personal history from the discussion. "Miss Bligh has limited experience and a tendency to argue with her superiors. The position may be above her touch."

It wasn't like Harper to speak ill of anyone without cause.

Marcus didn't want an incompetent dressing his countess. Especially *this* countess, who would need a skilled servant to make the most of her appearance.

He slipped the nightshirt over his head. "I will talk to her ladyship."

Harper bowed. "I'll leave these candles alight, my lord. For when you return."

Return? He wasn't going—

Blast! It was his wedding night.

Was that why Constance seemed nervous?

Or had he imagined her nerves?

Yet if her nerves were imaginary, the duty was very real.

A Brookstone never shirked his duty.

Marcus eyed the door that led to his wife's chamber. Renewed anger surged through him. Yes, she had been kind to his mother, but that didn't change the fact that the Somerton family had made a fool of him. He was in no way reconciled to the prospect of a lifetime with her.

Surely a man could be excused his duty when he had been duped into marriage?

Or should a man give his bride the benefit of the doubt?

By now, Marcus must be ready for bed, Constance decided. Perhaps he liked to read in bed, as she did herself. Maybe they would converse about books—though probably not tonight—and discover a shared interest that would strengthen the bond between them.

Would he stay the whole night with her? Her parents had always shared a room. She imagined it would be lovely to have a husband curled next to one in bed. Especially in winter.

Perhaps he won't stay. It may not be the accepted thing.

Perhaps he won't come at all.

He'd already said this marriage wouldn't be annulled. She was his wife; he would want an heir. She may not be as pretty as Amanda, but she was not repulsive. Her hair had sheen. Her eyes were attractive.

She felt a spurt of alarm that he may not have had time to notice her eyes, nor their well-shaped brows.

She thought back over the day. He had examined her when he'd realized she wasn't the woman he'd planned to marry, but that scrutiny had doubtless focused on her disadvantages.

His own eyes had been full of shock, then anger, yet she had still noticed their brilliant blue. Hers…oh, gracious, in the carriage her eyes had been awash with tears. No man was attracted to female tears…it was a known fact.

Constance groaned, beset by the fear that in failing to show off her best feature, her only good feature—*my hair also has sheen, but he won't have seen that, for it was pinned up*—she might have given her husband no reason to come to her tonight.

He is my husband; that is reason enough.

And her figure was good, as good as Amanda's. She must assume he'd noticed that.

She tried to calm her mind, to settle herself against the pillows. She'd never been so tired…but she mustn't fall asleep. She didn't want him to find her snoring, or worse, drooling. None of her sisters had made that complaint against her—Isabel was the only one who snored, a habit that took the tiniest gloss off her perfection and thus endeared her to her siblings. But Constance couldn't count on history. It would be cruelly typical if the drama and exhaustion of the day were to bring on a sudden bout of snoring and drooling!

So she stayed high on the pillows, where her hair caught the candlelight, reciting psalms in her head. When the psalms tended to have a lullaby effect, she switched to Proverbs, always improving to the mind.

How long had she been waiting? Surely he would come soon?

She prayed for patience.

She waited.

She prayed again.

He did not come.

Chapter Six

❦

Constance didn't fall asleep until dawn streaked the sky. As a consequence, she didn't wake until half past nine. She dressed quickly, refusing Miriam's offer of a more complicated hairstyle than her usual simple knot. That left time for a brief breakfast alone in the yellow-toned breakfast room—a footman informed her the earl had gone riding early—before Madame Louvier arrived.

The couturiere insisted that every one of the prevailing styles would suit Constance's "exquisite figure" to perfection. Constance had no idea of the prevailing styles, but was grateful.

The season's colors, were a different matter, the seamstress said with a very Gallic moue. "Not the best, *madame*. You are pale, which is good, but you are in danger of being washed out. If *madame* will pardon me."

Constance allowed the woman to guide her almost entirely, which delighted Madame Louvier, who departed with the promise to have the first day dress delivered by tomorrow morning. Then another day dress and an evening gown by Monday evening. The rest of the wardrobe would follow as soon as possible.

In the meantime, Constance wore her sprigged muslin,

a dress that had seen at least two years' service, to visit her mother-in-law, who seemed none the worse for her late night. That is, if one overlooked that a lady of not quite sixty years of age looked at least sixty-five.

The dowager began by listing all of Constance's new relatives and where they fit in the family. Lady Spenford was the daughter of a duke, so between her family—the Havants—and the Spenfords, there were an inordinate number of titles. Constance only managed to store a fraction of them. One name did strike a chord, that of Marcus's cousin Lucinda—one of the few people who used his Christian name.

"She's Mrs. Quayle, married to Jonathan, youngest son of the Earl of Hazlemere," Helen said. "I'd be surprised if Lucinda doesn't visit you today. She must always be in the thick of the news."

"I was under the impression the earl—er, Marcus—doesn't care for gossip," Constance said.

"True," Helen agreed. "But he and Lucinda spent a great deal of time together in their youth. Their closeness persists despite Lucinda's tendency to say too much. Now, my dear, am I right in thinking you have already been presented at Court?"

"Yes, Mama. My sister Serena and I were presented in the company of my aunt, Miss Jane Somerton, last year." Her aunt was currently traveling on the Continent, not expected back in London for at least a month.

"Then there's no reason why you shouldn't appear immediately in society. What a surprise you'll be to our friends."

Did she mean a good surprise, or a bad one?

"I only hope they take the shock as well as you have, Mama," Constance said, in an attempt at humor.

"Not a shock, my dear. Although—" she paused delicately "—I admit, this happened rather fast. It was only last Sunday

I told Marcus I'd love to see him married to a nice, Christian girl. He left the next day to see your father, and here you are."

That was such a ridiculously shortened version of the disastrous wedding story, Constance didn't know what to say. "You have a most obedient son," she managed.

Helen tipped her head back against her pillows. "He's perfect," she agreed gloomily.

Constance blinked. "I beg your pardon?"

"One thing you'll soon learn with Marcus—he always does the correct thing," Helen said. "He never makes a mistake. Never."

Constance could think of an enormous mistake Marcus had made yesterday at quarter past eleven. She chose not to mention it.

Helen must have sensed her doubts. "I'm not saying he's infallible. But Marcus sets such high standards for himself. His father was the same, devoted to his duty and the earldom."

"Those are good things," Constance reminded her.

"I used to think so," the dowager agreed. "But now…well, I've stared death in the eye over the past few months. Believe me, Constance, I don't worry about whether my life has been dutiful enough. I worry whether I've loved enough."

"Do you think one must choose between duty and love?" Constance asked.

"Not necessarily. But for Marcus…" Helen plucked at her blanket. "When he became heir apparent after Stephen's death, his father found him lacking in the qualities he considered essential—authority and bearing and dignity. Marcus wasn't to blame. I was too doting a mama, and he hadn't been groomed for the title from a young age, as Stephen had. I think sometimes the poor boy despaired of attaining what my husband considered the acceptable standard for an earl."

"So you think he became wedded to his duty to please his father?"

"I feel guilty," Helen said frankly. "I withdrew from his upbringing, believing it the right thing to do. But in becoming the perfect earl, he's grown intolerant of others' weaknesses. It stops him from getting close to people."

"You and Marcus are close," Constance reminded her. "And lovely though you are, I doubt you're perfect."

Helen chuckled. "Far from it. Luckily, the maternal bond seems to exempt me from his high standards. The thing is, Constance, I don't want to die knowing it's at least partly my fault that my son is unhappy."

"You think he's unhappy?" Constance asked.

"How can he not be? He's proud, and I believe he must be lonely. If nothing short of perfection satisfies him, he'll never find contentment in this earthly life."

Misgiving flooded Constance. He could never be content with *her*.

Helen glanced at the clock on the mantelpiece. "Gracious, it's past one o'clock. Luncheon will be served. You must go down." As Constance stood, Helen grasped her fingers. "Constance, my hope and prayer is that you will soften dear Marcus's heart."

Given pen and paper, Constance could list a dozen reasons why she wouldn't succeed in working such miracles on *Dear Marcus's* heart. Number one: he'd been duped into marrying the wrong woman.

But Helen's story had given her insight into why Marcus was so proud. The dowager's loyalty had been to her husband—it was perhaps too late for her to show Marcus another way. But Constance could teach him that other things were just as important as status and reputation. Even more important.

The sooner she started, the better.

* * *

The news that his cousin Lucinda had come calling made Marcus groan.

"Shall I tell her you're not available, my lord?" Dallow asked.

He'd have to face Lucinda sooner or later, but maybe he could deter her from meeting Constance before his wife took delivery of the dresses and other things that might make her look more countesslike. Marcus closed the accounts book on his desk—at least he had an excuse to stop staring at those depressing figures. "Where is the countess?"

"With Mrs. Quayle, my lord."

"What?" Marcus pushed his seat back quickly.

"Lady Spenford was just finishing a meeting with Mrs. Matlock in the small salon when Mrs. Quayle arrived." Matlock, the housekeeper, was doubtless ecstatic to have a new mistress to take an interest in the meals and the running of the house, something the dowager hadn't been able to do for some months. "Mrs. Quayle took advantage of the open door to, er, present herself to Lady Spenford," Dallow said.

Typical of his overwhelming, inquisitive cousin.

"I'll join them right away," Marcus said.

As he hurried upstairs, he inwardly cursed his own haste in telling Lucinda earlier in the week that he was about to marry. She'd hounded him for details and had been bemused to learn the new countess was a parson's daughter. Well-born, but cut off from her titled relations through some family rift. No fortune. "How *interesting*," she'd said. And Marcus, hating that she would be judging the new Countess of Spenford as an inferior creature, had declared, "She is a great beauty."

Which immediately made the countess acceptable in Lucinda's mind, and would have done so in the eyes of the rest of the ton.

If not for the obvious problem.

Lucinda would take one look at Constance and come to the only rational conclusion—that he'd married the wrong bride was *not* rational—that he'd fallen head over heels in love.

He shuddered as he stopped outside the small salon, his hand on the door handle. He needed to convince Lucinda that Constance was a perfectly eligible bride for him. Not some foolish love affair. Marcus closed his eyes, feeling the need for divine assistance. When he couldn't think of a prayer that didn't sound insulting, he gave up, and opened the door.

Lucinda shared a sofa with Constance, the two women angled toward each other. Lucinda looked...*stunned* was the best word for it. Her slightly sagging jaw and overbright smile said, *This is Marcus's idea of a great beauty? Has he gone mad?*

His cousin couldn't have been more different from his wife. Lucinda's flaxen hair and rosebud mouth had secured her dozens of suitors when she came out, and an early marriage proposal from the most eligible Jonathan Quayle. The dashing pelisse she wore—purple silk trimmed with black—was something only a supremely confident woman would wear.

Whereas his wife... Her appearance wasn't helped by that dowdy sprig muslin, but he suspected that even when Constance had her new dresses, she wouldn't carry them off with Lucinda's careless elegance. Her hair looked different today—softer, perhaps. But the plain style did little to become her.

She owed it to her position, and to him, to rise to the appropriate standard.

"Marcus!" Lucinda caught sight of him. "I've just been getting to know your bride." She almost managed to keep the surprise out of her voice.

Marcus kissed her cheek. "Good afternoon, Lucinda...

ma'am." The *ma'am* was to Constance. "How are you today?" He hadn't seen her, having breakfasted early and taken luncheon in his study.

As he sat in the chair next to her, something flashed in her eyes: an accusation of neglect? Then she seemed to pull herself into some kind of resolution—what a transparent face she had—as she spread her fingers on her skirt of her muslin dress and said, "I'm well, thank you."

The smile she gave him was oddly sympathetic. Not that she could know he was alarmed as to what Lucinda would think of her—and presumably she wouldn't be sympathetic if she did.

"Lady Spenford is telling me about her family," Lucinda said.

"Did she mention that her father, Reverend Somerton, is a nephew of the Duke of Medway?" Marcus asked.

Constance frowned. "Our Medway relations don't speak to us, apart from my Aunt Jane."

"The Reverend and Mrs. Somerton are most gracious," Marcus said. Constance's frown deepened, as if *gracious* weren't a compliment. Probably some ridiculous rectory prejudice. "It's important to marry into a family one likes." A flimsy argument in favor of wedding a plain-looking country girl, but Lucinda's own mother-in-law was a tartar of the worst order, so she might agree.

Indeed, his cousin nodded thoughtfully. Marcus began to feel hopeful he might pull this off.

"The Somertons have an unblemished reputation," he continued, pointing out an advantage Lucinda knew was important to him.

A muffled, high-pitched sound came from Constance. Possibly a squeak of outrage. She was intelligent enough to know he was making excuses for her. Too bad, it had to be done.

"My mother considered the match most eligible," he said.

Lucinda had a great deal of respect for her Aunt Helen's views.

Lucinda was nodding in an encouraging fashion. "Well, Marcus, all I can say is, your countess is delightful."

Marcus smiled.

Constance said politely, "I hardly think you know me well enough to reach that conclusion, Mrs. Quayle."

What on earth…? Marcus kept his gaze on Lucinda, while he slid his right foot toward Constance. He gave her slipper a sharp nudge.

Without looking at him, she moved her foot away.

Lucinda blinked twice. Then, thankfully, she giggled. "No, but I had to say it out of politeness, didn't I?"

Constance laughed. Marcus hadn't heard her laugh before—it was low, almost musical. Warming.

"In that case, you might need to teach me London manners," she said. "My father always exhorted me and my sisters to either speak the truth or say nothing at all."

Marcus groaned, foreseeing numerous awkward encounters ahead. Instead of looking annoyed, Constance gave him that sympathetic smile again.

He sensed it could soon become an irritant.

"You poor girl," Lucinda breathed. "That's just the sort of silly thing a parson *would* say. How on earth do you survive in society?"

"Mostly by saying nothing at all," Constance admitted.

Marcus's chuckle was drowned by Lucinda's peal of laughter.

"Well, that won't suffice in London," Lucinda said. "Now, Constance—you must call me Lucinda, by the way—I want to know all about you. How can I be your first friend here if I don't?"

"Don't tell my cousin anything you don't wish aired all over town," Marcus warned Constance.

"Marcus, I'm not *that* indiscreet." But Lucinda was laughing. "I try not to gossip," she confided to Constance. "But one sees and hears so much, one would burst if one tried to hold it in."

"I can see that would be most uncomfortable," Constance said.

At least, he noticed, Lucinda hadn't overwhelmed her. In fact, Constance hadn't been overwhelmed by any of the events of the past, tumultuous twenty-four hours. Perhaps she did have the potential to develop the dignity of a countess.

"I am quite discreet in winter," Lucinda offered in her own defense.

"When you're in the country, with no source of gossip, nor anyone to tell it to," Marcus retorted.

"The good thing is, I know everything about everyone." Lucinda ignored him. "So I shall bring you up with all the news before you meet the world, Constance. And I warn you—" she wagged a finger "—everyone is agog to meet the Countess of Spenford."

Not before she had her new dresses, and her maid had proven herself competent to present Constance the way his countess should appear, Marcus thought. No doubt Lucinda had already blabbed all over town that he was marrying an impoverished beauty—his own fault, he realized, cursing the moment of pride that had made him boast. As Constance looked now, she would be a lamb to the slaughter of razor-sharp tongues.

Constance's brow wrinkled. "There's nothing amazing about me."

"My dear, you've snatched the biggest prize on London's marriage mart. If that's not amazing…" Lucinda spread her hands as if to suggest that even Mr. Murdoch's invention of gas lighting couldn't compete with Constance's achievement.

"It doesn't seem right to think of a man as a prize," Constance said.

Marcus blinked. Of course he was a prize!

"Of course he's a prize." Lucinda saved him the need to state the glaringly obvious. "Constance, you can't be *that* rural. He's the Earl of Spenford."

"Which implies that if he were not the earl, people wouldn't like him so well. My father teaches never to judge a man by his status."

Marcus couldn't remember seeing his cousin reduced to stunned silence before. It would have been amusing, if it hadn't been at his expense.

"If he were not the earl, he wouldn't be the same person," Lucinda said at last. With a naughty grin at Marcus, she added, "But he'd still be as handsome. You do think he's handsome, don't you, Constance? I'm relying on you to speak the truth or say nothing at all," she teased.

"Very handsome," Constance agreed.

Marcus could not feel flattered: her tone implied his appearance wasn't important—no doubt another stricture of her father's—as well as, he suspected, a lingering doubt as to his likability.

Yes, all right, I should have bid her good-night last night. And good morning this morning.

"Marcus's address is beyond fault," Lucinda pointed out; she'd obviously discerned Constance's lack of excitement over his good looks. "His manner is so polished."

Constance looked confused. "Perhaps he has been…less formal in his manner to me."

Blast it, she was right. Marcus hadn't yet favored his wife with the polished address for which society knew him. He'd fallen short of his own standard.

"I dare say, since he was *wooing* you," Lucinda said with a relish that made Marcus wince. "And I'm sure he was too modest to tell you his many accomplishments." She tut-tutted at this oversight.

"Excessive modesty is not one of the faults I've discerned in him," Constance said with a slight smile.

She'd gone too far! Marcus shot her a quelling look, but since she wasn't paying him any attention, she remained un-quelled.

"Excellent," Lucinda said. "So he's told you he can fire a bullet through an ace at sixty paces—"

"Not in polite society," Marcus interjected.

"—and that he's never lost a curricle race," Lucinda said triumphantly.

"Most impressive," Constance murmured.

She fooled no one.

Lucinda set her teacup down with a rattle. "It seems none of the things our society holds dear matter to you," she said with uncharacteristic uncertainty.

In a different conversation, Marcus would have laughed to see her so confused.

"Would it be too vulgar of me to mention Spenford's for-tune?" Lucinda asked.

"Yes!" Marcus snapped.

"But, Marcus, Jonathan says no one manages financial af-fairs as well as you. His skill has made all the difference to the family fortunes," she told Constance. "One more reason why he's deemed such a catch."

"I don't calculate the worth of my husband in pounds and guineas," Constance said apologetically.

Marcus felt as if he'd stumbled into a back-to-front world, sense turned to nonsense. He had lived half his years as heir and then Earl of Spenford. Lived them right, and well, and properly. And now his *wife* was attempting to shred the very fabric of those years?

"Ah, my dear, I begin to understand." Lucinda recovered

her self-possession and shifted to the edge of her seat, eyes gleaming in a way that Marcus knew meant she'd just sniffed out a new piece of gossip and was about to pounce. "You chose to marry my cousin—but not for his looks, his manner, his sporting prowess or his fortune. Which can only mean—"

"Which can only mean you've badgered my wife more than enough," Marcus forestalled her.

"You're right, Lucinda," Constance said. "I married my husband for his kindness."

What?

Constance's chin—every bit as pointy as it had been yesterday—went up in the air, as if she was ready to defend her own. The way she'd defended her father to Marcus yesterday. She gave him a reassuring smile, which only worried him. From what, exactly, did she plan on defending him?

"To be sure, a man who is kind to his mama will also be kind to his wife," Lucinda agreed knowledgeably, giving Marcus a twinge of guilt that he didn't appreciate. "But that can't be—"

"I don't mean his kindness to the dowager countess," Constance said. "Though that's admirable."

"You actually admire me for something?" Marcus asked drily.

"I'm referring to an incident in Piper's Mead—the village where I grew up—some three years ago," Constance said.

Lucinda leaned forward eagerly. Marcus had no idea what Constance was about to say. Instinct told him to be wary, but short of clamping a hand over his wife's mouth, he couldn't stop her.

"I was walking to the village to buy thread when I encountered a group of youths who were—" Constance swallowed "—abusing a puppy. They were kicking it as if it were a—a ball."

Lucinda gave a squeal of revulsion.

"This is hardly fodder for polite conversation," Marcus said. He recalled the event, but hadn't recognized Constance as the young woman he'd found sitting in the roadway, the pathetic animal cradled in her lap.

"I dispatched the boys without much bother," Constance said. Marcus found himself wondering how she had achieved that. "But the puppy was near dead."

Lucinda moaned.

Marcus half expected to have to ring for smelling salts; this story wasn't fit for the drawing room. Constance would do better to extol his legendary largesse toward his tenants at Christmas. Generosity on an earlworthy scale.

"Spenford came along in his curricle," Constance said.

"I took up the dog and had my groom look after it," Marcus said quickly. "Anyone would have helped that wretched animal."

He remembered now that the girl—Constance—had bitten her lip fiercely, saying in the shakiest of voices that she didn't dare cry, or the dog might feel its pain more keenly.

Which made no more sense now than it did then. Nor did it make sense that she had taken his assistance so much to heart that she still remembered it with such clarity.

"Many men would have decided the creature was beyond help and would have put it out of its misery," Constance countered with surprising firmness.

"Better indeed to have ended its suffering." Lucinda cast Marcus a reproachful look.

Marcus couldn't remember why he hadn't.

"I was surprised he didn't," Constance admitted. "This was no treasured pet, Mrs. Quayle—Lucinda—escaped from Palfont or another estate. This was a mongrel of distinctly unattractive appearance and surly manner. But Lord Spenford used his handkerchief to clean the blood from its body—"

Marcus was oddly reminded of handing her his handkerchief

in the coach yesterday and her refusal to accept it "—and gave it water from his own flask."

Lucinda shuddered. Marcus shrugged apologetically.

"He took the puppy home and gave it to his stable-lad to look after."

"Kind indeed," said his cousin.

"And there ends the tale," he said heartily.

"Not quite," Constance contradicted him. What a surprise. "Your mother's stable-lad is the son of our gardener. I learned from John that the puppy didn't at first fare well. That unless you personally offered his food he wouldn't eat."

"A stubborn creature," Marcus said impatiently.

Constance turned to Lucinda. "So the earl took the puppy into his care, nursing it back to health."

"I had no idea you were so tenderhearted Marcus," his cousin said, astonished.

"Harper did most of the work," he muttered, not entirely truthfully. Harper had claimed the dog made him sneeze.

"Where is the animal now?" Lucinda glanced around as if she expected it to dash out from behind the curtains.

He lifted one shoulder. "When it was recovered I sent it to Chalmers. I was relieved to be rid of it." He heard the hint of defiance in his own voice. His father would have been appalled at the amount of time he'd devoted to a dog so unsuited to either a useful occupation like hunting, or the privileged life of a pampered pet.

"That's the most romantic story I ever heard," Lucinda said.

Marcus rolled his eyes.

"Romantic?" Constance queried.

"Quite obviously, Constance—" Lucinda paused for dramatic effect "—you fell in love with our tenderhearted earl."

No! Exactly what Marcus had entered this room to prevent: ridiculous conjecture about this being a love match. Now Lucinda would consider she had full justification to spread the story his countess was besotted with him. And he with her.

"Not at all," he said lightly. "Constance fell in love with the puppy. Isn't that right, er, my dear?"

He waited for Constance to agree.

Instead, he heard a choked gurgle. Turning, he found her face fiery red, an unflattering scarlet that bore no resemblance to the pink-tinged blush extolled by the poets. Her brown eyes were tortured as she stared at him in a mute appeal—distressed, but hopeful—that reminded him very much of that puppy.

Comprehension dawned. And with it, horror.

Lucinda was right. His wife had married him for love.

Chapter Seven

Why had Marcus reacted so oddly to a story that showed him in a positive light, Constance wondered as she lay awake early on Sunday. She was accustomed to early rising on this, the busiest day in her family's week. Bligh had not yet arrived with her cup of chocolate, an indulgence Constance was keen to enjoy again.

Marcus had bundled his cousin out of the house yesterday with a haste that would have been rude with a less intimate acquaintance. He'd informed Constance he would dine at his club, speaking with a rigid self-control she didn't understand. A footman had confided the earl was unlikely to return before the small hours of the morning.

"Very odd," Constance said aloud to herself.

Unfortunately, she didn't fool herself. She could no longer avoid the suspicion lurking in the back of her mind. That Marcus's ill humor was the result of Lucinda's suggestion that Constance was in love with him.

If only Constance had managed to come up with a lighthearted riposte that would have treated Lucinda's comment as an amusing joke. But the horror in Marcus's face had filled her with humiliation and she hadn't been able to say a word.

Instead, she rather feared her eyes had done the talking…
and that they'd betrayed her.

*It's not such a terrible thing, is it, for me to love my hus-
band? Awkward for me, perhaps, when my feelings aren't
returned, but why should it anger him?*

Besides, he might think she loved him, but he couldn't
possibly *know* it. And since he had such a big opinion of his
own worth already, it was probably best if he didn't.

Constance abandoned any immediate plans to "show
Marcus another way" to live. She would channel her energies into acting as if Lucinda had never said such a thing, as
if the embarrassingly desperate look Constance had given
him had been about something else entirely. That would be
more than enough of a challenge.

She adjusted her pillow so the morning sunshine stream-
ing through the double sash window didn't directly hit her
eyes. Once again, it was clear she had slept alone. Yesterday
had been excusable, after their long journey. But today…

Would it be very proud of her to hide the fact of her husband's lack of interest?

Before she could think too hard, Constance moved to the
other side of the bed and snuggled into the pillows there. She
squirmed about, then decided to stay where she was, since
the sun did not blind her in this position.

When Miriam arrived a few minutes later, both sides of
the bed looked well-used.

"Good morning, my lady." The tiniest flicker of the maid's
eyes took in the rumpled bedding.

Constance was glad she'd made the effort. Marcus should
be equally glad—he would hate to be the subject of gossip
below stairs.

"Have you found out where his lordship worships?" Constance had charged her maid with that task last night.

"It seems his lordship's church attendance is irregular. The dowager normally attends St. George's on Hanover Square, but in her illness she has a curate visit to conduct a private service." She proffered a folded sheet of paper. "Her ladyship has sent a note."

My dear Constance, I would be delighted if you would join me to hear Mr. Robertson preach at nine o'clock this morning. We will partake of Communion.

Perfect. Constance needed to find refreshment in the liturgies that put God at the front of her mind, in the quiet of prayer to restore her confused soul.

It was Miriam's day off, but before she left she arranged Constance's hair and helped her into her new day dress, delivered last night from Madame Louvier.

The modiste had chosen well, Constance thought as she surveyed herself in the mirror when she was alone. The cream-colored silk warmed her complexion, and the simple style displayed her figure to advantage.

As she picked up her Bible, her door opened and Marcus walked in.

"Good morning, ma'am."

Now he comes to my chamber.

As she returned his greeting, she tamped down a surge of embarrassment about yesterday. "Are you here to accompany me to your mother's church service?"

Worshipping together might be just what they needed.

"May we talk?" he said.

Talking was good, too.

"Of course we may," she said. Turned out his question had been rhetorical: he recoiled slightly, the way he did whenever she had the temerity to comment on his actions, or, in this case, to assume his words were a request, rather than an order. "Perhaps we could sit…" A quick glance reminded her there was only one chair and, worse, if he looked to his right, he might see she had rumpled both sides of the bed and guess her motive. "On second thought, I prefer to stand."

She took a quick step to his left, toward the dressing table, forcing him to turn to her. The morning sun struck his face.

"You look awful," she blurted.

He was pale, with deep shadows under his eyes, as if he hadn't slept. Exhaustion grooved the corners of his mouth.

"My compliments to you, too, madam." Who knew it was possible to bow sarcastically?

"Did you sleep at all?" she asked, in the hope a soft answer would turn away wrath, as one of the Proverbs she'd recited on her wedding night suggested. "It cannot be good for you to stay out so late."

"I spent much of last night thinking," he growled. "It's clear our situation cannot continue as it is."

"Whatever I said yesterday to distress you, I apologize," she said, still employing the "soft answer" tactic.

"Was Lucinda right?" he demanded. "Are you in love with me?"

So much for pretending it never happened!

"I—well—really!" she stuttered. Belatedly, she summoned her dignity. "That is an outrageous question, and it is none of your—"

"Speak the truth, madam," he said softly, "or say nothing at all."

Just like that, he doused her fire.

Constance had no choice. She clamped her lips together so hard, she forgot to breathe.

Marcus bit off an exclamation. "You made a fool of me," he said. "It's becoming a habit, and I will not tolerate it."

"Is this another example of your famous polished address?" she said shakily.

Unfortunately that came out more confrontational than soft.

A dull red seeped along his jaw, but he continued. "Imagine my shock to discover you have felt a—a tenderness for me ever since the incident you described to my cousin."

She tried to imagine shock, tried very hard, but could conjure nothing more dramatic than surprise. "So...you weren't flattered?" she suggested cautiously.

He reached her in two forceful strides. "For Lucinda, it's one short step from knowing you...you have feelings for me to deeming *me* in the grip of a wild infatuation. I believe she was already entertaining that view."

Constance snorted. "Why on earth should she think you're infatuated with me?"

Was it her imagination, or did he blush?

"And from there," he said, "it's an even shorter step to the world hearing her views."

Constance tightened her grip on her Bible. "You think you would look a fool to...to fall in love with a plain wife."

"I would be a fool to fall in love with anyone!" he barked.

It seemed that some small part of her had imagined he would say he hadn't noticed her lack of beauty, or that it was of no importance. His failure to do so left her unreasonably stunned.

He paused, as if she'd made some noise, then scrutinized her face. "You're not going to cry, are you?"

She shook her head.

With less than his normal certainty, he said, "You're not a beauty. I won't lie to you."

She was starting to wonder if honesty was always a virtue.

"But, er, you look well in your new dress." He fumbled for the words. "Your eyes are...expressive."

Constance found her voice. "Please do not exert yourself to such crumbs of consolation."

One side of his mouth almost twitched. "Your chin," he said, "is telling."

Telling? What kind of a compliment was that? An insult, more likely.

"I'm overwhelmed by your flattery," she said, and was happy with the briskness of her tone. "But I don't understand why you'd be a fool to fall in love with any woman."

He sighed. "Your father raised you with an unfortunate need to understand things."

"Unfortunate for whom?" she inquired.

His eyebrows drew together. Then he said abruptly, "My grandfather married for love. It was an obsession that caused him to neglect the estates, and to spend money recklessly."

"So you think any man who marries for love will lose all self-control?"

"His actions almost wiped out the family's assets. He exposed the Spenford name to ridicule. He lost the confidence of our tenants, our stewards, our bankers."

"And yet the earldom survived," she said.

"Only because my grandfather died," he said bluntly. "My father inherited the title and immediately set about restoring our good name. He had the sense to marry the daughter of a duke—"

"You're saying he married your mama for her money?" Constance asked.

He ignored her. "He set standards of conduct for himself and others that restored faith in the family. Even so, I inherited debts that, if called in, could ruin the house of Spenford."

"Perhaps you might have told me some of those details before I met your cousin and gave her cause to gossip," she said.

"Would it have made a difference?"

She couldn't honestly say it would, so she didn't answer.

His lips flattened. "More to the point, only rigid adherence to my father's practices will secure the earldom—I could have no better example than him for my own tenure as earl."

"I'm surprised you didn't marry for money yourself," she observed.

"If Mama had not been ill, I would have looked to contract a match as mutually advantageous as my parents'," he said coolly. "The circumstances that led me to offer for you—"

"For my sister," she corrected him.

"—were unusual. But acceptable. What is not acceptable is any suggestion that I've lost my head over you. Or you over me."

"Are you saying," she asked slowly, "you would rather I'd married you for your wealth and status?"

"A thousand times rather!" Distractedly, he picked up the jar of perfume she had used on her wedding night and turned it over in his hand, unseeing. He set it down again. "Madam, I would rather you had married me for something I am willing to offer you."

Constance pressed her Bible to her chest as if it could stem the steady seep of hope from her heart. "I...don't know what to say." Beyond, *I want to go home.*

He raised one eyebrow. "An unusual circumstance for you, surely?" When she did not respond to his inappropriate levity, he said gruffly, "I don't want my staff, or my tenants, or society thinking I have the same weakness of mind as my grandfather. You have twice made a fool of me—and your emotional attachment makes me wonder anew if you were party to your sister's scheme."

"I wasn't!" It came out weak, watery.

"You won't have a third opportunity to undermine me," he said. "I have decided on steps to preserve my dignity and my family's reputation."

A shiver ran through Constance. "What steps?"

"I believe my mother's health will continue to improve," he said. "As soon as she's well enough to travel, you will accompany her to Chalmers. She'll enjoy the country air, and it'll be an excellent opportunity for you to learn about the house and its running."

"And where will you be?"

"I shall stay here in London until the end of the Season."

This was wrong, all wrong. Constance set her Bible on the dressing table, and squared her shoulders. "I believe marriage is a commitment to a shared life."

"In the ton," he said, "it's not uncommon for a husband and wife to live separate lives. By doing so, we'll convince the world there was no wild passion involved in our decision to wed."

He needn't worry about that, Constance thought. If his manner in public was as it was now, the world would have no trouble believing he didn't love her.

"Separate lives…that's not how the Bible describes a marriage," she said. "My father told me you prayed about our union."

His chin, which she would not have described in such idiotic terms as *telling,* jerked back. "Is there anything your father doesn't discuss with you?" he demanded.

She eyed him steadily. "*Did* you ask God's guidance about our marriage?"

"Not…exactly." He ran a hand around the back of his neck.

"What *exactly* did you do?" she persisted.

"I agreed with God," he said, exasperated, "that if I married one of Reverend Somerton's daughters, He would heal my mother."

Constance gaped. "You can't bargain with God like that!"

"I realize that as the daughter of a parson you may feel you can lay greater claim to knowing God's will, but I'm afraid you're wrong." He took a step backward. Away from her. "My mother is improved to a near-miraculous extent. You will travel to Chalmers with her at her earliest convenience."

With another bow, he left the room.

Left Constance alone. Again.

She sank down onto the little stool at the dressing table and picked up in the small, ivory-framed mirror. She faced herself in the glass. Faced the truth, not some fantasy about warm eyes and shiny hair and a kind heart making Constance Somerton the treasure of the Earl of Spenford.

She had married a man she believed had chosen her above others. When that proved untrue, she'd clung to her "knowledge" that he was a kind man, a praying man, and the hope that those qualities could be the foundation of a loving marriage.

He claimed to have been made a fool of. Truth was, *she* was the fool.

Shame welled within her, shame that she'd been so naive. That she'd judged him a fine man on so little acquaintance. That she'd walked without question into the kind of marriage that was not what God could want—most certainly not what *she* wanted.

She would be overlooked once again, and it was her own fault.

The girl in the mirror mouthed a protest.

No more.

Her vehemence, the tremor of anger that shook the hand holding the mirror, surprised her. Constance thought for a moment. Then she spoke aloud, a new vow, and watched her reflected mouth form the words.

"He will not send me away. I will not go."

Chapter Eight

It was all very well to decide she wouldn't go to Chalmers. Conveying that decision to her husband was another matter.

For almost the next two weeks, Constance didn't see Marcus. He was always busy in his study, or out riding in Hyde Park, or some such thing. She didn't want to draw attention to his neglect by communicating through the servants, and he took care to avoid chance encounters. In the evenings, he went out in society, leaving behind a wife who owned six beautiful evening gowns but had yet to wear any of them.

Her new morning and afternoon dresses were wasted, too, because although she'd received several notes from society ladies welcoming her to London and expressing a desire to make her acquaintance, no one had called to see her. Protocol dictated she couldn't make calls until she'd been called on. Since she doubted every lady in the ton entirely lacked manners, she had to assume Marcus was in some way responsible for her being more or less ignored. Possibly he'd said she was busy nursing his mother.

She had attempted to call on Lucinda, at her mother-in-law's suggestion, only to discover Lucinda laid low by the influenza. A mild case, the butler had informed her, but Mrs. Quayle was not up to receiving visitors for some days. Constance had left a note of condolence. The next step was Lucinda's.

Now it was nine o'clock on Thursday evening. Constance had dined early with the dowager, had reread her mother's latest letter and written a reply, and was now sewing in the smaller of the two drawing rooms, with Miriam for company. Mr. Bird had at last given his approval for Helen to travel, and tomorrow, they were to leave for Chalmers—their trunks were packed. Unless Constance dug her heels in, she would be gone from here before nine in the morning. She contemplated the prospect of a last-moment standoff with her husband in front of Dallow and her mother-in-law, and wasn't certain she could carry it through.

She set down her stitching—a new embroidery of a Bible verse, to grace her new bedroom—with a sigh.

"My lady?" Miriam looked up from her repairs to a stocking. "Is there anything you need?"

A loving husband. "Nothing at all," Constance assured her.

"I hope you will like Chalmers," Miriam said tentatively. "'Tis a place close to his lordship's heart."

Constance had given up disordering her pillows after a few days, so she had no doubt the servants speculated about her marriage. She set down her needle. "Did you see much of Lord Spenford when he was younger, Miriam?"

The maid lifted her stitching to the light and appraised it critically. "Not exactly, my lady. He and Mr. Harper were friends—"

"He and Harper? His valet?" Constance couldn't imagine it.

Miriam nodded. "Mr. Harper's father is the head gamekeeper at Chalmers. Mr. Harper's just a year younger than his lordship, so as lads they used to go out shooting and fishing together."

"You must have been just a child," Constance suggested.

"I particularly remember Lord Spenford from when I was around ten, my lady, so he would have been fourteen."

"What was he like?" Constance asked.

"To be honest, my lady—" Miriam poked her needle into the stocking and set it down "—I mainly had eyes for Tom—that's Mr. Harper. Quite besotted, I was. But I will say his lordship was kind. He'd always give me a fish to take home, and he'd gut it first, which there was no call for him to do. My mother's a washerwoman. She does the laundry for Chalmers. On the occasions he saw her, Lord Spenford was always respectful."

"I'm glad to hear it," Constance said. *And surprised.*

"He was away at school, of course, but in the breaks he and Mr. Harper spent all their time together. I used to tag along behind them." She pursed her lips. "Until his lordship's brother died."

"Did the earl have more responsibilities immediately?" Constance asked. "He was only fifteen."

"His father decided his lordship—the current earl, I mean—was too soft. He took him in hand, so to speak."

Her mother-in-law had said the same, but Constance still struggled to picture Marcus as this gentle creature. "*Was* he soft?" She picked up her needle again.

"He was always looking after some animal or other," Miriam said. "And he was the sort of young man who, if he saw a woman struggling with her load, he would help her."

"Indeed," Constance said thoughtfully.

"The old earl wasn't keen on any of that, even for a young 'un. He was very firm about requiring the proper deference."

Constance snorted.

Miriam looked scandalized. "My lady, it may be true the young earl was better liked before his brother died, but he had to do what his father wished."

"I suppose." Constance set the last stitch in a crimson letter *E,* and knotted the thread. "Tell me about Harper—did their friendship end?"

"Yes, my lady," Miriam said simply. She handed Constance the scissors so she could snip her thread. "The old earl wouldn't countenance any more than a master-servant relationship. Neither would Tom or his lordship have as they got older, so at worst it ended maybe a year or so earlier than it would have. Tom wanted to be a valet, not a gamekeeper like his father, so his lordship arranged a footman position for him in one of the Spenford cousins' households. Tom worked his way up from there."

"How did he end up back in the earl's service?"

"He applied for the post, my lady, regular like. But of course he's not friendly with the earl now. Not even," she reflected, "as friendly as I hear some other gentlemen are with their valets."

If Marcus was lonely, as his mother suggested, wouldn't he be friendlier with Tom Harper? Maybe the dowager was wrong.

"Was…was his lordship happy as a boy?" Constance asked. Seeing her maid about to object, she added, "I know it's not for you to say, but I wish you to say it anyway."

Miriam nodded. "Very happy, my lady. But his brother dying, well, that was a tragedy. His lordship was never the same after that."

"Because he wasn't allowed to be," Constance said.

The maid looked uncomfortable, so Constance turned to a lighter topic. "What became of your love for Harper, Miriam? Do you still cherish a fondness for him?"

The maid pffed. "I hope I wouldn't be so stupid as to like a man who thinks I'm a lesser being than he is."

"Are you sure Harper does that?" Constance asked.

"He didn't used to." Miriam stared at the flames of the

dying fire, flickering in the grate. "When I was fourteen, he—" She colored, shook herself much like a dog emerging from a stream and gathered up her sewing. "The thing is, my lady, when Tom came back from his time away, he had the same stiff neck he does now. Only he was worse once he became his lordship's valet—he wouldn't give me the time of day. I could never want a man who had no respect for me."

For several minutes, Constance sat lost in thought. People changed, of course they did—just look what Miriam had said about Harper. So she shouldn't be surprised Marcus was no longer the man she'd believed him to be. But there was no reason a person couldn't change again. A man couldn't repress his true nature all the time. With his mother, and even with a country girl, as Constance had been when he met her with the puppy, his true self came out.

She wanted that man for her husband. Not the earl who considered love either beneath his touch or a dalliance with insanity. Not the man who put his consequence above all else.

Her heart broke for a boy who had been happy until he'd been taught that kindness and goodness and, yes, love, were a form of weakness. The very things the Bible declared to be fruit of the Spirit!

Resentment welled within her. Resentment toward the stiff-necked former earl who had equated tenderness with weakness and despised his son until he molded himself into his father's image.

Resentment toward Marcus for not having the sense to know better. For promising to love and to cherish Constance when he had no intention of doing so.

Someone needed to teach him how to be a husband.

Who better than his wife?

Constance stood. "Bligh, I need to go out."

"Out, ma'am? But you've just had tea." The maid pointed

to Constance's empty cup as if she might have forgotten the end-of-evening ritual.

"I must see the earl tonight." If she waited until morning, he'd be gone for an early ride or some such thing, and wouldn't show his face until the coach was loaded and she and the dowager were about to depart. "Do you know where he went?"

Most evenings he had at least half a dozen invitations of which to avail himself. Most of those invitations were also addressed to Constance.

"No, my lady." Miriam sounded scandalized at the very thought she should know the earl's whereabouts. "It's not right for a lady to go out alone so late."

Constance ignored that warning. "I'll ask Dallow if he knows Lord Spenford's plans. Ring the bell, please."

As Miriam tugged on the silk-tasseled rope, she said, "If Mr. Dallow doesn't know, Mr. Harper will."

Harper was summoned after the butler proved ignorant of his lordship's plans.

"Where is your master this evening?" Constance asked.

"He had several invitations, my lady," the valet said. He ignored Miriam, his childhood friend and admirer—he'd not so much as glanced in her direction.

"Which of those events did he plan to attend?" Constance asked coolly.

"His plans were not fully formed," the valet said.

Miriam gave a little cough.

"What is it, Mir—Bligh?" Constance asked. Just in time, she remembered to give her maid the consequence she was due, especially in front of the "hoity-toity" Harper.

"Perhaps Mr. Harper is ignorant of his lordship's whereabouts," the maid suggested.

A masterstroke. Harper swelled visibly. "His lordship is

mostly likely at the Rotheram supper dance," he said, disdain directed at Miriam.

Miriam colored, but she looked him in the eye.

"Thank you, Harper." Constance dismissed him. "And thank *you,* Bligh," she said, when he was gone.

The maid bobbed her head.

Supper dances typically started around nine o'clock, so to arrive this late would be unremarkable. "I need you to dress me," she told the maid, and through her worry and determination she felt a purely feminine thrill of excitement at the thought of wearing one of her fine new dresses. "I will join my husband."

An hour later, the Spenford carriage pulled up outside the Rotheram town house in Clarges Street. Constance dreaded having to walk in alone, a sentiment reinforced when the butler looked askance at her solitary arrival.

He masked it quickly as he bowed. "May I announce you, madam?"

"Miss—the Countess of Spenford."

He bowed lower. "Pardon me, my lady."

She nodded nervously. As the grandfather clock chimed half past ten, he ushered her to the salon. Though the receiving line had broken up to join the festivities, the butler announced, "Her ladyship, the Countess of Spenford."

If he'd announced the Man in the Moon he could not have had greater effect.

A hush fell on the throng near the doorway, those who had heard the announcement, then a buzz of curiosity swelled.

"Lady Spenford—" a woman wearing a mint-green dress with matching turban approached "—what a pleasure. I am Edwina Rotheram."

"Mrs. Rotherham." Constance made a small curtsy. "How kind of you to invite…us."

Where, precisely, was the other half of this marriage?

"I'm delighted to see you have recovered from your plague of headaches," her hostess said.

So that was how Marcus explained her absence from his side!

"I am quite well, thank you," Constance said.

As she spoke, the crowd parted, and there before her... stood Marcus.

Had she seen him in full evening dress before? Perhaps, during one of the soirees her family had attended at Palfont. But not when he was her husband, her equal in society.

She had never felt more inferior.

Her pleasure in her new russet-colored crepe dress with its hem trimmed in forest-green faded in the face of his dark blue coat, cut exquisitely to fit his shoulders, his perfect snowy cravat, his imposing bearing. He had the presence, the charisma, of a lion, a peacock, or some other animal that knew its rightful place at the head of its world.

While Constance clearly did not.

Marcus bowed over Constance's extended hand. "My dear, if I'd known you would join me I would have escorted you."

"Indeed?" she said with a tight smile.

Marcus didn't like her tone, or her smile.

He didn't like that she was here, either, but he was careful to keep that off his face. Tongues would be wagging enough as it was.

Why was Constance here? She must know it was entirely improper to venture out alone to the home of people she hadn't met. Around them, the crowd had grown silent. One more second and they would be whispering.

Hadn't she listened to a word he said about the importance of avoiding gossip? Probably not, he thought grimly. She seemed to listen to no one but her father.

And now, when she should be greeting him with the gracious pleasure of a woman who had snagged the best catch in the ton, she looked more likely to gut and fillet her catch.

Her chin was stuck in the air—if it hadn't been impossible from her inferior height, he would have said she was looking down on him.

"My plague of headaches has vanished as if it never existed," she said. Her voice was gentle, but held an edge that gave him cause for alarm. Who knew what she might blurt out next?

Marcus tugged her in his direction. "You are just in time to dance the waltz with me. After that, I'll introduce you to our friends."

Perhaps she'd wanted to attend one London party before she left for Chalmers. Moving with a determination that cleared a path, he led her toward the dancers. Finding a space in the crowd, he turned to face Constance, and set his left hand at the curve of her waist. The ease with which he found that curve through the fabric of her dress unsettled him. Her shiver reminded him it was the most intimate touch they'd shared…and it was in the middle of a crowded ballroom.

"I'm not very familiar with the waltz," she whispered urgently. "I've only danced it with my sisters, and have always taken the man's part."

"Which explains why your hand is at my waist," he said, relieved to pinpoint the cause of his feeling off balance. Quickly, she lifted her hand to his shoulder. "I will keep you on course."

Marcus swept her into the opening steps. For the benefit of their audience, he curved his lips as he gazed down at her.

She stumbled. "What are you doing?"

"I'm smiling at you." He steadied her.

"It gives you the appearance of toothache," she said.

He loosened his jaw, but kept the smile. "I find it strange

that you regularly question my manners, but appear to have none yourself. How dare you come here—"

She forced a public smile of her own—if his looked anything like hers, no wonder she'd found it alarming. "No, sir," she hissed through bared teeth, "how dare *you?*"

He faltered, then recovered. "Do you accuse me of something, madam?" he asked pleasantly, aware his tone, if not his words, would be picked up by others.

"How dare you make a vow in front of God to be my husband, then plan to send me away?"

They waltzed past Lady Jersey, the woman whose good opinion would influence the rest of society. Her eyebrows were raised in a way Marcus did not consider positive.

Constance noticed, and lowered her voice—he supposed he should be thankful for small mercies. "The Bible says marriage makes two people one flesh. We cannot be one if we're living in different parts of the country."

"That is irrelevant. You will leave for Chalmers in the morning," he said smoothly.

"I can't do something I believe is against God's design for our marriage. Before I left the house tonight, I informed Dallow and your mother's maid there has been a change of plans."

Marcus felt his jaw drop. He snapped it shut. "You promised to obey me," he reminded her harshly, the ability to feign delight in her company deserting him. He almost didn't care. "I'm telling you—I'm *ordering* you—to go to Chalmers."

"My first obedience is to God," she said. "So unless you want the indignity of physically carrying me and forcing me kicking and screaming into your carriage…"

Her words conjured the image; he shuddered. Surely she didn't mean her threat? His eyes narrowed as he assessed her countenance. The eyes were soft and warm, the nose unremarkable, the lips—he skimmed quickly over them—pliant. Nothing to suggest such outrageous rebellion.

But then, there was that chin.

"There is no purpose in you staying," he said as he swept her into a turn. She seemed to think he owed her explanations, and he could reason as well as anyone. "I want a wife who appreciates the honor and consequence of being the Countess of Spenford. Who'll assume the position with dignity and pride. Not someone who values an innkeeper's health over my needs, a puppy over an earldom."

"You're too proud," she agreed, as she smiled a greeting at Lucinda, whirling past in her husband's arms.

He came to a sudden, complete stop. Momentum carried Constance forward to crash into his chest. The momentary brush of her softness against him, before she drew back, contrasted so starkly with her direct words, he was peculiarly dazed.

"*What* did you say?" he demanded.

The spark in her eyes suggested that not only had he heard right, but she was willing to repeat her accusation. Marcus relinquished his dance hold, and grasped her elbow to steer her toward the balcony, where doors stood open to admit the evening air. He helped her over the threshold.

"Let us avoid any confusion," he commanded, as soon as they were clear of the ballroom. "You've made it clear you won't be the kind of countess I want. I will therefore settle for a countess who stays out of my way and does nothing to damage the reputation of my family."

A breeze lifted the hair her maid had arranged to curl at her neck. "Surely that's not enough," she said. "I presume you wish for an heir."

"I—that is—of course I do," he sputtered. "Eventually."

"I, too, wish to have children. Soon." She blushed furiously, but lifted her chin anyway. "I married you in good faith. You ought to come to my bedchamber."

Rigid with shock, Marcus couldn't even glance around to see if anyone had overheard.

"That's not all," she said. "I want a man, a husband, who will love me as he promised to at our wedding."

He recoiled, drawing the attention of old Colonel Barnett over by the balustrade, enjoying the company of the Duchess of Havant. Marcus's kind of people, who knew how the dance of London life should be played out.

Marcus focused on Constance, his wife, who had absolutely no idea how to live her position. "You're mad if you think I will be that man," he said bitterly. "You will leave tomorrow."

And as for the—the bedchamber business, *he* would decide when that should happen.

She said nothing. Her eyes gleamed in the moonlight.

"I am accustomed, madam, to getting what I want," he warned.

"I, sir, am not," she admitted.

It should have been a concession of defeat.

But it sounded very much as if the parson's daughter had just declared war on the pride of Spenford.

Chapter Nine

At quarter past seven the next morning, Miriam stopped in the doorway of the servants' dining room, just off the kitchen.

I can't avoid the man forever. She forced herself to keep moving forward. "Good morning, Cook, Miss Powell. Good morning, Mr. Harper."

Cook set down her teacup and returned the greeting, as did Miss Powell. Tom Harper looked up from his plate. He grunted.

"Did you say, 'Good morning, Miss Bligh?'" Miriam asked, as always unable to let him get away with his high-handedness.

Predictably, he scowled. It was all he ever did around her. Just as well, Miriam reminded herself, considering that Tom Harper's smile had been known to have a bad effect on the strength of her knees.

Far better that he should be a grunting, surly giant, with not so much as a polite word to say in the mornings.

Miriam helped herself to some of the ham Cook had set out for the servants' breakfast. The maids and footmen were still busy with their early-morning duties, but now was a brief chance for the more senior servants to eat before their employers woke, needing attention and food. Mr. Dallow arrived in the kitchen, sparking a round of greetings. Tom was perfectly civil to the butler, Miriam noticed.

She sat on the same side of the table as Tom, at the end unofficially reserved for female staff, across from Miss Powell. This way she wouldn't have to look directly at him. Not that he was still any kind of distraction.

Miss Powell pushed her chair back from the table. "Time I went to lay out my lady's dress. You said the coach would be brought around at nine o'clock, Mr. Dallow?"

"Did you not see the note I slipped under your door, Miss Powell?" Dallow said. "Their ladyships won't be traveling to Chalmers, after all."

"Her ladyship was restless, so I slept on the truckle bed in her dressing room," the older maid said. "They're not going? You're certain?"

"His lordship didn't say anything," Tom objected.

"I left you a note, too." Dallow tut-tutted at this wholesale ignoring of his written missives.

Cook stood up as she gulped the last of her tea. "Are you saying I'm to cook for the whole family today, Mr. Dallow?" she asked, neatly converting her curiosity into an inquiry about her work.

"That's right," Dallow said.

"Did his lordship require his mother to stay here?" Tom said, confused.

"My lady doesn't wish to leave London," Miriam explained. "It was her decision." She realized immediately that in her attempt to show off her knowledge to Tom, she'd overstepped propriety. A good lady's maid didn't share her mistress's rebellion with other servants.

Harper's frown deepened. Which Miriam would have said wasn't possible.

On her way out the door, the cook tsk-tsked. "It's not my place to comment on Lady Spenford's behavior," she began.

"Indeed it is not," Mr. Dallow said frostily.

"But any Christian knows a wife must obey her husband," she called over her shoulder.

The nodding of heads around the table supported her assertion. Mr. Dallow couldn't argue with so plain a truth—he had to satisfy himself with a quelling look. *Miriam* couldn't argue, not in her heart. She'd been as shocked as anyone at her mistress's outright disobedience.

"No one knows what goes on between a man and his wife," she ventured in the countess's defense.

"Will your mistress be nursing the dowager countess?" Miss Powell asked.

"I believe she'll be going out and about more," Miriam said, more hopeful than certain.

"If that's so, you'll need to do a better job of dressing her," Tom said.

Hoity-toity, just like she'd said.

"Her ladyship looked lovely last night," she said defensively.

His pursed lips suggested he didn't agree.

Miriam stifled a sigh. It would be easier to establish her reputation as a superior lady's maid if the countess was prettier; Lady Spenford would be a test of any maid's abilities.

"Her ladyship is most refined," she pointed out. No one could fault the countess for her manner—not proud, but not familiar, either.

"As I see it," Tom said bluntly, "she does Lord Spenford no credit."

The judgment was a slap on the face. And an impertinence to the mistress of the house.

But it wasn't to Tom that Mr. Dallow directed a disapproving look as he pushed his plate away. Miriam squared her shoulders under his scrutiny. The butler wasn't her master, but he did like to have his finger on the pulse of the household. Who knew if he might take it into his head to mention to the earl that she wasn't up to scratch in her work?

It was rare that a washerwoman's daughter should end up a lady's maid in a fine house in London. Miriam might be too ambitious, as her mother liked to say, but having come this far, she'd do whatever it took to stay. Which was why she couldn't entirely disapprove of whatever rebellious spirit had come over the countess. Her ladyship had also come a long way, and she refused to be relegated.

Mr. Dallow stood and left the table, doubtless for his daily conference with Mrs. Matlock, the housekeeper. Miss Powell followed him out.

Alone with Tom—Miriam didn't count the clattering of the cook at the stove in the kitchen, or the kitchen maid's industrious sweeping—she chewed on her piece of bread, her eyes fixed on a knot in the pine table as she considered the challenge of turning a plain-looking bride into a fine countess.

"You need to do better, my girl," she murmured to herself.

"Maybe," Tom said, "this isn't the right position for you."

She'd forgotten how sharp his hearing was. Which she shouldn't have, considering it was a whispered word from her, not intended for his ears, that had encouraged him all those years ago to— *Don't think about that.*

"No one's perfect in a job right from the start," she said. But her defense lacked fire. The countess probably did need a more experienced maid. Miriam could ask Miss Powell's advice, but the older woman was hardly original, or daring. Dressing a dowager was nothing like dressing a young bride.

The only other person in the household with such expertise, and a younger personage to dress, was Tom. The Earl of Spenford was arguably the best-turned-out gentleman in London. Thanks in no small measure to his valet.

Asking Tom's advice would only reinforce his sense of

superiority. But if she didn't improve in her work, she might not keep her position.

Miriam swallowed her pride. "Mr. Harper, who would you say are the finest ladies in London this Season? Those who wear their clothes the best?"

For a moment she thought he wouldn't answer. Then: "You mean, whose lady's maid does the best job?" He saw immediately where she was going.

She nodded.

"Mrs. Quayle can seldom be faulted," he said. "Her grace, the Duchess of Lewisham. Lady Bartlett and Lady Mottram."

"Thanks." Beyond Mrs. Quayle, Miriam had no idea how she was to observe those ladies. She could only hope they would call on her mistress, and Miriam could get a glimpse. Perhaps the earl would host a supper party...

"I'd better deal with his lordship's boots." Tom wiped his mouth with his napkin and stood.

Now that he was looming right next to her, she couldn't help looking at him. And to look at Tom Harper was still a mouth-drying experience. At twenty-five, Miriam was no longer young enough to think the sun rose and set on him...but what girl wouldn't have her head turned by such a physique—broad shoulders, flat stomach, long legs? Hurriedly, she raised her gaze. And encountered another problem: his eyes. Dark as coal, but with a gleam in them that unsettled her.

She wondered why he wasn't married. Maybe because it was all but impossible to remain a personal servant once you were married—not if you ever wanted to see your spouse. Maybe because he hadn't met the right girl...but she'd seen the flirtatious glances the housemaids slid in his direction. If it wasn't strictly against house rules, he could take his pick of any one of them.

Maybe he's courting one of them on the sly. Just thinking

it made her feel as if she'd sucked on a lemon. "Where were you last night, that you missed seeing Mr. Dallow's note?" she blurted.

His gaze slid away. Did that mean he *was* courting?

"That's none of your business, Miriam Bligh."

He was right, of course; she didn't know what came over her. He looked her up and down, and she was conscious of her odd figure, all angles and sharpness where a woman should have curves and softness. His jaw firmed, as if he saw nothing to please him. "Why don't you just admit you can't do this job, give the countess a chance at making something of her looks with a *real* lady's maid, and go home?"

He might as well have punched her in the ribs, she felt such a shaft of pain.

"This *is* my home now, Tom Harper, as much as yours," she said, anger strengthening her voice. "You telling me I'm no good doesn't make it true. It just makes you the kind of man my father was."

It was the worst insult she could think of, and anyone acquainted with the Bligh family knew it.

Tom's face turned a deep, brick-red.

"That might have been an exaggeration," she muttered.

Too late—Tom had stalked from the room, surprisingly light on his feet for such a big man.

Miriam smacked her forehead with her hand. Why had she gone and said that? Few men were as bad as her father, who'd taken every penny Miriam's mother ever earned, doling only the occasional farthing back to her. He'd been more than generous with his insults—"You're worthless" being his favorite—with a backhand across the cheek if the mood took him. Which it regularly did. The day he'd run off with the baker's wife had been Miriam's happiest moment.

To compare Tom to him…she'd just mortally offended the

one person in this house who might offer some useful advice for her work.

And she liked to think she was clever!

Constance lay abed for some time after she woke, in no hurry to descend to breakfast. Savoring her victory. She had defied Marcus, and had won!

"Are my trunks still unpacked, Bligh?" she asked, on a sudden spurt of fear that Marcus might have devised a way to get her into that coach.

"Of course, my lady." Finished with brushing down a morning dress of rose-pink muslin, Miriam shook out the dress. "Did you want them packed again?"

"No, no," Constance assured her. "We're staying here."

But now that she'd triumphed, what next? She'd told Marcus she wanted a real marriage, and children. Over the course of a long night spent tossing and turning, she'd realized just how far she was from that goal. Although she'd fancied herself in love with Marcus, she barely knew him—and he knew her even less. To talk of building a marriage on such ignorance was stupidity.

She and Marcus needed to spend more time together. But he would still be fuming from last night—any request for his company would likely be rebuffed. The only thing that might bring him to her side was a fear she might embarrass him.

Constance pushed her blankets aside and stepped out of bed. "Bligh, I suspect I shall receive a few morning callers today. But later, I'd like to go riding. Could you tell Dallow to have a horse readied for me at four o'clock? Nothing too frisky." Beyond walking in the garden in the center of Berkeley Square, she'd hardly been outdoors since she arrived in London—suddenly, she craved fresh air.

"Yes, my lady." Miriam helped her into the muslin dress. "Will I set out your new riding habit?"

Constance nodded. "I'll also need you to give Harper a message for Lord Spenford." She thought for a moment. "Tell him I plan to ride in Hyde Park at four. And tell him my riding skills are not the best."

If she knew her husband, the prospect of her tumbling from her horse, and thus embarrassing the precious name of Spenford, was just the thing to guarantee her Marcus's company.

Chapter Ten

Marcus was already waiting when Constance stepped through the front door at four o'clock to greet the groom who held the reins of an exceptionally placid-looking bay mare. Her husband's black steed was dancing with impatience.

"Good afternoon," Constance greeted him cheerfully, as she stepped onto the mounting block.

Marcus did not appear to be finding the afternoon all that good. He inclined his head in a cold nod. "You look tired, madam. Did you sleep badly?" He had the nerve to sound hopeful.

How rude!

"I slept like a baby," Constance assured him. Which was true, because in her experience babies never slept at all. She didn't know where that ridiculous expression came from.

The groom helped her onto the horse. "Minerva here won't give you any trouble, my lady," he assured her, as he adjusted the single, larger stirrup that came with her sidesaddle.

Her pale blue kid half boots peeked out from her blue cotton nankeen riding habit. Constance sat tall—easy enough since the horse wasn't moving—knowing the slightly military tailoring of the fitted jacket showed her figure to advantage. She patted the bay's neck. "I can tell she's very good-tempered. Just like Lord Spenford."

The groom smothered what might have been a cough, if one was to give him the benefit of the doubt.

"Shall we go?" Marcus snapped. Without waiting for a reply, he set off.

Confident that even she couldn't go wrong with a horse this placid, Constance spurred Minerva into a walk.

Marcus didn't speak to her as they rode, though he returned the greetings of several other riders. Constance didn't mind; she was too busy concentrating on steering her mount along the busy street. With five sisters and only two horses in the family, she seldom rode in Piper's Mead.

"Good girl," she murmured to Minerva. "Lovely, steady girl."

Marcus cast her an impatient look. "There's nothing *lovely* about that plodder. Now Sheba here is an elegant mount." He patted his horse's neck. Sheba tossed her head.

Constance peeped up at him around the feather that curled somewhat distractingly over the brim of her hat to sit just within the edge of her vision. "I can't think why anyone would prefer that high-strung creature to my sturdy Minerva." She paused. "Though perhaps you choose your horses on the same criteria as you choose your wife."

He barked a laugh. "That was an outrageous thing to say, madam."

"No one heard," she comforted him. "The Spenford reputation is still intact."

He rolled his eyes. "Here we are, Hyde Park." He gestured with a sweep of his arm. "Where did you wish to ride?"

"I don't know the park at all," she admitted. "I shall follow your recommendation."

He muttered something that might have been, "That'll be a first." Then he tapped his horse's flanks with his heels and headed along a wide bridle path at a trot that wasn't too fast for her. Making sure her crop was tight in her grasp, she rode alongside, aware of his regular glances to check she wasn't about to disgrace him with her lack of horsemanship.

When they pulled up in the shade of a stand of oak trees, Constance took the opportunity to survey the people around them. This, she knew, was the time of day to see and be seen, hence the park was filled with carriages of all kinds: curricles, phaetons for the more sporting men and a few daring ladies, more sedate barouches for the older ladies. Here and there, riders like her and Marcus conversed in groups.

"Do Mr. and Mrs. Quayle ride in the park?" she asked, to break the silence.

"It's more common to ride with one's friends than with one's spouse," he said.

"How odd. My father spends most of his time with my mother, except when he's writing his sermons," Constance said. "He says there's no company he'd prefer."

A heavy sigh reminded her Marcus didn't find stories of her father terribly fascinating.

"I've been thinking," she said.

"I wish you wouldn't."

Before she could stop herself, Constance spurted a laugh.

"I am perfectly serious, madam." But the corners of his lips tugged.

"I cannot believe an intelligent man like you would wish for a wife who never thinks," she said.

"*Now* you acknowledge me to have a virtue," he said. "When Lucinda tried to enumerate my charms, you wouldn't agree with any of her suggestions."

"She didn't mention your brain," Constance pointed out. "Which I have concluded is very fine."

Their gazes met, caught.

"I felt it only fair to say so," she said awkwardly.

"I appreciate your fairness," Marcus said. After a moment, he added, "You said you've been thinking?"

Constance almost didn't share her idea—they seemed to be in unusual accord, and it seemed a shame to disturb the peace. "I wish to go out with you in the evenings."

"I'm afraid my club isn't open to ladies."

"With the obvious exception of your club," she said patiently. "Marcus—" at his start, she realized she'd addressed him by his Christian name "—it's not right for you to go about as if you're still a single man. I intend to claim you as my husband in the eyes of the world."

"*Claim* me?" He wound his reins around one hand to steady his horse. "I'm not some newly discovered island full of barbarians to be colonized."

He *was* something of an island, Constance reflected, the way he refused to open his heart. But as the poet Mr. John Donne said, *No man is an island entire of itself.* "You are already excessively civilized," she agreed.

He narrowed his eyes. "There is no such thing as *excessively* civilized. I might have guessed you didn't know that."

"From now on," she said, "I'll accompany you to all the evening events to which we are both invited. During the day, I will pay and receive calls, as befitting my position as your wife. I had three callers today—I don't believe I disgraced you with any of them."

"Did you tell any of your callers you don't consider my wealth and status to be of any importance?" he queried politely.

"I managed to restrain myself," she assured him.

"If you wish to accompany me, you will need to behave in a manner befitting the Countess of Spenford," he warned. "No going out alone at night to the home of people you haven't met."

"I needed to find you," she said defensively, aware in the

cold light of day that her excursion to the Rotherams' had been eccentric, to say the least.

"You could have sent a messenger—do you think I would have refused to return, when my mother could have been ill?"

Was he saying he wouldn't have returned just for her? Inadvertently, her hands tightened on her reins; Minerva danced a little. Constance slackened her grip. "I didn't think of that. But that reminds me—I thought your mother looked rather pale this morning, didn't you?"

"No, I did not. Do I have your word you will behave correctly?" he asked. "If you're uncertain of anything, ask me, or my mother, or Lucinda. But as a first point, remember that London ways are a good deal more restrictive than country ways."

"You have my word," Constance said.

How much further should he push this? Marcus wondered. He rapped his knuckles against the pommel of his saddle as he thought. He couldn't very well refuse to take her out with him, when half the ton had seen her perfectly healthy at the Rotheram soiree last night. But it was important to do this on his terms…even if it meant covering a subject he had no wish to discuss.

He cleared his throat. "And, er, you will make every effort to hide your, er, *infatuation* with me?"

He judged that look in her eye to be a desire to slap him. Good thing she'd just vowed to behave correctly. And that, as he'd pointed out the day they married, she wasn't the slapping sort.

"No need to hide it," she said airily. "It's over."

It took a moment for her words to sink in. "I beg your pardon?" Marcus said.

She combed her fingers through her mare's mane. "After much thought, I have concluded you were right. My feelings for you were a childish infatuation based on a perception of virtues you don't possess."

"What do you mean, I don't possess them?" And how did she manage to couch her insults as good news?

"Not that you don't have other virtues," she assured him.

"You're too kind," he said tightly.

"After all, we have already agreed you are intelligent. And…well, I'm sure there are others," she finished briskly.

"How sure?" he asked.

"My point is," she said, "a childish infatuation is no basis for a marriage."

"No." That was unarguable.

He bit down on the urge to argue.

"Therefore, I have relinquished it." She snapped her fingers. "It's gone."

Marcus should have whooped for joy. "How can it be gone?" he asked.

"It simply no longer exists. It was a figment in the first place, and now it is nothing."

"You're saying you were in love with me," he said, "but now you're not?" The sense of offense that came over him was most peculiar.

"I *thought* I was in love," she corrected. "But as you pointed out, it was absurd."

"Quite," he agreed. Yet somehow, agreeing it was absurd for her to be in love with him didn't feel right, either.

"I wish to start again," she said, "in building a more realistic emotion toward our marriage."

"That is excellent news," Marcus said mechanically, still trying to rid himself of a sense of rejection. "Marriage should be founded on respect and duty." Perhaps he shouldn't have said *duty*—she might bring up the bedchamber again.

"Marcus," she said, "I believe that if you and I both work hard, a true and deep love can grow between us."

"A true and deep *regard,*" he amended.

"Love," she countered. "I intend to love you, Marcus. I intend for you to love me."

Marcus flinched. "But you just said—"

"A mature love," she interrupted. Marcus could never remember his mother interrupting his father, but *his* countess thought nothing of it. He blamed the Reverend Somerton. For the interruption *and* the mature love idea.

"My position hasn't changed from last night," he informed her. "I do not plan to love you. I don't see love as an admirable quality, and I have loftier concerns to occupy me."

For a moment, she looked daunted. And with those circles of exhaustion around her eyes, unexpectedly frail. He had an odd urge to reach out and grasp her fingers. To transmit some strength to her.

Then she said, in that sermonizing way of hers, "Time will tell. And time is the one thing we do have in our favor."

If she had any more strength, England could have sent her off to battle Bonaparte single-handed.

"You do as you wish," he said. "So long as your behavior in public is entirely correct, I don't care what fantasies you entertain."

She paled, swallowed visibly. Perhaps he had been too harsh, Marcus thought uneasily.

"Look, there's Mrs. Rotheram." He pointed out their hostess from last night riding toward them in her barouche, in company of Lady Mottram. A welcome distraction. "Did you send her a card of thanks this morning?"

"Of course I did," she said coolly. "But I shall go and talk to her now—it will be nice to converse with her in less awkward circumstances."

Before Marcus could instruct her further as to what she should or shouldn't say, his wife dug her little heels into Minerva's obliging flanks and trotted toward Mrs. Rotheram.

Marcus caught her up just as she joined the women.

"My dear Lady Spenford," he heard Mrs. Rotheram say. "I was just telling Lady Mottram what a pleasure it was to meet you last evening."

Marcus gritted his teeth. More likely, she was telling Sarah Mottram how Constance had arrived alone. How she had been witnessed dancing rather tensely with her husband. How the Spenfords had left early, before one o'clock, and neither bride nor groom had held a honeymoon look in their eye.

"The pleasure was mine, Mrs. Rotheram," Constance said with a demureness Marcus couldn't fault. He could only wish that demureness could be directed at him.

He introduced Constance to Lady Mottram, and they exchanged the customary pleasantries.

"Spenford, how is your dear mother?" Lady Mottram asked.

"Very well, ma'am," he said.

"Actually, she seemed somewhat fatigued today," Constance said.

Had he specifically said, *Do not contradict me in public,* or had he foolishly assumed that was obvious? "My mother is better than she has been in weeks, but still has moments of fatigue," he said pleasantly.

Constance pursed her lips, but didn't argue.

"Are you going to Viscountess Lynley's ball this evening?" Lady Mottram asked.

Neither Constance nor Marcus answered.

Marcus knew why *he* wasn't talking. This was where he would have to commit to spending his evening with his unworldly, argumentative wife.

Lady Mottram cleared her throat in further inquiry.

"I think not," Constance said. "I must admit, I'm rather tired. It was so hot last night."

"My dear, you said you slept like a baby," Marcus reminded her.

Her eyes narrowed.

For the first time since he'd woken up from his own troubled sleep fuming at his wife's outrageous behavior, Marcus sensed he had the upper hand.

"Certainly we will attend the viscountess's ball," he said. "Though we'll arrive late." In his mind, Marcus ran over the stack of invitations he had sorted through over the past week.

"How late?" Constance asked.

"Not before midnight, I imagine," he said carelessly. "Remember, my dear, we're to dine with Admiral Ferguson—" he must send a card informing the admiral his wife would accompany him "—then to attend a music performance at the Finches'."

Constance had paled, the circles beneath her eyes growing visibly darker. Marcus hoped her maid had some trick for concealing them.

"Three events in one evening," she said.

"I don't think we'll be able to squeeze in Mrs. Robson-Burke's card party, my dear," he said regretfully. "But you'll be pleased to hear Viscountess Lynley is known for the excellence of the breakfast she serves."

"Breakfast!" Constance exclaimed.

"At four o'clock," Marcus said affably. "The Lynleys' ball is a famously late night, and the viscountess doesn't like to send her guests home hungry."

"It's true," Mrs. Rotheram assured Constance. "My husband rates it the best breakfast in London."

It was, of course, quite disgraceful for Constance to whimper. But in a spirit of magnanimity, Marcus forgave her.

He found himself in a much more cheerful frame of mind as they rode home. Constance would have no chance of a restoring nap before their evening activities. Tomorrow would be the same, as would the day after that. With the Season in full swing, Marcus gave his exhausted wife a week, at most, before she *begged* to be sent to Chalmers.

Chapter Eleven

I have nothing to complain about.

If Constance told herself that often enough, maybe it would sink in. After all, she'd insisted Marcus take her with him to Society events, and for the past two weeks he'd done exactly that.

With a vengeance.

She stifled a yawn and forced her tired eyes to focus on the soloist singing on the stage below their theater box. It was the first act of the Italian opera that was their first engagement of the evening, barely seven o'clock. Tonight wouldn't end until the small hours—they had a card party and two suppers to get through first.

Goodness, that singer had a piercing voice! Constance rubbed her temples.

Observant as ever, Marcus noticed her discomfort from where he sat on the other side of their hostess, Lady Annabelle White, in the slightly curved box. His forehead crinkled in concern. Constance forced a smile. His mouth tightened, but he turned back to continue his discussion with their host, Sir Hugh, of something called the Coinage Act, a piece of legislation apparently designed to define the value of the pound relative to gold. Fascinating.

She supposed it was kind of him to look worried. But spending so much time together, he'd had every opportunity to develop some affection for his wife by now.

She had married a slow learner.

Constance dragged her attention back to the ladies, who were chatting alternately about the performance and about Lord Byron's latest bizarre behavior. Lady Annabelle kept twisting to talk to the two ladies behind her, in the second row of the box. It seemed attending a performance in London was as much about talking as watching and listening. Constance ventured the occasional opinion—on the opera, not Lord Byron—but constrained as she was by her promise to Marcus to say nothing improper, she didn't dare be as blunt as she'd like. Small wonder the ladies didn't find her conversation interesting.

Realizing her eyelids had drifted dangerously downward, Constance fanned herself with her new silk-and-ivory fan in the hope of creating a rousing breeze.

It was a beautiful fan. Her wardrobe of clothes and accessories had grown significantly to keep up with the round of parties, suppers, concerts. Her hours of sleep had decreased markedly.

Every night, as they drove home from the evening's entertainments, Marcus asked her if she was ready to travel to Chalmers for a rest. Every night, she told him no…then fell asleep in her corner of the carriage, not waking until he touched her shoulder as they arrived home. It was an odd ritual that had developed between them.

Constance realized the conversation around her had moved on. Lady Annabelle was talking about her much-loved aunt.

"She has undergone the most miraculous recovery under the care of a new physician," Lady Annabelle said. "Her heart palpitations have almost entirely ceased."

"Which physician is that?" Constance asked, with more

enthusiasm than she should probably display. "The Dowager Countess of Spenford is in the care of Mr. Bird."

Constance had formed no good opinion of Mr. Bird. He may be the finest doctor in London, but his manner was stiff and prescriptive. He preferred to make his own assessment rather than engage in discussion with his patient. He certainly brought no cheer to the sickroom.

Although her mother-in-law had seemed much improved immediately after Constance arrived in London, Constance felt her condition had deteriorated. She'd told Marcus of her fears for his mother's well-being. But he was so convinced his "bargain with God" would keep Helen safe, he wouldn't take her seriously. Mr. Bird had said the dowager might get worse before she got better, so Marcus saw her worsening condition as a positive sign.

"This new doctor is a younger man, Mr. Gerald Young," Lady Annabelle said, "newly returned from Paris. His specialty is heart illnesses."

"Marcus—" in her excitement, Constance leaned across her hostess "—Lady Annabelle is telling me about a new physician, Mr. Young. He may be able to help your mother."

The lift of his eyebrows pointed out that she'd used his Christian name in public. Which she wasn't to do unless they were with close friends. She suspected he'd rather she didn't do it at all.

"Mr. Bird is the finest of his kind in the country," he said. "I doubt there's anything this other fellow can do that Mr. Bird hasn't thought of."

"I am sure you know best in the matter of your mother's treatment, Lord Spenford," Lady Annabelle said coyly. "My dear aunt is an eccentric, so she had no hesitation consulting Mr. Young, but I believe much of his practice is among the lower classes."

Exactly the wrong thing to tell Marcus.

Lady Annabelle fanned her face with subtle grace. Constance had heard of "the language of the fan" and its flirtatious messages, but she needed an interpreter. She suspected Lady Annabelle's fan was saying something more than *Look at my fine eyes and charming pout*.

Constance sighed. *Here we go again*. She'd stopped being shocked by the willingness of the ladies of the ton to flirt with other women's husbands, but it still made her crazy.

She told herself they meant nothing by it. An accepted part of the "fun" of an evening like this was flirting with members of the opposite sex. She doubted *all* these women wanted to start a full-blown affair with Marcus.

The only saving grace was that Marcus did not flirt back. Ever. Constance wasn't sure why—if she had to guess, she would say his pride stopped him from unbending enough to flirt. Who would have thought Marcus's self-regard would have a positive aspect?

She was relieved he was nothing like Sir Hugh, currently peering through his opera glasses at the rather lovely young singer on the stage. Constance suspected there was more that interested him than her soprano voice.

Sir Hugh had made no attempt to flirt with Constance. No one ever did. And although she was grateful—she would have no idea how to respond, beyond a clumsy set-down that Marcus would doubtless consider rude—she also felt the snub to her lack of beauty and charm.

What would Isabel do? Her sister always knew how to behave, delivered every line perfectly. She would be amusing and gracious and astonish every man here with a fineness of mind that matched her fineness of face and figure, all without overstepping the mark of flirtation. *Ah, well*.

Lady Annabelle tapped Marcus's knee with her fan—goodness knows what that meant—as she made some coquettish remark. The woman was quite beautiful. Only a year or two older than Constance, but with a sophistication that must surely draw the interest of any man.

Marcus laughed at something she said, and his face broke out of its stern lines. Lady Annabelle looked as if the goose had just laid a golden egg at her feet.

She leaned in closer to Marcus, affording him an excellent view down the front of her low-cut dress, had he been looking.

He wasn't looking.

If Marcus did feel an attraction to another woman, he wouldn't reveal it in public, Constance realized miserably. He would visit the woman in the security of her own home....

Was that how he spent his days? Was that why he was yet to consummate their marriage?

Marcus is a Christian, she reminded herself. Albeit a Christian who let his faith serve him, rather than one who served his faith.

I shall not judge my husband. It is wrong.

But it was hard to hold that thought as Marcus grew more animated in his conversation with the other woman. More animated than he ever was with Constance...if you didn't count their arguments.

"Are you unwell, Lady Spenford?" Lady Annabelle asked. "Your color is high."

Constance found herself the scrutiny of all in their box. Knowing how unfavorable the comparison between her scarlet face and Lady Annabelle's porcelain complexion must be, she fidgeted with her program. "I am quite comfortable," she said.

Marcus nodded approval—he wouldn't like her to make a fuss.

Constance blurted, "Lady Annabelle, may I lend you my cloak?"

"I beg your pardon?"

Constance's voice quivered, but she wouldn't stop. "I assume it is for warmth that you lean so close to my husband."

A gasp from the woman behind her. One of the other gentlemen gave a strangled laugh. Sir Hugh lowered his opera glasses. His gaze traveled over Constance—she wanted to apologize for drawing attention to his wife's misconduct. But when he spoke to his wife, he was all amiability. "By George, the countess has you there, my dear."

Lady Annabelle had straightened away from Marcus, whose countenance resembled a thundercloud. "Your company is so refreshing, Lady Spenford," she said.

Constance winced, then decided to take the compliment at face value. "You're too kind, Lady Annabelle." She had the pleasure of seeing a look of impatience cross that woman's face and of hearing a faint, stifled snort from Marcus. "What a remarkable player the first violinist is," she continued, and turned her attention to the orchestra below.

After the opera, the card party and the two suppers, Marcus and his wife traveled home in the Spenford carriage, the usual three feet of space between them. Rain beat down on the roof, its din closing them in their own little world.

Though it was almost two o'clock in the morning, Marcus felt unusually alert. Constance's chastising of Annabelle White had turned a dull performance into one of the more entertaining evenings he could remember. Though he shouldn't see it like that.

"Do you plan ahead how you will draw unwelcome attention to yourself?" he asked her, more curious than annoyed. "Or does inspiration strike you in the moment?"

"The evidence of my eyes strikes me," Constance said. "That woman was flirting with my husband."

"Lady Annabelle was being friendly. She meant no harm."

"She was leering at you in the exact same way her husband was leering at that singer."

"She was perhaps a little forward," Marcus admitted. "But as the daughter of a duke and heiress to a fortune of imposing dimensions, no one will judge her." Whereas they wouldn't hesitate to judge Constance in her attempt to castigate Annabelle. Which, he had to admit, was unfair. "I didn't respond to her approach," he pointed out.

"I appreciate that," Constance said. "But frankly, Marcus, I'm sick of women fawning all over you every time we go out."

"That's your parsonage upbringing talking," he said uncertainly. Uncertain, because a part of him was flattered at what looked much like jealousy. Even though he disapproved of jealousy as a petty emotion suited to the lower classes.

"Their behavior is improper," she said. She added a muttered, "And inexplicable."

He surprised himself by chuckling. "Ah, yes. You find me so proud, such poor company, it must seem strange when other women show interest in me."

"I've noticed that by and large they're not women of sense," she said.

He laughed. "I'd thought you might be too tired to lance me with one of your insults." Even he found their current schedule punishing. But he had a point to make: however determined she might be, Constance did not fit in with ton ways. Tonight was just one more example. Life would be easier for both of them if she would give up this idea she had of building some romantic bond with him.

She yawned, only just managing to cover her mouth with her hand in time. Her eyelids drooped. Another few seconds, and she'd be asleep. Marcus had grown accustomed to the slight frown she wore in her slumber, which contrasted with the softening of her mouth. He was used to the occasional incoherent murmur passing her lips—clearly, sharing a bed with her, a man would have no rest from her conversation!

"Perhaps if I looked more imposing, more like a countess, those women wouldn't chase after you," she murmured sleepily.

"I doubt it would make much difference," he said drily. Constance's appearance had improved in her new clothes, and her maid was obviously making an effort with her hair. But she would never look imposing.

"Men might flirt with me if I did," she said, yawning around the words and not even trying to cover her mouth. "I suppose you'd say that was harmless fun?"

Something tightened between Marcus's shoulder blades. "Of course," he said lightly.

A moment later, her lids settled more firmly on her cheek; she'd fallen asleep.

The carriage jolted through a rut—this rain would turn it into a hole by morning—and Constance's head banged against the back of the seat. Her frown deepened in her sleep.

Marcus moved across the seat toward her, close enough that he could settle her head on his shoulder, so she shouldn't be disturbed by any more ruts.

As he half closed his eyes, he realized he'd omitted to make Constance his usual offer of a trip to Chalmers to relieve her fatigue.

Chapter Twelve

Tom had made good use of the time Lord and Lady Spenford were out. He'd cleaned his lordship's brushes and mixed up a batch of his own special boot polish, which would set him up nicely for tomorrow. He'd need a good setup, since he'd be tired after another late night.

Tom clasped his hands behind his head, trying to relieve the aching muscles in his neck. He ached all over—he hoped he wasn't sickening for something. *A cup of tea, that's what I need.* The kettle would still be hot over the remains of the fire.

In the kitchen, deserted except for the scullery maid sleeping on her cot in her corner, he poured a pot of tea. Not boiling, but it would do. He waited for it to brew, then poured out a cup. He carried it through to the servants' dining room to drink it…and saw someone else had the same idea.

Miriam sat at the pine table, a cup in front of her, a candle guttering in its saucer next to a stack of periodicals.

She was asleep, her head pillowed on her arms, which were folded on the table. In the last light of the candle, her hair looked darker than it was, her face paler.

Tom quashed the familiar stirring of his senses. He shook her shoulder, aware of the hard ridge of bone beneath her dark-colored dress. "You'll burn the house down," he growled.

Miriam jerked upright. "What? Oh, Tom, it's you."

The drowsiness in her voice as she said his name made him want to blow out that flame, take her in his arms, kiss her.

Deliberately, he pushed the candle beyond her reach, beyond the pile of periodicals that could easily catch fire. He glowered down at her—he knew he shouldn't, but he couldn't help it. As always, the mess of feelings she produced in him couldn't be accepted with any pleasure.

Miriam yawned, and pushed her hair back off her face. She reached up to adjust the position of a hairpin. "Don't be daft, Tom. I wasn't about to set fire to anything."

"Better safe than sorry, Miss Bligh," he said, hearing the starch in his own voice, seeing how it stiffened her spine and erased that drowsy softness from her face. *Good.*

He busied himself finding another candle on the shelf, lit it off the remains of hers, then set it on the table.

When the flame was steady, Miriam leaned forward and blew out the old candle. Tom schooled himself not to look at the pursing of her lips. Lips he could still remember the feel of after so many years. Which made him a right bufflehead, as his mam would say, should he ever choose to share that memory with her. Which he wouldn't.

He sat down opposite Miriam, too tired to exercise sense and resist the lure of her presence. Weeks now, he hadn't been able to go wherever he pleased in this house, without having to think first whether she might be there.

Miriam's gaze dropped to his jaw—self-conscious, he ran a hand over the barely visible growth of new beard.

She looked away, yawned again.

"You've been overdoing it," he said. Ever since he'd suggested she wasn't up to the job, she'd been constantly on the go. He felt like a brute.

He always felt like something less than civilized around her.

"Or—" she said, glancing at the clock that hung above the doorway that led upstairs "—it's two o'clock in the morning and I'm naturally tired. I assume there's no sign of our lord and lady?"

He shook his head. "But Lord Spenford said they won't be very late."

Miriam's *humph* told him she considered two o'clock to fall firmly into late territory.

Tom watched a lick of wax form down one side of the candle. "I'm sorry for what I said. Last time. I didn't mean to bully you."

She spread her fingers on the tabletop. They were a little work-roughened, but even just a few weeks as lady's maid had softened her hands. Tom was glad.

"I shouldn't have said you were like my dad," she said. "Few men are that bad, thank God."

"So I'm bad, but not as bad as your father?" he clarified ruefully.

She grinned, but it turned into another yawn. "Though maybe you were right about this job being too much for me. I feel like a wrung-out dishcloth, and there you are looking as prime as one of his lordships grays."

She thought he looked prime? Tom had to work hard not to puff out his chest. His gaze traveled over her, over her angular face and what he could see of her slender figure. "You're skin and bones, Miriam." Blast it, that wasn't what he meant…but he wasn't about to fix it with a compliment. That would be asking for trouble.

The warmth in her eyes faded.

"I meant you've got thinner," he said awkwardly. Ah, why

did he even bother? He was a blundering idiot in the words department, and never more so than when he was talking to Miriam Bligh.

He shouldn't even be noticing her figure in the first place, let alone its shrinking. But that would be like expecting a dawn fisherman not to notice the sunrise.

She heard the concern in his voice and relaxed. "I may be a few pounds lighter—with these late hours, I often don't have the energy to eat. I didn't realize the earl and countess would go out quite so often."

Tom rested his forearms on the table. "Aye, I must admit, his lordship wasn't quite so sociable before he was wed. They haven't been home before two o'clock any night this week."

Miriam groaned. "Don't remind me. Last week was just as bad." The thought provoked another yawn; she pressed her fingers to her lips. "Do you think it'll always be like this?"

Her gloom made him smile. "Until the Season ends. Once we're back at Chalmers we'll be right."

Her head drooped. With an effort she raised it. "I shouldn't complain. I wanted this job, wanted the extra money."

Tom felt himself blush and hoped she couldn't read his mind. To think, he'd wondered if she'd sought the position in an attempt to be close to him! A futile attempt, it would have been, but he was still contrarily disappointed to know it hadn't even been made.

"I didn't pick you as the mercenary type," he said.

"If you mean you thought I'd be content to let my children grow up not knowing where their next meal is coming from…"

"What children?" he asked. "Are you planning to marry?" With difficulty, he kept his voice light. He tried not to think about her marrying, having another man's children. As if not thinking about it could prevent it!

Her cheeks pinkened. "Not at this stage."

"You won't ever, if you stay in this job too long," he warned. "Look at Powell." Her shoulders stiffened, and he realized how that sounded—his cursed clumsiness with words again. "I'm not trying to tell you to give it up," he assured her.

She relaxed again. "What about you, Tom?" she asked. "Are you promised to anyone?"

He shook his head. She'd implied more or less the same question a few weeks ago, when she'd asked his whereabouts the night the countess had decided to stay in London.

Now, at the news of his ongoing bachelorhood, a little smile curved her lips. Did she remember that kiss? She'd been fourteen, he'd been seventeen. That's where it began— if you didn't count the weeks before that he'd spent just noticing her—and there it had to end.

If ever he doubted that it had to end, he only had to imagine telling her the whole truth to be convinced again.

"Do you have a plan for making the countess more presentable?" he asked, more harshly than he intended.

The smile dropped from her lips. Businesslike, she pulled the pile of periodicals toward her. The topmost was open at a page with pictures of ladies in various dress styles.

"I've been reading these," she said.

"Fashion magazines?" Tom asked.

"Summer Fashions from Paris."

"What's wrong with English fashions?"

She rolled her eyes and pushed the periodical toward him. "Look." She indicated the caption beneath a drawing of a lady wearing a green coat and a hat sporting far too many— in Tom's opinion—matching feathers. "Pelisses of embroidered silk organdy are all the rage in Paris for evening dress. I should think they'd be too delicate to last more than a few months, not to mention completely impractical, but isn't it beautiful?"

Tom glanced briefly at the page, then pushed it back toward her. His head had started to ache, right on the very top, as if someone had conked him on the noggin with a hammer. It was warm in here, warmer than you'd expect given the fire had died down some hours ago.

"Being a good valet, or a good dresser, isn't about aping a picture in a magazine," he said gruffly. "It's knowing what works for your master. Or mistress. Instinct—either you have it, or you don't. Then it's about attention to detail."

"So you're telling me you take no interest in the fashions," she said, disbelieving.

This was why he hadn't wanted her here—she'd never been able to let things rest. To accept that not everyone did things her way.

From upstairs, he heard the unmistakable sound of the door knocker hitting the front door. Then, the night footman hurrying to open it.

"They're home," Tom said unnecessarily.

Miriam was already feeling for the pins in her hair, making sure she wasn't disarranged.

As Tom headed up to the bedchambers, he heard her boots on the servants' stairs behind him.

He climbed faster, making sure his longer legs increased the gap between them with every step.

From the landing, Constance saw Marcus talking to Dallow in the entrance hall. She wasn't entirely sure how they'd left things last night. She'd dozed off in the carriage… was he angry with her for her words to Lady Annabelle at the opera, or not?

Her stomach growled a reminder of the need for breakfast, so she grasped the stair rail and began her descent.

"Good morning, Marcus," she said when she reached the bottom.

His head jerked around, as if it still surprised him to discover every day that he had a wife.

Perhaps his memory wouldn't suffer such a lapse if he spent part of the night in her bed, she thought tartly.

To her astonishment, after handing her a small pile of letters from her family, Marcus followed her into the dining room. Usually, he breakfasted before her.

As Constance helped herself to some ham from the platter on the side table, she darted a curious look at him.

Catching her in the act, he grimaced. "You're right," he said, "my boots are below their normal standard. Harper is ill." He served himself some ham, about triple the quantity Constance had. "Gregory, the footman, did my boots."

"Is Harper's illness serious?" she asked. She wondered if Miriam knew Harper was sick. If her maid was worried.

"I don't suppose so." Her husband added a slice of rare beef to his plate. "Dashed inconvenient, though. Gregory is a long way off Harper's standard."

Constance inspected his Hessians and found them as glossily perfect as always. "How awful for you," she said. "I do hope Harper will be well enough to clean your boots soon."

He reddened. "He's not on his deathbed. Someone would have told me."

"I gather you didn't ask?"

He ignored that and pulled out a chair. Seated, he served himself a slice of fresh-baked bread. "I have a meeting with my bankers today. If ever there was an occasion where I should look every inch the imposing Earl of Spenford…"

"Oh." Constance could understand that. "I don't suppose it would help if I said you always look splendid."

"Not at all." Then he added gruffly, "But thank you."

They ate in silence for a minute or two.

"I tried to look in on your mama, but Powell said she's still sleeping," Constance said. "She seems more tired lately."

"Sleep is part of the healing process. Her condition seems much the same to me."

Constance bit her lip. No doubt he *wanted* it to be the same, or better. But in her view, the dowager was getting weaker—one had only to hold her hand on a regular basis to detect a failing grip.

An idea struck her. Really, a very naughty idea…but also a very good one. "Have you summoned a doctor for Harper?"

"Dallow gave no indication that he needs one," Marcus said. He suddenly looked genuinely concerned. "Do you have reason to think Harper is seriously ill?"

"There are conditions going around," she said vaguely. "I don't like to think of him suffering if a doctor might help."

Marcus leaned back in his chair. "Yet again, you lavish your concern on a servant. Would you worry this much if *I* were ill?"

"Far more," she blurted, her heart thumping in fright at the thought of him feverish, or in pain.

He set down his bread and stared at her. The room was silent, except for the muffled rumble of carriage wheels in the street outside.

"You're my husband," Constance said feebly.

"So…your concern would be the sort of good work one would expect of a Christian wife." It was as if he could think of no other rationale. Was it really so long since anyone other than his mother had cared about him for himself?

Afraid she would show pity, and embarrass him, Constance chose to joke. She said thoughtfully, "If you'd wanted a wife devoted to good works, I'd have recommended my sister Isabel."

He gave her a warning look, though his mouth twitched.

"She's a little young," Constance said, "but I know that doesn't—"

He cleared his throat ominously, and she subsided.

She returned to her food, satisfied she'd made it plain that if he were to fall ill, her concern would not be born of Christian goodness.

After a moment, Marcus said abruptly, "You may tell Dallow to summon a doctor for Harper, if you wish."

She fought the urge to beam. "The sooner your boots are restored to their former glory, the better," she agreed.

He chuckled, shook his head at her deliberate misinterpretation. Then he picked up the newspaper the footman had set next to his place.

Constance watched him read, watched the intelligence in his eyes, the absorption in his face.

The silence now was warm…could even have been companionable.

If Constance hadn't felt guilty.

She was truly worried about Harper, she assured herself, and would like to think she would summon a doctor to him regardless of her other motives.

What mattered was that she had carte blanche to summon a physician of her choosing. As soon as Marcus left for his club, she would pen a note to Mr. Gerald Young asking him to see both Harper and the dowager.

What harm could there be to request a visit from a respected physician recommended by so notable a person as Lady Annabelle White?

Except…while Marcus hadn't forbidden her to consult Mr. Young, he'd made it plain he didn't want her to. And now, just as he'd softened enough to show his concern for Harper, and to tolerate the possibility of Constance caring for her husband, she was about to do something that would displease him.

Chapter Thirteen

To Constance's chagrin, Mr. Young didn't arrive within the hour. He sent a note to say he would attend toward three o'clock, after he finished his rounds at St. Mary's Orphanage. A part of her approved of his refusal to rate a wealthy patient ahead of his poorer ones…but another part of her wanted to assert privilege and insist the man drop everything for the Dowager Countess of Spenford.

Constance sat with her mother-in-law, penning a letter to her family, then working on her embroidery. A few more weeks and the verse would be finished. She was considering giving it to Marcus…but she wasn't sure if he would appreciate its sentiment. Every so often she set down her work and clasped the dowager's hand on the counterpane. The return grip was feebler than it had been last week. Feebler still than the weeks before that.

When Dallow knocked on the door to announce Mr. Young's arrival, the dowager was enjoying a much-needed nap. Constance instructed Dallow to take the physician first to Harper. Thankfully, Marcus usually stayed at his club until at least five o'clock. It would be easier if he didn't come home while the doctor was here.

When the butler knocked again, she sprang to her feet

with relief and went to greet him at the door of the dowager's room. She was equally relieved to find the doctor appeared perfectly normal, dressed in a dark coat and a white shirt almost as immaculate as her husband would wear. He looked in no way a quack.

"Thank you for coming, Mr. Young." She shook his hand. "How is Tom Harper?"

The man smiled his approval of her concern. "A middling case of influenza. His fever is high just now—I've given instructions to your housekeeper for how he's to be nursed. He won't be fit for duties for another week, at least. A few weeks for full recovery."

Constance foresaw another three or four days, at least, of Miriam being so distracted she'd lay out odd slippers for Constance or forget her gloves. Her maid hadn't taken the news of Tom Harper's illness well—so much for her insistence she had no further interest in the man.

"Mr. Young, allow me to introduce you to the Dowager Countess of Spenford." Constance led him into the room.

After greetings had been exchanged, she prepared to leave.

"My dear, please stay," Helen said. "I'm not—not quite strong enough to explain myself today."

"Of course." Constance squeezed her hand. At Mr. Young's request, she told him as best she knew the treatment Mr. Bird had decreed. Helen filled in the gaps.

"In the past week or so, her ladyship's symptoms have worsened," Constance concluded.

"Mr. Bird says my condition will continue to fluctuate," Helen said. "I may feel much better next week. But…it would be nice to have a clearer prognosis."

"We shall see," was all Mr. Young would commit himself to. From his bag, he pulled out a long wooden tube with a kind of cup on the end.

"What's that?" Constance asked, alarmed.

"A new invention by a colleague of mine in France, Mr. Rene Laennec." Mr. Young handed the device to her for inspection, with a reverence that far exceeded the value of its materials. "He calls it a stethoscope. It's for listening to the patient's chest. Mr. Leannec has been besieged by doctors wanting the device—I'm honored he chose to send me one."

"Indeed," Constance said doubtfully. "Will it hurt?"

"Not in the least," Young said.

She moved to the window while he conducted his examination. She didn't hear any murmur of pain from Helen, so had to assume the stethoscope was causing no harm.

"The heartbeat is irregular, and much too fast," Mr. Young announced.

Constance turned from the window, where she was watching the street for any untimely return by Marcus. "Can you help us?"

"My examination isn't yet concluded." The doctor smiled briefly before turning back to his patient.

Constance liked him. Unlike Mr. Bird, he did not address his patient as if she had no understanding. He didn't issue expressionless orders, as if he didn't care about their outcome. And now, when the dowager spoke, her sentences broken by her need to catch her breath, Mr. Young listened patiently. He seemed to absorb what he was told into his assessment, rather than assuming he knew everything already.

Please, Lord, let him help.

Informed by a footman that his wife was with the dowager, Marcus headed upstairs. Typical of Constance to be attending his mother, he thought. She was kindness itself.

Was it pure kindness that would guarantee her attention to him if he were ill? She'd suggested not. The thought of excessive tenderness being aimed in his direction should repel him. And yet…he'd found himself drawn back to his home. To his wife. He'd left his club early, much to Severn's disappointment—normally they would play snooker until it was time to go home to change for the evening's entertainments.

Marcus knocked once on his mother's door, then pushed it open.

Constance stood by the window, fingers pressed to the pane—she spun around, and when she saw him gave a gasp of shock.

"Is something wrong?" Marcus walked swiftly toward her. From the corner of his eye, he registered another presence. A man, looming over his mother. He changed course.

His mother smiled weakly at him; she didn't appear to be in any danger. Marcus offered her a perfunctory greeting.

"Who are you?" he demanded of the stranger. "And what is *that?*"

That was a bizarre wooden tube, with a kind of bowl on one end.

The stranger bowed. "Mr. Young, my lord, at your service. This is a stethoscope, a new invention for listening to a patient's heart and lungs."

Marcus whipped around to face Constance. "Mr. *Young?*"

She had the grace to blush. "This is the physician Lady Annabelle White recommended."

He realized he was about to argue in front of a stranger, and instead strode to the window.

"After I expressly told you *not* to?" he demanded, in a low voice.

"You didn't actually say not to. Besides, I—I called him in to attend Harper." But she looked as guilty as a poacher caught with a skinned rabbit.

Marcus was turned to the doctor. "You may leave," he said coldly. The sooner he got Constance alone and gave her the scolding she deserved, the better. To think, he'd hurried home to her. *Wanted* to see her.

"Mr. Young." She had the nerve to address the physician. "Can you help her ladyship?"

About to order her to keep quiet, Marcus took stock of Young's grave expression. A chill struck his heart. He glanced at his mother, really looked at her this time. She lay still, her eyes closed.

Marcus found himself unable to shove the interloper from the room.

Young joined them over by the window. "Lady Spenford's condition is severe," he confided. "The rapidity of her pulse, its irregular nature…those things are taking more of a toll on her energies than I would expect. Which suggests they're a symptom of an underlying deterioration of the heart."

"What are the implications?" Constance asked.

"Her weakness is so severe, my own estimate is that without intervention, she has only days left to live."

Blood rushed in Marcus's ears, drowning the doctor's next words. His vision swam—to clear it would require a handkerchief, he realized, appalled. He clenched his eyes shut.

And felt a hand—Constance's—steal into his.

Wanting to thrust it aside, he found himself clutching it. He gave up the attempt to let go of her, and ducked his head, as if to glare at the inferior polish of his boots.

"I believe Mr. Bird's opinion as to her ladyship's fluctuating condition is overly optimistic," Young said.

Marcus wanted to punch him. "What makes you more qualified than an esteemed physician like Mr. Bird?" he demanded.

"Is there nothing to be done?" Constance asked. "You mentioned intervention?"

Young chose to answer Constance, rather than Marcus. "There is a new medicine that helps regulate the pulse. Devised by a Mr. William Withering, an extract from the fox-glove plant."

"Foxglove is poisonous," Marcus snapped.

"Many varieties are toxic," the physician agreed. "But *digitalis purpurea* has proven effective in the treatment of heart complaints. Folklorists have long known it but the medical profession is newer to the remedy."

"Folklorists!" Marcus practically choked on the word.

"You think it could help Lady Spenford?" Constance asked.

"For some patients, the effects have been remarkable," Young confirmed. "Something close to full health has been restored with ongoing treatment. In Lady Spenford's case, I would hope for at least a recovery from her excessive fatigue, and an easing of the strain on her heart. Whether *digitalis* can strengthen a deteriorating heart, such as I suspect your mother has…" He clearly didn't know the answer.

Quackery, Marcus thought. "If such restoration was possible, Mr. Bird would have said." Although Mr. Bird did not, as far as Marcus knew, have a steth—whatever that device was.

"Not all physicians favor the remedy," Mr. Young said. "Careless preparation reduces its efficacy, so some haven't found it useful. I don't employ a chemist to prepare my medicines. I make them myself to ensure they're up to standard."

Reassuring words. But…his mother couldn't be as ill as Young claimed; just two days ago Mr. Bird had said he could see no reason why Marcus's mother shouldn't continue on as she was, improving and declining by turns.

Marcus realized now he'd ignored the *declining* and focused on the *improving.* He'd seen Bird's uncertainty as confirmation that everything was in God's hands…and he had every reason to believe God would keep their bargain. He'd chosen to ignore Constance's warnings about his mother's deterioration. If Mama died now…

"How do you wish to proceed?" the doctor asked Marcus. "My own recommendation is we discuss this with the dowager countess. Don't be afraid, my lord, that you will shock her. She knows the severity of her condition."

Unable to speak, unable to find a more palatable alternative, Marcus jerked his head toward his mother's bed in agreement.

The quack was right; his mother seemed unsurprised to learn of her limited time remaining on this earth. She must feel worse than she'd admitted.

His mother listened carefully to the doctor, and asked a breathless question or two.

"I wish to try this new medicine," she said at last, with sudden strength. "It may be a slim hope, but that is better than no hope."

"You have only this man's word that there's no hope," Marcus reminded her quickly.

The physician nodded at the dowager. "I will return this evening with your first tincture. Then each day until we determine if it is helping." He addressed Marcus: "I trust that meets with your approval."

His mother didn't need his consent for medical treatment, unlike his wife. But Marcus knew that if he decreed against it, she would follow his wishes.

He'd never felt such shocking responsibility. Not even when news of his brother's death had been brought to him, and he'd known he, the inadequate second son, would one day have to step into his father's shoes. Not even when his father had died and made that prospect a reality.

Nothing came close to this.

Please, God, tell me what to say.

Clear, divine instruction was not forthcoming. Marcus

cleared his throat. "Very well," he said. "It can't hurt to try a new medicine."

Mr. Young's gaze didn't waver. "All medical treatment carries a risk, my lord. It's essential to calculate the correct dose of *digitalis* for each patient. Too little, and it won't work. Too much, and the heart will slow too far—to the point of death."

"No!" Marcus exploded. *This* was God's answer? It might work, or else it might hasten his mother's death? "My mother will not take a drug that might kill her."

His mother looked shaken.

"Mr. Young says she has only a few days in any case," Constance reminded him. "If she still wishes it..."

"Mr. Bird has given no cause for such alarm," he said. "Mama, I forbid you."

Silence fell over the group.

As Marcus watched, what little light remained in his mother's face went out so suddenly and completely, it was as if someone had extinguished a lamp, leaving them in gray, featureless twilight.

"Mama?" he said uncertainly.

"Are you certain I must not take it?" she asked. The hand she extended trembled, and Marcus enfolded it in his.

"It's dangerous. You could die," he said.

"Marcus," she said, "every breath is harder than the one before. Every word brings pain."

"Then don't talk," he urged her.

"There are things..." She beckoned Constance, standing behind him. Constance moved closer. "I fear each word will be my last and I will not have said the most..." She closed her eyes. "I love you, Marcus."

"Mama, don't!" He chafed her hand. She hadn't said that since he was twelve years old—to say it now could only mean she was losing hope.

"Forgive me, I must speak plainly," she said. "This is too

important. Marcus, I know you're unhappy." She clutched a fistful of blanket in her left hand. "Forgive me for not having had the—the strength to teach you what matters most."

"There's nothing to forgive," he said, horrified. She was ill, her mind was doubtless wandering.

Constance started to weep. Marcus wished he could do the same. To think his mother had been facing her own mortality, had been terrified at the prospect and hadn't said a word. Had he been so intent on having his way, on curing her through prayer and the attentions of Mr. Bird, that she'd been unable to tell him how she felt?

"You feel ill right now, but wonderful things can happen," he said desperately. "God works in mysterious ways."

There was still time for the Almighty to uphold His end of their bargain.

Constance hiccuped, then cleared her throat. "Can mysterious ways include sending a new physician with a new treatment?"

His head snapped around; he stared at her.

She cannot die, he told her with his eyes.

Have faith, he fancied her steady gaze transmitted in reply. But if that was her message, even she didn't look entirely convinced. She couldn't promise Mr. Young was sent by God, and Marcus knew it.

His gaze measured her. Measured his mother's frail form. Measured the hours of life that remained…if Young was right.

"Very well," he said to Young. "We'll try your treatment."

Her eyes still closed, his mother smiled.

Chapter Fourteen

Marcus sent his apologies to the Quayles and the Mottrams, both of whom expected to see him and Constance that evening. Their absence at their other engagement—the Duchess of Havant's ball—wouldn't be noticed.

At seven o'clock, Mr. Young returned as promised with the medicine. Marcus supported his mother with an arm around her shoulders while she swallowed it.

If the dose was incorrect, any adverse effect would likely be experienced tonight, the doctor said. Though there was always a risk, every time she took it, the risk was greatest the first time.

"I'll stay with her," Marcus announced. He turned down Constance's offer to sit with him. Whatever happened would be on his head.

The next day, Sunday, Constance pulled on her morning dress, asked Bligh to hurry up with the fastening and went straight to the dowager's rooms.

"She's sleeping," Powell said in answer to Constance's light rap on the door with her knuckles. Then, a half smile broke the severity of her expression, telling Constance all she needed to know.

When Constance clasped Powell's hands and squeezed them for joy, the maid blinked away tears. "Don't dither in the doorway, my lady, go on in," she scolded. "The patient slept better than you did, by the look of you."

As Powell had said, the dowager lay sleeping. Marcus dozed on the chair next to her.

It was the first time Constance had seen him asleep.

He looked…maybe not exactly tranquil…but his forehead was clear, his strong mouth a little less intimidating in repose. He'd loosened his cravat; she could see the column of his bare throat. His vulnerability struck her, reached into a place in her heart.

Perhaps she made some small noise, for his eyes opened.

It took a moment for him to focus on her. Then he jerked upright. "Mama…"

"She's sleeping," Constance assured him. "It's morning, past nine o'clock."

He yawned. Then ran a hand around the back of his neck to ease cramped muscles. The movement emphasized the breadth of his chest.

Constance transferred her attention to the bed. "She's breathing more easily." The dowager's lips were pink, without the blue tinge that so often framed them.

Marcus moved to stand at her shoulder, displacing cool air with his warmth. Constance's skin prickled.

Under their combined scrutiny, his mother woke up.

Her eyes widened. "You'll have me worried I'm about to die, standing there like a pair of mourners at a graveside," she said.

"You're not about to die," Marcus said firmly.

Constance smiled. "You seem well, Mama." She wondered if Helen remembered what she'd said last night about Marcus being unhappy. He'd been visibly shocked, but no trace of that showed in his face now—only relief.

Hearing her mistress's voice, Powell hurried in from the dowager's sitting room. "My lady, how are you?"

"I feel…" The dowager stopped. She pressed a hand to her chest. "I feel…*easier* here. Powell, I do believe I could manage some breakfast."

The maid raced off before her mistress could change her mind. A few minutes later, wary of tiring the patient, Marcus and Constance left, too.

"I know one night is too soon to talk of miracles," Marcus said as they walked downstairs together—like a true husband and wife, Constance thought. "But…"

She murmured her agreement. It was tempting to hope.

Marcus stopped, a stair below her, so the difference in their heights was greatly reduced.

"I have you to thank," he said. "Believe me, you have my sincere gratitude."

His *gratitude* wasn't what she wanted. Maybe, if she'd allowed Bligh a few minutes to style her hair more becomingly… Too late now. "It's Mr. Young who deserves your thanks," she pointed out.

"He will have them," Marcus said. Almost, but not quite, humbly, he added, "I apologize for doubting you, Constance."

She almost tripped and fell down the stairs. Not at the apology—he had called her Constance! Although he'd referred to her by her Christian name to his mother, he'd never directly addressed her thus.

Marcus grasped her elbow. They finished their descent of the grand staircase joined like that.

The following Sunday, Marcus decided his mother's continued improvement required suitable thanks to the Maker. He would attend the worship service held in Mama's bedchamber each week. He'd never particularly enjoyed the sermons of Mr. Robertson, the curate from St. George's who came in to preach and administer the sacrament. But an hour of tedium, even one starting at the surely ungodly hour of nine o'clock, was a small price to pay: his mother felt so well, she'd declared her intention of coming downstairs one day soon. Mr. Young had been visiting daily, and according to his stethoscope, the dowager's pulse had slowed almost to normal. Even the fact that Mr. Bird had washed his hands of his patient when he'd heard of her experimental treatment couldn't dampen the mood of optimism.

Marcus arrived in his mother's room to find Constance there already. He was almost accustomed now to having her around the house, and accompanying him in the evenings. He nodded a greeting, not wishing to interrupt the curate's conversation. She did have a nice smile, nice lips, he observed. Some people might think her bottom lip should be fuller, but he liked its ready curve. He found himself smiling back at her.

"If your lordship is ready, we will begin." The curate glanced at his watch, as if they were all champing to say their prayers.

Pestifying man—he had such an air of zeal about him. Marcus formed a reply that would set him in his place…but then he noticed the cocking of Constance's head. She was probably expecting him to deliver a snub, and would use it to confirm her outrageous view that Marcus was too proud. "By all means," Marcus said with extreme grace.

Constance dropped her gaze to her Bible. Ha!

The warm glow of defeating his wife's expectations sustained Marcus through the first prayers, including the reciting of the Lord's Prayer. Constance had a fine voice, he noticed. Clear and warm. No wonder his mother liked to have her at her bedside.

Then it was time for the sermon. The curate set down his prayer book. "If it pleases your lordship, in recent weeks we've taken the liberty of dispensing with a formal sermon, and instead discussed the reading from the New Testament."

That must be Constance's doing. Any woman who could convince a preacher to forgo a long-winded sermon was a jewel in Marcus's estimation. "By all means," he agreed.

"My lady, will you read the verses to us? Here, use my Bible. It's open at the correct place." As the curate handed his Bible to Constance, his fingers brushed hers. Constance seemed oblivious, but Mr. Robertson blushed.

Blushed?

Marcus's gaze sharpened on the man as Constance began reading. The curate's eyes were fixed on Marcus's wife. Twice, he closed them briefly, as if transported to some delightful place. A spiritual place, Marcus assured himself. The curate could have no interest in the countess.

Half an hour later, he revised that opinion. The curate was more than interested in the countess. He hung on her every word as if she were wisdom personified. Constance did have some interesting views on the scripture under discussion. Irritatingly interesting—Marcus had no firm opinion of his own to defend, and didn't want to discuss something of which he wasn't entirely certain.

No doubt Constance would deem that a sign of his pride.

He rolled his eyes as the curate entreated her to see his point of view. If the man had more gumption, Constance would be less inclined to question him! Though perhaps that wasn't true—she questioned Marcus all the time.

"Sir, I cannot," she said with good humor. "I wrote to my father after we talked last week, and here is his reply." She pulled a folded piece of paper from a pocket concealed in the rose-pink silk dress that suited her complexion, and handed it to Mr. Robertson. "I hope you don't mind my asking his opinion?"

"My lady, I'm honored that you considered my views

worthy of bringing to your esteemed father's attention," Mr. Robertson said.

Sycophant! Marcus thought. What was Constance doing, writing to her father about the preacher, anyway? Did she write about Marcus, her *husband,* too?

If so, what did she say?

Suddenly, Marcus wasn't sure he wanted to be the subject of her letters.

The curate had an annoying habit of soundlessly mouthing the words as he read. Marcus tried not to watch. When the man had finished, he looked up, smiling.

"What a wonderful mind your father has, my lady."

"He certainly does," the dowager agreed from her bed. Her voice grew stronger every day.

Constance glowed. "Thank you, Mr. Robertson, you're very kind."

Marcus scowled. The preacher couldn't have chosen a better way to win Constance's favor.

"If we could discuss how your father's views affect our understanding of today's passage," the curate prompted.

Constance needed no encouragement to talk about her confounded father—in moments, an animated debate was underway. Marcus's mother took part, and it was a thrill to see her so alert. Which she had to be, since if she hadn't forced herself into the conversation, all the curate's attention would have gone to Constance.

The man should be ashamed of himself—how dare he make eyes at another man's wife?

Marcus couldn't fault Constance's behavior. She was doing nothing to attract the clergyman. Indeed, there was nothing in her to attract the man. Unless he had a weakness for a fine figure and a stubborn chin.

And a sweet smile.

And an inquiring mind.

And a kind heart.

Entirely possible, Marcus conceded. Constance had probably been reared to make an excellent wife for a churchman.

He can't have her. The moment of possessiveness surprised him. But it was only natural, he decided. He hadn't taken his vows lightly, despite what Constance might think.

"You have an excellent mind, your ladyship." The curate was now groveling as he closed his Bible. The service was over, Marcus realized.

"You're too kind, Mr. Robertson." She extended her hand to him in farewell.

For one shocked moment, Marcus thought the man would kiss her fingers, necessitating his swift ejection from the house.

But it turned out Robertson was only after an innocent handshake. Marcus was disappointed.

The curate took his leave of the dowager. Marcus stood at the top of the stairs as Dallow bowed the man out, and felt better once the curate was off the premises.

He pondered his reaction to the man's behavior as he headed for the stables for his morning ride. Constance had asked if he would object to a gentleman flirting with her. He'd said he wouldn't. But now… *The curate's not a gentleman,* he told himself. *He's not Constance's equal, which is why I was disturbed.* He felt vaguely uncomfortable declaring one of God's workers to be unequal. Scripture probably had something to say about that, and no doubt Constance could quote chapter and verse on the subject.

So if the curate *was* her equal…did Marcus object to the man flirting with his wife?

He did, as it turned out.

Rather strongly.

"I think I'll pay a visit to Tom Harper," the countess said.

Miriam felt the blood leave her face. She set down her ladyship's hairbrush. "Why, my lady, have you heard that he's worse?" She'd been worried sick, ever since she'd heard Tom had influenza.

Lady Spenford met her eyes in the mirror as she said calmly, "No, Bligh, I believe he is much improved. But I doubt Lord Spenford has found the time to see him, and one of us should."

Miriam pressed a hand to her chest, trying to still its panicked thudding. "May I come with you, my lady?"

She'd been touched by Tom's apology to her last time they spoke, and she'd never showed it. And to think, he'd been worried about her health, when he must have been feeling rotten himself. That wasn't the behavior of a man anything like her father.

"You realize Harper is still in bed?" the countess asked.

"I've done plenty of nursing of my brothers, my lady."

"And Harper is like a brother to you?"

It took Miriam a moment to realize her employer was teasing.

Certain she was blushing rosily, she said, "Not exactly, my lady."

"I shouldn't tease," Lady Spenford said. "I know you've been worried, Bligh. It's partly for your benefit that I'm planning this visit."

If that didn't prove the countess was a true lady, Miriam didn't know what did.

And so, on their way out to the shops, dressed in their outdoor clothing—Miriam with a shawl over her gray dress and Lady Spenford wearing a dark red spencer over a white muslin dress—they made their way to the male servants' basement quarters.

Miriam had never been down here before—and now she had, she was very pleased to be female. Better a poky attic room with some natural light than one of these dark spaces.

And she knew from the other servants that this was a modern town house, with better servant accommodations than most.

There was nothing improper about her visiting a male servant with Lady Spenford, but still, Miriam felt awkward as they crossed the threshold of Tom's room.

Until she noticed the chair next to the bed was occupied by one of the junior housemaids—a girl Miriam judged too forward by half.

"Mrs. Matlock asked me to bring some soup down to Mr. Harper," the girl defended herself, correctly interpreting Miriam's squint.

"You may go now," Lady Spenford told her. She stepped forward. "How do you do, Harper?"

Tom shuffled higher up his pillows. He looked as if he would dearly love to get out of bed and bow. "Well, thank you, my lady. And thank you for asking Mr. Young to visit. I believe my recovery was much quicker thanks to him."

Not a word to Miriam. Which, strictly speaking, was proper in the presence of the countess, but it still miffed her mightily.

"You'll see I've brought Miss Bligh," Lady Spenford said. "What's that you have pinned to your wall over there, Harper? May I look?"

"Yes, my lady. It's a sampler. My sister stitched it for me. Psalm 23…"

Miriam snickered at Tom's bemusement as the countess, a parson's daughter who likely knew the twenty-third Psalm backward as well as forward, crossed the room and focused intently on reading the unframed sampler he'd pinned up.

She wondered what Tom would say if he knew Lady Spenford considered herself to be acting as chaperone. For Miriam. With Tom.

He'd probably be horrified. She sighed.

"What is it, Miriam?" he asked in a low voice.

Better not give him a relapse. "Nothing," she said. "Are you sure you're all right?"

"Tired." He pressed back into the pillows. "Feel like I've done ten rounds in the boxing ring in an unfair fight. But I'm getting better." He watched her face. "Were you worried about me?"

"I had a sister die of influenza," she muttered.

"I remember," he said. "Little Katherine."

She nodded, surprised. "I know how quickly it can turn lethal."

"Mine wasn't that severe," he assured her.

"I—I've been wanting to tell you I appreciate your apology. You know, for saying I was no good at my job."

He paused. "You must truly have been worried about me."

Miriam glanced at the countess, and decided to pretend her mistress's feigned deafness was real. "I didn't want you to go to your grave with me angry at you, so I forgave everything you've ever said or done to hurt me."

Too late, she realized she'd as good as told him how much she cared about him...for if she didn't care, how could he hurt her?

In for a penny, in for a pound, as her mother would say. "If we both put the past behind us," she said, still unsure where his resentment of her lay, "maybe we could start afresh."

Even through the lingering pallor of his illness, Tom looked stricken, flattened against his pillow as if he'd just done an eleventh round in that boxing ring.

Not at all as if he felt the same way about her.

Miriam choked on a sob of humiliation—she sounded like a mouse caught in a trap. She ran from the room, startling the countess out of her contemplation of the comfort provided by the Lord through the Valley of the Shadow of Death.

Chapter Fifteen

For Tuesday morning, Lucinda organized an excursion to Richmond Park. A small group—ten or twelve people—would stroll the park then enjoy a picnic. With the dowager doing so much better, Constance was eager to have a day outdoors; she accepted the invitation without consulting Marcus.

To her surprise, her husband came, too. Presumably for the pleasure of his cousin's company, rather than his wife's.

Apart from Lucinda and Jonathan, Constance didn't know the other members of the party well. She'd met them at various ton events, but considered them mere acquaintances. Yesterday's rain had left the sky a clear, clean blue, and the temperature not too hot—perfect conditions. They began their stroll on the broad sweep of the Queen's Ride. Narrower paths branched off either side into the Duchess Wood. There was no wind; deer grazed peacefully on lush grass beneath ancient oaks.

"Beautiful," declared Major Price-Chorley, a bachelor gentleman who'd attended Eton with Jonathan. "'Mongst boughs pavilion'd where the deer's swift leap," he quoted, "'startles the wild bee from the foxglove bell.'"

"Mr. Keats's poem is an ode to solitude," Constance pointed out. "I fear you'll be horribly crowded by us today."

"You know the poem?" Major Price-Chorley moved around Lucinda so that he was walking alongside Constance.

"I read it a few days ago in the *Examiner*," she said. "I believe it's Mr. Keats's first published work?"

Marcus watched his wife become engrossed in conversation with the major with a sense of mild shock. He'd never heard of this Keats fellow—not surprising if he'd only managed to write one poem, he supposed—and since when did Constance read a liberal magazine like the *Examiner?* Marcus didn't allow the thing in his house— *Ah.* The Reverend Somerton, no doubt, had been sending such "literature" to his daughter.

Marcus answered a question from Lucinda about his plans for a summer house party at Chalmers—he had none. They moved on to other people's house parties and which would be worth attending...a light enough topic that Marcus could keep one ear trained on Constance's conversation. The major seemed to think Keats would be a tremendous hit. The more lines he quoted, the less Marcus agreed.

After half an hour, they came to a deep rut in the road, filled with yesterday's rain. Fortunately, it ran only half the width of the road, so they could walk around it.

"I declare, Lady Spenford," Major Price-Chorley said, "I've a good mind to lay my cloak down over this puddle for you. It's only fitting, for a lady as poetically minded as yourself."

Marcus gave him an incredulous look.

"I hope you'll do no such thing," Constance retorted. "Your poor valet would be faced with an impossible job to clean it, and all for some silly notion of gallantry."

The major appeared to lose the power of speech at this forthright opinion of his chivalry. "Your ladyship is so thoughtful," he managed to say as Constance walked around the puddle.

Humbug! Marcus excused himself to Lucinda and rejoined his wife. "There is a charming copse down the path to your left," he said. "It's home to some uncommon birdlife. Will you come with me to see it?"

"Of course."

A moment later Marcus was bundling her down the path, away from Major Price-Chorley, as fast as propriety allowed.

When they rounded a bend, he slowed.

"How far is the copse?" Constance asked.

"Perhaps five minutes' walk." He hadn't been there in years; he hoped it was as attractive as he remembered. Now that he had her to himself, he wasn't sure what to say.

"I can tell by your boots that Harper is back at work," Constance said.

Marcus cast a satisfied glance at his gleaming Hessians. "It was nice to see his face this morning," he agreed.

"Did you tell him so?" Constance asked.

He gave her an impatient look. "I didn't ask how he's feeling, either. Because *you* will ask him, so all I need do is ask you."

She chuckled at his logic.

The foliage was denser here, sunlight breaking through in dappled patches. The leaves had protected the path from yesterday's rain; it was dry beneath their feet.

"Lucinda's friends are a nice group," Constance said.

Marcus grunted.

"You don't like them?" she asked.

"It's more that I didn't think you would like them," he said. "I know you disapprove of flirts."

"Who was flirting?" she asked.

He took her elbow to help her over a fallen log. "When a gentleman offers to lay down his cloak for a lady to step on—"

"That was a joke," she said. "And you'll have noticed I

scolded him about his lack of consideration for his valet. Marcus, the major wasn't flirting. It's just that he appreciated that I'd read Mr. Keats's poem."

"I think you'd agree," he said, "that I have far more experience than you of ton life."

"Of course," she said.

"Then I suggest you trust my judgment where the major is concerned. And where the curate is concerned."

Her brow crinkled. "Mr. Robertson?"

His plan, if it could be glorified with such a title, had been to provide some gentle guidance, the kind a husband should offer his less sophisticated wife.

Instead, he snapped, "Yes, Mr. Robertson. The man was flirting with you, blushing like a schoolboy."

Her jaw dropped. "I shall pretend you never said such an outrageous thing."

"I accept that you didn't intend to encourage him," he said. "But your admiration for his theology may have given him the wrong message."

"Mr. Robertson is a man of God. He was *not* flirting." The pink in her cheeks was more vivid out here than indoors. "I hope he enjoys our discussions of Bible doctrine, but more likely, he humors me out of good manners. For you to suggest…I would *never* indulge in a flirtation."

"I'm not accusing *you*…."

She swept past him. Then the extravagant song of a lark halted her. "Marcus, listen!"

Her outrage forgotten, she tilted her head to one side, much like a bird herself. He'd once thought of her as a sparrow, Marcus recalled.

"I hear it," he said. It had been years since he'd paid attention to birdsong. Years since he'd marveled at the genius of the Creator.

When the song died away, they moved on.

"Even if I were not a married woman, I would have no idea how to flirt." Constance resumed her defense of herself.

A wife who didn't know how to flirt—Marcus had made a wise choice in his parson's daughter. Not that he had *chosen* her, of course. The thought crossed his mind that Amanda had known how to flirt. For the first time, he felt he had the better end of the bargain.

So he was shocked to hear himself say, "Perhaps I should teach you."

"*What* did you say?" Constance stared, her lips softly parted.

"It would help you recognize inappropriate behavior among those of your acquaintance," he said, aware he was talking nonsense.

Her eyes narrowed. "I had no difficulty recognizing that Lady Annabelle White was flirting with you at the opera. Might I point out, her behavior bore no resemblance to the curate's, which *was not flirting.*"

"Lady Annabelle was unsubtle," Marcus said. "You need to be able to identify more intelligent flirtation."

"You are accusing Mr. Robertson, a curate, of *intelligent flirtation.*"

"More intelligent than Lady Annabelle's," he said.

"Anything would be," she agreed.

He smiled.

The catch of her breath told him his smile affected her. Which in turn piqued his own attention. He found his senses on alert, and had to feign relaxation.

"So," he mused, "where shall we start?"

"I have no desire to indulge in such behavior," she said, pleasingly short of breath.

Marcus realized he was enjoying himself…and he was very much looking forward to flirting with his wife.

"We'd better not attempt too much to start with," he said. "After all, you're the daughter of a country parson."

"Hopelessly rustic?" she suggested.

He scanned the elegant green silk of her dress. "Not hopelessly."

"You're too kind," she murmured.

"My point is…" He had to think for a moment to recall his point. Something about his wife's wide, warm eyes was distracting him. "My point is, if you can't recognize the cleverer kinds of flirting, you may inadvertently yield to it."

"Thus damaging the Spenford reputation," she suggested.

"It's possible." Though in truth he hadn't thought of that.

"Men don't flirt with me, Marcus."

"The curate did." He saw a gleam of annoyance in her eyes, and hurried on. "So did the major. You dance with men at the parties we attend. Are you telling me not one has complimented you on your appearance?"

"They're only being courteous," she said.

He didn't know whether to be relieved that gentleman paid her compliments, or annoyed.

"Has anyone ever complimented you so as to make you feel uncomfortable?" he demanded, momentarily dropping their game.

"I did have to tread on Lord Atherton's toes at the Ballys' rout," she reflected.

Marcus laughed. Old Atherton had a shocking reputation; he was glad she'd put him in his place. "Anyone else?"

She shook her head. "The gentleman I stand up with most is Lord Severn, and he's never too forward."

Severn? My best friend? Come to think of it, Marcus had noticed his friend dancing with his wife once or twice. Severn wasn't a man who danced with women out of charity. Or out of politeness.

"So…you enjoy Severn's company?" he asked.

Constance considered the question; Marcus found himself on tenterhooks.

"He is always interested to talk to me, or at least he gives that impression," she said. "And his temperament is sunny."

Marcus made a noise in his throat suspiciously like a growl. No one had ever called *him* sunny.

Thankfully, Constance didn't appear to hear. "Perhaps Lord Severn is a little *too* sunny," she reflected.

"An excess of sunniness can be irritating," Marcus agreed.

"He doesn't appear to think very hard," Constance continued.

"You get that with these sunny fellows," Marcus said, blithely ignoring that Severn possessed one of the sharpest minds in England. If his friend chose to conceal his intellect beneath a frivolous attitude, he must suffer the consequence.

Marcus made a note to watch his friend when he danced with Constance in the future.

As they walked, he allowed his fingers to brush hers. She drew in a sharp breath.

Marcus stared straight ahead as he said, "You should be aware that when a gentleman touches your hand, like this—" he did it again, producing another little indrawn breath "—he is flirting."

"I see," Constance said, her voice strangled.

They walked on. Occasionally, Marcus's fingers brushed hers. The air between them seemed heavy. Marcus, who always knew the correct thing to say, wondered where this conversation was going…and why his brain was sluggish, his tongue too thick in his mouth to form graceful words.

They stumbled across the copse when he thought it was still a few minutes away.

He'd been both right and wrong remembering it as special. The foliage was identical to every other copse in the park— oaks and pines, bluebells growing at their base. And yet…

"These trees are older," Constance said. "Look how thick they are, how high the canopy."

Marcus nodded, pleased. "The place feels somehow majestic, doesn't it? Inspiring."

"Inspiring?" She grinned. "Does this mean you plan to quote poetry, like the major?"

"*Some* men use poetry as a flirtation device," he said dismissively.

"I like poetry," Constance admitted.

"Others find a well-placed compliment allows a more personal approach."

"Too easy to veer into flattery," she disagreed. "If a man should wax lyrical over my beauty, I should consider him a fraud."

"You mustn't speak of yourself that way," Marcus said, shocked.

"You consider it too self-effacing for the Spenford pride?" she asked lightly.

"No!" He stopped, forcing her to do the same. "Constance, you are the woman God made you. You're not a famous beauty, but you have charms that anyone can see."

She blinked. Her mouth opened, as if to speak, then she closed it again.

Somewhere above them a bee buzzed lazily. The sweet scent of bluebells, mixed with crisp pine, hung in the air.

"If you were flirting," Marcus prompted her, "you would ask me to list those charms."

His eyes held hers, and he was conscious of a strange sense of anticipation. She licked her lips.

"Will you?" she asked, her voice barely a whisper. *Will you list those charms?*

His head swam, as if the heat of the sun had blasted its way through the canopy. It felt as if the words he chose now would mean something far more than the combination of vowels and consonants. *Lord, may I choose well.*

He scrutinized Constance's face. "Your forehead is clear and honest."

No mistaking the flash of disappointment.

"A wonderful attribute in a chambermaid," she said.

She was right. He grimaced, and tried again.

"Your wit is sometimes subtle, sometimes not, yet always intelligent."

Her eyes widened. "Thank you." She would have walked on, but he held up a hand to stop her.

"A list is more than two items," he said. He settled on her visage again. "Your eyebrows have a fine arch. Your eyes are expressive, as I have told you before. They convey warmth and compassion, two qualities that are very appealing. Your nose is straight and true—neither too big nor too small." He considered it, then nodded once. "All in all, I consider it a fine nose."

"Thank you." Her lips curved, drawing his attention.

"Your mouth has proven adept at delivering the set-downs you deem necessary to keep a man's pride in check," he said. "But when I look at your lips, I see…softness."

"Oh," she said.

"Then I glance just an inch or two lower, and encounter that chin." He touched his thumb to her chin. She stilled. "So much stubbornness, so much determination in one little chin," he mused.

"Stubbornness is not considered an attractive quality in a woman," she said. "Not by most men."

"Yet some men," he said, "might find the contrast between such a chin and the soft lips above it intriguing."

Her entire face reddened. "You—you are indeed an accomplished flirt, sir."

Marcus didn't feel accomplished. He felt like a boy just out of the schoolroom, with no lessons learned that could help him here.

I will kiss her. Had he known all along, deep down, that this was his plan? Marcus couldn't say—he only knew that he had to kiss her right now. He settled his hands at Constance's waist, anchoring her. Her eyes widened. He lowered his mouth to hers.

Sweet was the word that filled his head, like the swell of flutes in a Mozart concerto. After a moment of shock, she responded, and *sweet* became *seeking* and *finding.*

Right.

When Marcus lifted his head, he was shocked to find himself none too steady. Constance quivered in his hold.

"Marcus?" she whispered.

He cleared his throat. "We'd best return to the others. They'll be wondering where we are."

She nodded.

He took her fingers, and they started on the way back, her slender hand tucked tight in his.

As they walked, Constance hardly dared breathe. That kiss…so tender and yet underpinned by some stronger emotion. Her mouth still tingled.

And now, Marcus held her hand…. She curled her fingers more tightly in his, as if to convince herself the contact was real.

It felt like a miracle. As if God had answered her prayers and opened her husband's eyes to the possibilities of a true marriage. To kiss her like that, he must feel something for her. At least the seeds of love that might grow into something as strong and dependable as these ancient oaks.

Please, let it be so.

"Constance," Marcus said suddenly. He stopped, and his grip on her hand forced her to stop, too.

When he said no more, just stood staring down at her, she asked, "What is it?"

His gaze alighted on her lips, as if he might kiss her again. Instead, he took her other hand in his.

"It is time…" He hesitated. "I am your husband, you are my wife. Do you understand what I am saying?"

Yes! He was saying he cared for her, and now he wished to make their marriage real!

Overwhelmed, she nodded.

Pleasure, and gratitude, filled his face. He lowered his mouth toward hers.

"There you are!" Lucinda exclaimed, as she and Lady Bracken emerged around a twist in the path, closely followed by Lord Bracken and Jonathan.

The whole party came to a halt as Marcus sprang back from Constance.

"Oh, my," Lucinda trilled. "We're intruding on the lovebirds."

"I say, Spenford," Lord Bracken said, "can't go treating your wife like some little housemaid."

His ribald comment—and the suggestion a gentleman could force his attentions on a servant—made Constance flinch. Marcus's face had darkened—he was equally outraged. Constance reached for his hand—the eyes of everyone in their party moved to their joined fingers. She didn't care. Marcus had claimed her as his wife with that kiss.

"Surely, Lord Bracken," she said, "a husband and wife may show their natural affection for one another."

Lady Bracken tittered. Constance waited for Marcus to deliver one of his ever-so-polite set-downs.

With what seemed to her showy deliberation, he pulled his fingers from hers.

No! Constance's gaze flew to his face…and found it stony. *Don't do it,* she cajoled him silently.

"My wife is young," he said, his tone languid with disinterest. "It does no harm to humor her."

Constance's jaw sagged; quickly, she snapped it shut.

Humor her? He had kissed her with such tenderness, held her hand with affection, and now he dared claim he was humoring her?

I am his wife! I am entitled to his affection!

That, it seemed, didn't matter. When they returned to the lawn where the groom was setting up the picnic, Marcus joined the men and was in no time engrossed in a discussion of some upcoming horse race. The women, treating Constance with amused but nonmalicious pity, engaged in an animated conversation about the latest styles in half boots.

Constance stood alone. Dismissed.

They ate a quiet dinner at home that evening. Marcus had planned to attend the Travers's rout, but those plans had changed. Constance agreed with his decision to stay at home, as he expected. After all, she had told him as plainly as a lady could without uttering indelicate words that she wished their marriage to be established *completely.*

As did he. More than he would have believed possible, he wanted to be in union with his wife.

All through the long ride home from Richmond Park, the men on their horses, the ladies in the coach, Marcus had remembered that kiss. And thought of where it would rightly lead. He'd pictured Constance in the coach, talking with the other women, her mouth smiling, her brown eyes warm, her thoughts elsewhere. She'd been quiet when he'd handed her into the vehicle—as distracted as he, despite Bracken's tasteless comment necessitating a sharp rebuff.

It is time, he told himself, as he ate the dinner Cook had prepared with less than his usual interest. They had committed to a lifetime together, committed before God.

When Constance went upstairs early, at nine-thirty, Marcus took his cue from her and followed soon after.

Anticipation fizzed in his veins as he prepared for bed.

"That will be all, Harper." He dismissed his valet.

It seemed to take an age for the man to leave the room. It had required all Marcus's willpower to keep his gaze from the door that connected his chamber to Constance's, from making his intention embarrassingly obvious.

Once he was certain Harper wouldn't return for some forgotten item, Marcus took a step in the direction of her door. It occurred to him to ask God's blessing on the union…but he was at the door now, and he didn't want to waste another moment. His wife would doubtless have done all the praying they needed.

He pictured her waiting for him. Innocent and eager. Anticipation rose. It was past time for this.

The door handle was cool beneath his grip. Marcus turned it, and pushed.

The door didn't open.

Odd. Still, it hadn't been used in years; perhaps the wood had swelled in the damp of many winters. He pushed harder; it didn't budge. He didn't want to do anything so undignified as put a shoulder to it…or so embarrassing as summon a servant to help.

Then it dawned on him. It may be locked. Having been unused so long, there was every chance it had at one stage been locked and left that way.

Marcus rapped his knuckles against the door.

"It's locked," Constance said, so close to the door that he jumped.

"Is the key in the lock?" he asked in a low voice.

"Yes."

Knowing she was only inches away had set his heart

thumping. "Can you turn it?" The words came out slightly hoarse.

"I can," she said.

He waited.

"But I won't."

LIH-EC-11C

HOW TO VALIDATE YOUR
EDITOR'S FREE GIFTS!
"THANK YOU"

1. Peel off the FREE GIFTS SEAL from the front cover. Place it in the space provided at right. This automatically entitles you to receive two free books and two exciting surprise gifts.

2. Send back this card and you'll get 2 Love Inspired® Historical books. These books are worth $11.50 in the U.S. or $13.50 in Canada, but are yours absolutely FREE!

3. There's no catch. You're under no obligation to buy anything. We charge nothing—ZERO—for your first shipment. And you don't have to make any minimum number of purchases—not even one!

4. We call this line Love Inspired Historical because every month you'll receive books that are filled with inspirational historical romance. This series is filled with engaging stories of romance, adventure and faith set in historical periods from biblical times to World War II. You'll like the convenience of getting them delivered to your home well before they are in stores. And you'll love our discount prices, too!

5. We hope that after receiving your free books you'll want to remain a subscriber. But the choice is yours—to continue or cancel, anytime at all! So why not take us up on our invitation, with no risk of any kind. You'll be glad you did!

6. And remember...just for validating your Editor's Free Gifts Offer, we'll send you 2 books and 2 gifts, *ABSOLUTELY FREE!*

YOURS FREE!
We'll send you two fabulous surprise gifts (worth about $10) absolutely FREE, simply for accepting our no-risk offer!

The Editor's "Thank You" Free Gifts Include:

- Two inspirational historical romance books
- Two exciting surprise gifts

YES!

PLACE FREE GIFTS SEAL HERE

I have placed my Editor's "thank you" Free Gifts seal in the space provided above. Please send me the 2 FREE books and 2 FREE gifts for which I qualify. I understand that I am under no obligation to purchase anything further, as explained on the opposite page.

102/302 IDL FH7E

Please Print

FIRST NAME

LAST NAME

ADDRESS

APT.#

CITY

STATE/PROV.

ZIP/POSTAL CODE

The Reader Service—Here's How It Works:

Chapter Sixteen

Constance pressed her palm to the door to steady the tremor in her hand. Beyond these two inches of wood was her husband. Wanting admittance to her chamber. The admittance she had by implication agreed to grant.

"Is there a problem?" he asked, his voice low and intimate.

He hadn't even realized how he had hurt her! He was insufferable.

"I've changed my mind," she said.

"What?" The door handle rattled. "Constance, open the door, so we can talk."

"No," she said. "And the door to the landing is locked, too, so don't bother trying that."

A muffled imprecation told her she'd thwarted his next strategy. "Constance, what's going on?" he said, impatient.

She bunched her nightdress between her fingers as she pressed her mouth to the crack where the door met the jamb. "You dismissed me as of no account to your friends today."

"What? When? I didn't—" he broke off.

So, he remembered.

"That wasn't dismissing you," he said gruffly. "It's no one else's business that my wife and I kissed."

"You made me look stupid. You made it clear my feelings

are not yours, that they're of less importance to you than your pride and your reputation." Even now, she found herself blinking back tears.

Again, a bitten-off oath from Marcus. But he didn't argue. Because they both knew, those things *were* more important to him.

After some moments, he said tightly, "I apologize for hurting your feelings."

"Is your jaw uncomfortable from gritting your teeth so hard?" Constance inquired.

She was rewarded with a thump on the panel nearest her ear.

"You are my wife," he said. "You wish to have children, and so do I. This is our duty before God."

She pressed her lips together. Nothing worse than having one's own words thrown back at one. "Did you consult God at all in this matter?" she asked, aware she sounded priggish.

His silence was her answer.

Then he said, "You promised to obey me. As your husband, I command you to unlock this door."

A part of her dearly wanted to. She wanted to be a true wife, to comply with her vows. If she unlocked the door, Marcus would come in. He would kiss her again, and she would not be able to resist.

In the end, she would give herself to a man who did not value the gift the way he should. The way God intended.

And yet…he was right. She had promised to obey. A physical union was part of marriage, and Marcus had every right to demand it.

Guide me, Lord, please.

The door handle rattled again.

Constance grasped the key. "Very well," she said, "I will open the door if you wish."

He muttered something that might have been, *About time.*

"But let us be quite clear," she said.

He groaned.

"You are ordering me to obey you."

"That's right," he said with a patience she knew was feigned.

She half turned the key. "So you understand I am opening the door out of obedience?"

"Yes." But he sounded uncertain.

"And nothing more," she said.

A pause. "What do you mean?"

"I will be united with you as your wife out of obedience. If that is enough for you, then so be it."

On the other side of the door, Marcus paused. He'd been about to issue an order to open up immediately. But what was Constance saying? And why had he married such a devious woman whose every utterance required careful interpretation? Who took such easy offense.

Though, perhaps he had not been entirely considerate in his choice of words earlier.

Still, he was her husband. And right now, he was expected to tolerate a wife with strong views—regularly expressed—as to his deficiencies, while enjoying none of the pleasures of the married state.

It wasn't fair.

He'd kissed his wife today and realized he wanted to know her the way only a husband can. Right now, with the moonlight slanting mysterious and silver across the room, with his wife, and the marriage bed, just inches away, that interest became urgency.

He would have her.

Constance had said she would obey. That was enough. Wasn't it?

Marcus recalled her sweet, willing response to his kiss. And realized he would not wish for less than that willingness.

Confound it!

"Marcus?"

Her anxious query told him he'd thumped the door with his fist. He dropped his hand to his side.

"Your obedience is no longer required," he said.

Silence.

He pressed his ear to the door.

There came a faintly discernible, "Why not?"

Now she wanted to talk about it?

"I shall not trouble you on this matter again," he said against the wood. He imagined the words vibrating into her little ear. And suddenly, he couldn't bear to leave things there. "If you wish me to come to your chamber," he said, "you will need to invite me."

A part of him hoped she would invite him that very moment. Not out of duty or obedience, but out of... *Not love.* He didn't want love. But more than obedience.

"Good night, Marcus." The farewell seemed right against his ear where it pressed the wood.

Marcus sighed. He spread his fingers on the panel, imagined her fingertips against his. "Good night, Constance."

He lingered there another moment, but there was only silence.

He hoped she was satisfied.

Because he most certainly wasn't.

Chapter Seventeen

Miriam directed the chambermaid to hurry about her work making the countess's bed.

"I have three changes of clothes to lay out for the day," she scolded the girl, who was being remarkably slow. "You're in my way."

"Sorry, Miss Bligh," the girl muttered, her accompanying glance more resentful than regretful.

Miriam puffed out a breath. "No, *I'm* sorry. I'm a regular grouch this morning, Katie. Don't mind me."

Katie grinned. "For a moment I thought you were turning all high-and-mighty on me, like Mr. Harper."

Miriam shuddered. "Heaven forbid. No, my problem is lack of sleep, that's all."

"Still, at least with Mr. Harper, it's the face of an angel scolding you," Katie said dreamily. "You can forgive him anything."

"Whereas I have the face of a bran-cake, I suppose," Miriam said tartly.

Katie clapped a hand over her mouth, not fast enough to hide a giggle. "No, Mir—Miss Bligh, I didn't mean that."

Reluctantly, Miriam smiled. Katie was one of the Chalmers staff who came up to London for the Season, so they knew each other well. "There are more important things than looks, Katie. A kind heart, for one. That's what God sees."

Prompted by her own lecture, she held the door open for Katie.

"Thank you, Miriam." Katie didn't notice she'd let the name slip, and Miriam didn't remind her.

The maid left the room, freeing Miriam to select Lady Spenford's afternoon and evening attire. She liked that her mistress trusted her judgment, accepting Miriam's recommendations for her toilette and hairstyle. She only wished she could be certain the countess's faith wasn't misplaced.

Hmm, the sprigged muslin walking dress had a tear in its white flounce. Miriam examined it. She could fix it in a jiffy—she patted her pocket for her needle case. Not there. She must have left it out last night after darning her stockings. She'd been so tired, she could have *slept* on the blighted needle without noticing.

She grimaced at the thought of trudging up two flights of stairs just to fetch a needle. Maybe Powell would lend her one, if she wasn't busy with the dowager's mending. Or maybe…Miriam glanced at the door connecting to the earl's chamber. Tom Harper would have a needle and white thread.

She hadn't spoken to Tom since that day Lady Spenford had taken her to visit him.

When she'd betrayed her feelings for him.

She'd seen him, of course, at mealtimes. But they hadn't talked.

The longer she left it, the harder it would be. This was the perfect excuse to speak briefly to him, to show she didn't feel any awkwardness—though that last might take a miracle.

Her stomach churned as she turned the handle of the connecting door, and pushed.

It didn't move. She pushed again.

How odd that it should be locked. She turned the key and

found it stiff with disuse. Eventually, it yielded, and she was able to open the door.

Tom stood at the other side of the earl's bed. Like her, he was engaged in the task of laying out his employer's wardrobe for the day.

"Can I help you, Miss Bligh?" he asked stiffly.

In the servants' dining room, she hadn't allowed her gaze to rest on him. Now, she noted, he was paler than he used to be, maybe thinner around the jaw. She had a stupid urge to fatten him up.

"I'm after some white thread and a needle," she said. "I left mine upstairs."

Without speaking, he fished in his pocket and pulled out a needle case much like hers. As she took it, her fingers brushed his. She pulled quickly back.

"Are you all better, then?" she asked.

He shrugged. "I don't feel so knocked about as I did, but every so often I feel like I might keel over. The doctor says I need more sleep to recover proper, but that's not going to happen."

"That doesn't sound too good." She scrutinized him. She'd show the same interest in anyone newly recovered from influenza, she told herself.

"Maybe if you asked the earl for some more time off..." she suggested.

"What, and risk my job?" he said scornfully. "His lordship doesn't have much time for malingerers, even them that are truly ill."

Miriam could imagine.

"If I was to take off much longer, I'd get back here and find some footman lording it in my position," Tom said.

"Then you can't do that," Miriam agreed.

"I'd best get back to my work." He picked up the brush Miriam assumed would be used on the earl's coat.

She turned to go, more miserable than she'd ever been. A glance back at Tom told her he was just as miserable. Because of his illness, or was there more to it?

Lady Spenford had been unhappy this morning, too. Miriam would swear she'd been crying. And she'd heard a sharp tone from the earl through this very door earlier.

Something was wrong around here.

"Tom, did you notice," she blurted, "the door between these rooms was locked?"

He looked up from the coat, brush in hand. "Couldn't help but notice, with you rattling at the keyhole."

Uneasy with the subject, they eyed the door, rather than each other.

"Lady Spenford doesn't seem happy," she said. "She puts a brave face on things, but…"

Harper looked around, as if someone might overhear. "His lordship doesn't have the air of a happy bridegroom. Especially not this morning—never seen him in such a stinking mood."

She could tell he was as appalled by his own indiscretion in discussing such a thing as she was by hers.

But it needed to be discussed. Almost every waking hour of Miriam's life was spent in Lady Spenford's service. It was the same for Harper. If their employers were unhappy, that was bound to rub off. Besides, Lady Spenford had tried to help Miriam, taking her to see Tom. She deserved the same consideration in return…even if it was presumptuous.

Tom swayed slightly on his feet.

Miriam darted forward and grasped his arm, as if that could stop him falling over. Despite his illness, the flesh beneath his jacket seemed firm. Muscled. "You're not well." She pointed to a carved mahogany chest at the end of Lord Spenford's bed. "Sit there."

That he didn't argue, merely sagged onto the chest, was a sign of how ill he felt.

"Will you sit with me?" he asked. "There's room for two."

Miriam hesitated a moment before she joined him. She reminded herself her improved status meant that even if someone were to catch her sitting here, it would be no crime on her part.

Tom shuffled along to make room for her. He was certainly broader than the lad she'd kissed ten years ago. She hadn't been this close to him since then. If she turned her head to the right he could kiss her, soon as look at her.

Why would he kiss me, when he made it plain he considered it a big mistake the first time around? She'd been fourteen years old, newly employed at the big house. He'd been seventeen. Already a man in his own mind, but she still saw the boy she'd tagged after.

When he'd kissed her as they walked home from church, she'd thought life couldn't get better than this. She'd thought it meant he loved her.

Stupid. As they walked, she'd prattled on about anything and everything, certain he was hanging on her every word the way she hung on his. And the next day, he'd been so cool, so distant—it was if their lips had never touched. He'd never looked at her with that particular warmth in his eyes again.

Soon after that, Miriam had learned to read—she'd spent most of her hard-earned wages, the first year, paying a senior housemaid to teach her, believing that if she could read, she'd have more chance of advancement. As she improved, the dowager had lent her some books, romantic stories, and Miriam learned that the world was full of girls who naively thought men had love on their minds, rather than something baser. She would not be so easily fooled again.

Except…with Tom this close, his mouth right in her line

of vision, her pulse had taken off on an unseemly romp. His eyes held hers, and that familiar gleam warmed her up.

"Are you feeling better for sitting?" she asked quickly.

"Much." Yet he sounded hoarse.

Instinctively, she reached out to touch his forehead.

He froze.

His skin was a little too warm, though not dangerously so. "You have a slight fever," Miriam muttered, feeling rather feverish herself, all of a sudden.

He gave the barest nod. "Doctor said I'd have a few more turns afore this got better."

Miriam removed her hand from his brow. She didn't bother suggesting again that he ask the earl for more time off. But in her head, she most disrespectfully castigated Lord Spenford for his *intransigence*. She'd read that word in a book last week, and when she'd mouthed it aloud, the way she thought it should be said, it had felt perfect.

Tom shifted, as if he was about to stand.

"Maybe if Lord and Lady Spenford were happier in their marriage," Miriam said quickly, with a meaningful glance toward the connecting door, "they might not stay out so late at night. Then we wouldn't be so tired, and you wouldn't be ill."

"No point wishing that," he said. "Not when they're unequally yoked."

"They're what?" Miriam knew the scripture reference, but couldn't see how it applied here.

"How can a marriage work when a man and a woman are so different?" he said.

"They're of the same class," Miriam said. "They're both Christians."

"He's the Earl of Spenford," Tom said, as if that made any amount of intransigence acceptable. "He heads one of the noblest families in England, presides over large estates, has all the bearing of his station. She is the daughter of a parson, country-raised, without fortune, without presence."

"What does that matter?" she demanded. "We're all equal in God's eyes. You, me, the earl, the countess."

He drew in a shocked breath. "You'll not go setting yourself up the equal of your mistress."

"Not in this world, no," she agreed. She grinned. "But in the next…just watch how I swan around in my fine white robes!"

He shook his head, disapproving, but amused.

"We can't do much about the countess's lack of town polish, or noble lineage—though she's wellborn enough," Miriam added. "But her presence—that's my job." She admitted the truth: "I'm not good enough."

"You put things together not too badly," he said.

It was such faint praise, yet more than she deserved. Miriam didn't know whether to laugh or cry. She settled on a watery chuckle.

"Her ladyship's hair could be more artful," Tom said. "Trouble is, you're never going to turn her into a beauty. You need to find something that's her special thing. Like taking snuff."

"The countess won't take snuff!"

"Not that, ninny, since Lady Mottram already does it. And Mrs. Deveril drives that canary-yellow phaeton and Lady Chivers takes that pet monkey everywhere."

"So I need something that will make Lady Spenford stand out from the crowd," Miriam said thoughtfully. Far easier said than done.

"There's lots of ladies that aren't beauties, but they still command the attention of a room full of people," Tom said. "Like yourself."

Miriam's head whipped around. "Beg your pardon?"

Tom looked as if he'd like to bite off his own tongue.

"Nothing," he muttered. "You're not even a lady. You're a lady's maid."

"I don't command the attention of a room," she said. "I've never done so in my life."

He pffed. "It's been that way since you were fourteen years old." His jaw reddened.

So he did remember that kiss! Miriam held tight to the knowledge, stored it in her heart to examine later.

"All the men, the servants, like you," he said.

"They all like Becky," she retorted. Miriam's face might be pleasant enough, but Becky, a junior housemaid, had fair hair, rosebud lips and curves that a beanpole like Miriam could only dream of.

"'Course they fancy Becky," Tom said, scotching what she now realized was a hope that he'd say he found her much prettier than the other girl. "But you were wondering if a woman can hold people's attention without being a raving beauty, and I'm telling you she can."

"Thank you," she said through gritted teeth.

He eyed her in confusion…then burst out laughing. "I'm not saying *you're* plain like the countess, Miriam."

"I don't care if you are."

More seriously, he said, "You're pretty enough. But more important, there's something about you, a kind of energy. Every servant in this house would be thrilled for you to bestow a smile on him, Miriam."

She didn't care about any other servant, though it would be hard to look any of them in the eye after the nonsense Tom was talking. "Even you?" she asked.

Their eyes connected, held.

He cleared his throat. "I'm saying, there are ways you can help the countess make more of herself."

His firmness told her she wouldn't get more out of him.

They sat in silence for a moment or two.

"Those cravats won't starch themselves," Tom said after a while. But he didn't move.

"That ruffle won't mend itself, neither," Miriam added. And didn't move.

Tom's knee shifted slightly so that it almost, just a hairbreadth short, touched hers.

"Maybe there *is* something we could do," Miriam said.

He looked at her knee. "What do you mean?"

"To help the earl and countess."

"Oh. That." He sounded disappointed.

"Maybe if you say nice things to Lord Spenford about Lady Spenford…help him see she's a good countess."

"My opinion won't count for naught."

"You and his lordship used to be friends," Miriam said. "If he's feeling unsettled, he might be willing to remember that. I've heard of some masters who are right good friends with their valets."

"The Earl of Spenford isn't that kind of gentleman," Tom said. "He likes me to know my place, and I like it, too."

Infuriating man! "Do you know the word *intransigence?*" she asked Tom. "It means stubbornness, I think."

He rolled his eyes. "What do you want me to say, that you're clever as well as striking?"

"I *want* you to say you'll give my idea a try," she said.

They were glaring at each other when the door opened and the earl entered.

Funny how a moment ago Miriam had believed sitting on a carved chest in the earl's bedroom was no great crime. Funny how she could boldly declare to Tom that they were all equal in God's eyes, and now find her palms sweating as she jumped to her feet, an apology tripping on her tongue. Tom was a little slower getting to his feet, but equally embarrassed.

The earl definitely had mortal eyes, which did not embrace equality among God's creation. Those eyes narrowed on them. "Harper, if you have nothing to do, perhaps you could have my curricle brought around. I'm going driving with Lord Severn—I'll wear the dark blue coat."

"Yes, my lord." Tom discreetly hid a cough that revealed his lingering illness.

The earl had dark circles beneath his mortal eyes, Miriam noticed. She seldom got this close to the master of the house, but now she could see small lines at the corner of his mouth. Not worry about his mother, she suspected, since the dowager was doing nicely, but his marriage.

The earl was staring at the open door between the two bedchambers as if he'd never seen it before. Miriam gave Tom a significant look, and jerked her head in the earl's direction.

Tom cleared his throat. "Miss Bligh, with regard to that matter we were discussing, I will be happy to assist."

"Thank you, Mr. Harper." She returned to the countess's room, pulling the door closed behind her. Conscious of all the awkwardness of the situation, she waited until she heard the earl leave his room before she locked the door.

Chapter Eighteen

$\sim$

There could be nothing more embarrassing, Constance felt, than facing one's husband the morning after denying him access to the marriage bed.

She had some morning calls to pay this afternoon—she still found it odd that in London, "morning" calls invariably took place after midday—but she planned to remain sequestered until then. Miriam Bligh had brought mending; Constance had her embroidery. They would sew quietly in the small salon.

"I'm thinking, my lady—" Bligh pulled her thread taut after a stitch "—we need to develop a particular style for you. Something that draws attention and establishes you as a leader of fashion."

"Given that my looks will never do so," Constance said.

She could see Bligh about to issue a polite denial. Then the maid said, "That's pretty much the way of it, my lady."

"Is this for the sake of your ambitions?" Constance asked, a little hurt. She knew how important it was to Miriam to do well in this position.

"No, my lady, for yours." Bligh held her gaze with a frankness that would usually only be tolerated between mistress and maid after many years' service.

"You think I have ambitions?" Constance asked.

Miriam nodded. "Where his lordship is concerned."

Constance was so surprised, she jabbed her needle into her thumb. "Ah!" She sucked the tiny droplet of blood, staring at Miriam.

The maid didn't elaborate.

Constance inspected her thumb. "What a pair we are, Bligh. Wanting men who don't seem to want us."

"I'm sure there's no man I want, my lady," Miriam said stiffly.

Constance rolled her eyes. "Strength and honor should be the clothing of a virtuous wife," she said, referring to the book of Proverbs.

"As well as silk and purple," Miriam said.

True, those words were in the chapter, as well.

Constance sighed. "If you can find an equivalent to 'silk and purple' that will make me distinctive, by all means do so."

At eleven o'clock, Dallow brought a message from the dowager, inviting Constance to visit her room.

Constance gave a cry of delight to find Helen sitting in a chair next to the window.

The dowager beamed at her. "I know, my dear, isn't it wonderful? I feel strong as a horse."

"Just so long as you're not planning to jump fences," Marcus said from behind Constance.

She froze. *I will not look at him.* Already, her cheeks were heating. The dowager must have called for him, too.

"Marcus, darling, you're here." Helen stretched out a hand to him. He was careful not to brush against Constance as he went to kiss his mother.

"You do look well." His voice was deep with satisfaction.

"If I died tomorrow I'd be happy for having had a day out of bed," Helen said.

"You're not going to die tomorrow," Marcus chided her.

She patted his cheek. "Certainly not, my love. It would be most rude of me to die before the ball and plunge you all into mourning."

"What ball?" Constance asked, at the same time as Marcus.

"Sit down, my dears." Helen indicated the chairs either side of hers. When they were settled, she continued, "I plan to host a ball to welcome Constance to the family."

"That's not necessary," Constance said quickly. Part of her delighted in the prospect of a ball given in her honor. But that was foolish pride…and pointless if her husband wouldn't share her enjoyment. Right now, he looked determined never to enjoy her company again.

"Mama, you're not well enough to dance," Marcus said. "Let alone to organize a ball. These things take weeks."

"This ball shall take only three weeks," his mother declared. "I'm thinking an Indian theme—we still have all those wall hangings and the like that my brother brought back from the Subcontinent." She patted Marcus's hand. "And of course I won't dance. I'll delegate you and Constance to dance for me. I shall sit in a corner with my dearest friends and we'll gossip about the young misses and their marriage prospects, and which bachelors are fortune hunters." Her blissful sigh told them how much she missed those pastimes.

"You know I would deny you nothing," Marcus began.

"I'm delighted to hear it," Helen said.

"But this will be too much of a strain on your health."

"I assure you I won't do any actual work," Helen said. "Marcus, I see this as a fresh start for our family, a public declaration to our friends that the Spenfords are alive and well. And happy."

Marcus flinched, obviously recalling what she'd said about his unhappiness the day of Mr. Young's first visit.

His mother colored slightly. "I mean, I have a new daughter—" she reached over and patted Constance's hand "—which makes me happy. And day by day, my health is being restored."

"I'll help you in any way I can," Constance said. She rather enjoyed Marcus's frown of displeasure.

"I knew I could rely on you, my dear." Helen glanced up at her son. "You had best accept this plan of mine, Marcus. It will happen."

The steel in her voice made Constance smile. So, Marcus's pigheadedness wasn't all from his father's side!

"Only if Mr. Young says it won't be too much for you," Marcus said.

"I'm sure he will concur," Helen said. "Constance, I can't wait to watch dear Marcus whirling you around our ballroom."

Dear Marcus looked distinctly unenthusiastic.

"I'm sure it'll be wonderful," Constance said stoutly. Was that a snort from her husband? Couldn't he see that his mother was so happy at the prospect of this ball, it could only be good for her?

"Perhaps you and Constance could discuss which of your friends you'd like to invite," Helen said.

"Actually, Mama, I'm traveling to Chalmers today," Marcus said. "In fact, I'm departing imminently."

Since when had he planned this? From his carefully bland expression, Constance knew the answer. He'd planned it after last night. This was his strategy for avoiding her. An excellent one, she had to admit.

"Jeffers needs some guidance about the repairs to the tenants' homes," he continued. "Since you're so much better, I thought I might take a few days to give my advice in person."

"Of course you must," Helen said. "You've neglected your

business too much on my behalf as it is. I wish you God-speed, my son."

"Thank you." He kissed her cheek as he stood up. He slipped his hand into the pocket of his coat, and pulled out three envelopes. "Before I forget, these arrived for you in this morning's post—" he handed her two letters "—and one for you, too, Constance."

Constance recognized her father's squarish hand on the sealed missive.

Marcus was halfway to the door when his mother said, "Marcus, you outrageous boy! You've forgotten to kiss your wife goodbye."

Constance turned her head quickly before Helen saw her dismay.

Marcus came back. "How careless of me."

Constance stood and offered him her cheek. The brush of his lips felt like a whisper of disappointment.

"Goodbye, Marcus," she said.

When he left, something went with him—some kind of motivating force. Without it, Constance felt irritatingly lethargic.

"My dear, will you sit with me awhile longer?" Helen asked. "Perhaps we can read our correspondence together."

"Of course." Constance resumed her seat. She prized open the wax seal on her letter and began to read.

"From your father?" Helen asked.

Constance nodded. "Mama has added a message, too."

"What news of your family? If you don't mind my asking?"

"Isabel has joined the board of the local orphanage," Constance said. "She has a remarkable penchant for doing good works without being the least sanctimonious."

The dowager chuckled.

"Papa says Serena isn't writing from Leicestershire as

often as she used to, and asks if I have any news of her. Which I don't."

"And what of that pretty little minx, Amanda?" Helen asked. Something must have flickered across Constance's face, for Helen said, "Is something wrong? Is Amanda ill?"

"She's well, as far as I know," Constance assured her. The dowager's raised eyebrows told her she couldn't end there. "She and I had...a disagreement, that's all."

"Oh, my dear. It's not good to allow family disagreements to lead to estrangement." Helen's hand covered hers.

"I'm sure you're right," Constance said formally. She hurried to read on. "Papa says—oh!" She clapped a hand to her mouth.

"What is it?" Helen asked.

"Papa has been invited to meet with the archbishop here in London on the twenty-second of May, to discuss his views on social equality. I expect the archbishop plans to scold him—his views are rather unorthodox," she explained.

The twenty-second was next week.

"I imagine they are," Helen said appreciatively. "Much as I like to hear them, I know I'd be most uncomfortable if some of Reverend Somerton's views became reality."

Constance read on. "He says Mama will accompany him if I can assure him I will be in London—my mother suffers badly from travel sickness."

Helen clucked in sympathy. "But how wonderful that you'll see them. You must miss them."

"I do." Constance chewed her lip. A part of her longed to see her parents...but not here, not now. They were both far too perceptive. They would see in five minutes that all was not well in her marriage—even with Marcus away at Chalmers.

Constance would be mortified. That was the nub of the

matter, she realized. Her pride, in this respect at least, could rival Marcus's!

But she couldn't help it. Her mother had questioned Marcus's suitability as a husband and Constance had blinded herself to the truth of her mother's insight. Her father had faith in her to build a godly marriage, and she'd let him down. That he wouldn't hold her to account for the failure was irrelevant.

And what if they mentioned to Constance's sisters, to Amanda, that things were going badly? It was awful enough that Marcus had wanted to marry Amanda. Constance couldn't bear the thought of her sister knowing she hadn't been able to win the interest of her husband. Then she remembered last night's conversation through the locked door, and blushed.

"My dear, you don't seem pleased at the prospect," Helen said tentatively.

"I do want to see them," Constance said. "It's…well, it's complicated."

Helen set her own letters down. "My dear, I'm not your mother and never could take her place, but will you tell me what's bothering you? I noticed the moment you walked in that you looked unhappy, and it's not the first time."

"Ma'am, I wouldn't worry you for the world. I'm sorry."

"No need to be sorry," Helen said. "I know what it's like to be a young bride married to a man one doesn't know very well. I may be Marcus's mother, but believe me, my dear, I'm on your side." She smiled. "Will you tell me? Because Marcus doesn't look happy, either. You'll be doing me a favor if you could cast some light on his inner state."

Talk to Marcus's *mother* about her marriage? Constance shook her head, before she did something dreadful like blurt out her woes.

"Am I right in thinking you don't wish your parents to visit?" Helen asked.

Ashamed, Constance said, "I feel it would be awkward."

The dowager stared out the window for a few moments. "Would your parents wish to stay here?" she asked.

Constance skimmed the rest of the letter. "Papa says if it's not convenient for us to host them, they will stay with my Aunt Jane. She's been on the Continent these several months, but returns this week."

She winced. Aunt Jane would doubtless call in Berkeley Square soon. Her aunt—her father's youngest sister and the only member of his family still to communicate with him— was every bit as observant as Constance's parents. Constance sighed.

"Ah, yes, Miss Jane Somerton. A very *intelligent* lady." Helen appeared to doubt the usefulness of Aunt Jane's intellectual prowess in the current situation. "You know, my dear, whatever your problems are, I don't believe they are insurmountable."

"Pardon me, ma'am, but how could you know?" Constance asked.

Her mother-in-law smiled. "I detect a softening in Marcus's face when he looks at you."

To her annoyance, Constance's heart fluttered in hope.

"I believe if anyone can pierce his armor, it's you, with your gentle spirit."

"I haven't been particularly gentle in some matters," Constance confessed.

"I should hope not—Marcus would ride over you with all the finesse of an overloaded stagecoach if you didn't stand up to him," Helen said. "It seems to me, you two need more time to work these things out."

Constance had told Marcus time was the one thing they had on their side.

"I can see why you're reluctant to see your parents. I know from my correspondence with your father that he has the most disconcerting habit of seeing right through one's words in a letter. And the gift is far more potent face-to-face."

"It is," Constance agreed feelingly.

"Do you know, my dear," Helen said, "I have just developed the most intense longing to visit Chalmers." She paused and said innocently, "What a shame we won't be here when your father comes to London." She reached for the handbell on the table next to her, and rang it to summon Powell from her dressing room. "At least we'll have spared your mother the horrors of the journey," she said complacently.

"Really? We can go to Chalmers?"

"Certainly. Not tomorrow, but the day after," Helen said. "I'll tell Powell to organize us."

As Constance left the room, the only thing that curbed her urge to skip was a pang of guilt that she should be putting off a meeting with her father…and the thought of Marcus's reaction when he learned that the wife who'd refused to go to Chalmers was now pursuing him there.

Chapter Nineteen

So much for the healing properties of country air, Tom Harper thought as a wave of nausea swept through him—they'd been at Chalmers two days and he had yet to step outside. He swallowed the threatened reemergence of his breakfast and focused on the sporting coat he was holding out for Lord Spenford to ease his arms into the sleeves.

"Your father tells me the trout numbers are high," the earl said. "I'm looking forward to getting down to that river and casting my line."

"Yes, my lord." Tom's father, John Harper, was still head gamekeeper, despite his advancing years.

"Did you see your father when he came up to the house last night?"

Harper brushed a speck of lint off his lordship's lapel. "I saw him in the kitchen, my lord." He was barely listening. He was too busy thinking on his promise to Miriam that he'd say something nice about the countess to the earl. So far the opportunity hadn't arisen.

"By the way, my mother wants some Indian artifacts taken up to London for the ball," the earl said. "I believe they're in the attic. Could you tell Buddle?"

Buddle had been the butler here at Chalmers since before

Tom was born. You didn't *tell* Buddle anything—you laid a few words out and the butler decided if he would pay them any heed.

"Certainly, my lord."

Lord Spenford picked up a piece of paper from his dressing table and read from it. "Her ladyship specifically mentions some rugs, and a pair of wall hangings. Also some lanterns, brass candlesticks and a set of stacking bowls." He offered Tom the paper. "You'd better take this list."

"I can remember, my lord." Blast it, Tom was going to have to force a comment about the countess into the conversation, and somehow make it sound natural. He'd never been good at that kind of thing. But it was the least he could do for Miriam…and since he wasn't prepared to offer her anything else, he *would* do it.

"I, er, I've noticed before that you have a remarkable memory, Harper." The earl sounded stilted.

Was he *complimenting* Tom?

Tom didn't know where to look. "Too kind, my lord," he muttered. The earl looked just as embarrassed.

The awkward compliment could only be the countess's influence. Tom should grasp the opportunity to keep his promise to Miriam.

"It will be nice to see a ball in the London house again," he said. "Lady Spenford will be a most gracious hostess."

When Lord Spenford stiffened, he realized he'd said it all wrong. It wasn't for servants to pass judgment on their master or mistress. The fact that every servant in the land did so regularly and brutally in the privacy of below stairs made no difference.

"Beg pardon, my lord," he said, aware of sourness welling inside him. He knew other valets who were close to their masters. Servants who knew their place, of course, but that place was one of more-than-servant. A more-than-servant could have made the comment Tom just did without causing offense.

Tom had more reason than most to be on close terms with his master—for years, he'd missed their boyhood friendship—but Lord Spenford maintained a strict distance.

Tom had been thrilled to be offered the position of the earl's valet. Now, though he'd never give it up, it wasn't enough to make him happy. A man's job couldn't be his whole life; he needed connections with others. But the connections that, apart from his parents, had meant the most to Tom—the friendship with young Marcus Brookstone, and his stupidly tender feelings for Miriam—were beyond his reach.

Watching Tom gather gloves and a hat, Marcus wondered why his valet had turned so morose. This was what Marcus got for trying to cheer the man up in a misguided attempt to be more Constance-like in his attitude to his servants: an even worse fit of the sullens.

He felt rather sullen himself, but he wasn't about to show it. He had no reason for dissatisfaction; he was an earl in possession of his noble estate—even if yesterday's meeting with his manager had covered difficult ground. The discussion of the tenants' rents and the shortfall between them and the cost of repairs would depress anyone.

Occasionally, at times like this, Marcus's responsibilities weighed too heavily.

He reminded himself how peaceful it was here. No troublesome wife popping up to ask awkward questions or blurt out some insult…or to deliver the ultimate snub of locking her bedroom door against her husband….

He quashed that thought and instead focused on the more positive fact that these days he didn't have to worry about his mother. From the day of his marriage, that burden had been lifted. First by knowing Constance cared almost as much as he did for his mother's well-being. Then by the improvement Mama had shown under Mr. Young's care. *Thank You, Lord.* He surprised himself with the spontaneous prayer.

He wondered what Constance was doing right now. Writing to her precious papa, or stitching that Bible verse, most likely. He wondered which verse she'd chosen—he hadn't wanted to ask in case it was something intended for his improvement. He hoped she hadn't taken a chill—it was noticeably cooler today than yesterday.

Beyond the window, the skies were a pale, cloudless blue that promised a return to summer's heat in the afternoon. She would probably be fine.

"If you could stop staring at that hat and hand it to me, Harper, I'll be on my way," Marcus said.

"Certainly, my lord." Harper passed him the hat. The valet had worn a glum expression ever since they left London—anyone would think he'd be glad to come to the country, after his illness. Marcus would have liked to scold him out of his doldrums…but doubtless Constance would tell him he was inconsiderate, that something must be bothering Harper for him to drop his usual prompt, respectful manner.

Marcus wouldn't put it past her to somehow guess that he'd scolded his valet—with her tender heart, she'd expect him to find out what bothered Harper, then to sympathize.

Much more practical to tell the man that if he knew what was good for him, he would pull himself together. Except, Marcus had the uneasy feeling that God might not like the more high-handed approach, either.

He didn't appreciate having his conscience pricked by anyone other than himself—an invisible God and an absent wife should not exert such influence. But, dash it, he couldn't stand another moment of his valet's dark mood.

"Is something wrong, Harper?" he asked reluctantly.

In the moment before his poker face descended, his valet looked alarmed. "Nothing, my lord."

There. Marcus had done his best. He'd inquired, and been rebuffed. Even Constance couldn't expect more than that.

"Pleased to hear it!" Marcus cringed at his own false cheer.

"Indeed, my lord."

Blast. Marcus was fairly sure Harper wasn't even aware of that plaintive note in his voice, but try as he might, he couldn't ignore it.

Ask Harper to go fishing with you. Marcus started at the sound of Constance's voice in his head, clear as if she was right here in the room.

Certainly not, he retorted silently. No one would expect a gentleman to take his valet fishing.

But now the thought had occurred to him, he suspected his absent wife would plague him all day.

Of course, if he did ask Harper to accompany him, Constance would be impressed. Very impressed. Images flashed through Marcus's mind—her warm eyes, her sweet smile, her neat figure, that door between their chambers... He pulled his mind back to the matter at hand. It was pure fancy to assume that unbending toward Harper could somehow result in the unlocking of a door.

Still, he liked the thought of telling Constance he'd issued the invitation, if only to see the surprise on her face. That would teach her to judge him as too conscious of his own status! "How would you like a day of fishing, Harper?" he murmured. There, he'd said it. If he'd spoken so quietly that the manservant wouldn't hear, well, Marcus was sure that wasn't his—

"Is your lordship suggesting I should accompany you on your fishing expedition?" Harper said.

Dash it all. His bat-eared valet had heard. Marcus resigned himself to the inevitable.

"Your father would surely appreciate spending some time with you," he said.

"I shall be pleased to accompany you, my lord."

If Marcus had expected his offer to transform his servant's lugubrious expression, he was disappointed. By the time Harper had stumped down to the river with him, looking about as happy as a trout on a hook, Marcus was regretting the invitation. He consoled himself with the thought that his wife would be extra delighted—not only had he issued the invitation, he'd implemented it—and imagined dropping the news into casual conversation on his return to London.

John Harper met them on the north bank of the river, at the spot where Marcus and Tom used to fish as boys.

"Tom, lad, I didn't know you was coming." The delight in the gamekeeper's smile took Marcus aback. Even Tom cheered up, acknowledging his father with a grimace that if one squinted might pass for pleasure.

Soon their lines were in the water, and the main part of fishing—the waiting—began. Old John landed the first fish, a trout Marcus estimated at five pounds.

"Cook'll be pleased to see that," John said.

"Why don't you take it home to Mrs. Harper?" Marcus suggested. It was an instinctive offer, one he'd made frequently when he fished here as a young man—it had felt a good thing to give away the first fruits of his fishing or hunting expeditions.

His father hadn't agreed—he hadn't approved of allowing servants to make free with the bounty of the estate, believing it encouraged them to take liberties. Marcus strongly doubted his wife would agree with that view.

"Thank you, my lord. She'll be very pleased," John said. "And when the womenfolk are happy, we men are happy, right?" He winked, the familiarity born of his long tenure and a history that included scolding Marcus forcefully for failing to throw back a too-small fish when he was twelve years old. "Never let your pride in your catch outweigh your fairness to the battle," he'd said.

Advice Marcus liked to think he'd taken to heart in other aspects of his life. He thought about his battles with Constance, and hoped his pride hadn't let him override her sensitivities.

One second's reflection was enough to tell him this wasn't one of his many faults. Constance was more than strong enough to stand up to him—it was one of the things he liked about her. Except when her strength reinforced her belief she had the right to lock her door against him.

Marcus realized John was eyeing him expectantly, waiting for a reply about the importance of pleasing womenfolk.

"I'm sure you're right." Marcus realized he had no idea what would make his wife happy. Beyond a husband who loved her, which wasn't one of the options.

But John had a point. Perhaps this nagging discontent Marcus felt stemmed from the fact Constance wasn't happy. It made him feel guilty, and a man couldn't relax when he felt weighed down by guilt. If Constance were happier—and her smile more frequent—might Marcus feel more content?

"So, you're saying a husband who's a good provider makes a woman happy?" he asked John. Because if that was all it took, Constance had nothing to complain about. Harper, the son, gave Marcus a startled look, clearly surprised at the intimacy of the discussion.

The older man peered at the current, trying to see beneath the surface. "Well, she won't be happy if you're *not* a good provider, that's certain. But it takes more than that. This fish here—" he jerked a thumb toward the trout still flapping in the tin bucket on the bank "—is more than a meal. It's what my missus calls a nice surprise." John swooped down with his net and came up with a cluster of wriggling silver sprats. "These'll make good bait," he observed, tossing them into the bucket.

"And surprises are good," Marcus said doubtfully.

John chuckled. "For the womenfolk. Not for us men."

Marcus couldn't agree more—since he'd married, he'd had enough surprises to last a lifetime, starting when he lifted his bride's veil. Surprises were overrated.

Even Harper forgot he wasn't listening and grunted agreement.

"Fat lot you'd know about it, our Tom," his father joked. "You don't have a lass, let alone a wife."

"I know that women get maggoty ideas in their heads, and then they go changing everything and then a man doesn't know where he's at—or at least, he does know where he's at and it's not where he wants to be," Harper muttered.

Marcus eyed him with interest. Harper had summed up the conundrum of male and female relationships rather well.

"Got your eye on someone, have you?" John Harper asked. "Your ma'll be pleased."

"No, I don't," Harper said, with what Marcus considered unnecessary force. "I don't hold with a man and a woman being unequally yoked."

Marcus's jaw dropped. Was Harper talking about him and Constance? If so, his valet could start looking for another position right now. Then he realized Harper's expression was far too miserable for him to be speaking of his employer. He was referring to his own romance. The one whose existence he'd just denied.

Marcus snickered sympathetically. Unequally yoked, eh? Poor Harper, losing his heart to a woman either too far above him or too far beneath him. Marcus might have married a woman whose equality was debatable in society's eyes, but at least his heart was in no danger.

"Doesn't matter what you think on the matter," John told his son. "If a woman wants you and she's determined, you might just have to plan on walking lopsided the rest of your life." His smile said he knew something Marcus and Harper didn't. Perhaps that the fairer sex was worth all the trouble. "But that's why you need your little surprises. Keep 'em on their toes."

There was some wisdom to that, Marcus thought. Hadn't he just been planning to surprise Constance with his consideration for his valet? She was too quick to think she knew him, too quick to make assumptions.

Though she would be happy to hear he had taken Harper fishing, that act wouldn't benefit her directly. He realized he was eager to do something for her. After all, she deserved it—she was the one who had introduced Mr. Young to his mother.

What did Constance like? She doted on that father of hers, of course. She liked the countryside. She liked poetry, apparently.

He continued to think up and discard ideas for "surprises," as they fished. By the time he and Harper headed back to the house, they'd caught five trout between them. Servants and master alike would dine on fish tonight. A good provider, indeed!

Before they packed up their gear, Marcus insisted on gutting the largest trout for old Mrs. Harper. He had a feeling she'd appreciate the boyhood courtesy.

He and Harper walked back to the house, parting for Harper to take the catch directly to the kitchen.

Marcus entered through the front door…and something leaped in his chest.

Constance was there. In the entry hall, talking with

Buddle. She'd not been here long. She still wore a traveling dress of dark blue; the color brought out a chestnut tinge in her hair.

Buddle saw Marcus, bowed and excused himself.

Constance turned. She colored, and it flooded back to him, the memory of standing the other side of her door, practically begging her to admit him. The memory of her refusal.

"Your mother wished to visit Chalmers," she said defensively. Her chin went up in the air.

"Did the journey tire her?" he asked coolly. But not with the glacial cold he'd have liked. Yes, he was mortified, frustrated, by her rejection...but that odd jolt he'd felt at the sight of her had tipped him off balance. Familiarity, he supposed it was.

One thing he knew, though—he wouldn't bother to check the status of the connecting door between their chambers here at Chalmers.

"Mama is fine," Constance said. "We left early and took the journey slowly, hence our late arrival."

An awkward silence fell.

"I've been fishing," he said. He wished he was carrying the string of fish, so she would see his prowess. See the provision he'd made for their meal.

"How nice."

More silence.

Hang it, he'd forgotten to mention he'd taken Harper fishing. It would sound contrived to do so now.

"The estate looks very beautiful, driving up the avenue," Constance said.

"It's regarded as one of England's finest." And he didn't care if that sounded proud; he *was* proud of Chalmers. "But it's also my home," he added, "and I love it for that."

"Home is a wonderful thing," she agreed.

She smiled and her eyes warmed, and Marcus couldn't look away.

In that moment he knew just what he should do for her, by way of a surprise.

Chapter Twenty

It was such nice weather, the dowager had suggested sitting in the rose garden. Servants had carried out chairs and a table, and lemonade, setting them in the shade of a copper beech. Lastly, two footmen had carried out the dowager countess herself, an undignified process she'd forbidden Constance to watch.

Once they were settled, Constance was quite content sitting with her mother-in-law. Despite previously having refused to rusticate here, she'd fallen in love with Chalmers. The home was much grander than she considered necessary, even for an earl, but it felt welcoming. As for the grounds... if she tried to imagine the Garden of Eden itself, it could not look too different.

She sat back in her chair, eyes only half-open, listening to the chattering song of a sedge-warbler lurking among the shrubbery. The bird reminded her of home, of summers spent in the rectory garden with her sisters. She felt a pang of homesickness.

"Good afternoon, ladies." Marcus entered the rose garden from the west portal.

"Marcus, my dear." His mother stretched out a hand. He squeezed it, but moved swiftly on to Constance. Taken by surprise, she was a moment late in extending her fingers. She received the same squeeze, but it seemed to her his hold lingered.

She still felt awkward facing him, having refused him his conjugal rights. And she was still *hopping mad,* as her sister Charity liked to say, that he'd denied having any feelings for her in the presence of his friends in Richmond Park.

"Such a scowl," he murmured, and she realized those sentiments were written all over her face. "Would it help if I told you I have a surprise for you?"

Constance should say no, of course, but she hadn't received many surprises in her life. "Perhaps," she said grudgingly.

His mouth twitched.

Before she could ask what the surprise was, a dog of indeterminate hue raced through the west portal, and ran right up to Constance, where it began an enthusiastic sniffing of her slipper. Instinctively, she reached down to scratch its ears; it promptly turned its tongue to her hand.

Something about its multicolored face and eager eyes struck her as familiar. "This is the dog you saved those three years ago!" she said. "Marcus, what a wonderful surprise."

"Yes," he said. "And no."

Still rubbing the dog's ears, she looked up at him.

"Yes, it's the same dog," he explained. "But this isn't the surprise—he must have followed me from the stables. Go away, boy." But he didn't sound particularly anxious to be rid of the dog, which ignored him.

"Clever puppy," Constance crooned. The pup lay down, rolled on its back, begging to be petted. Constance obliged. "Aren't you a beautiful boy?"

Its tail thumped the grass.

"Constance, dear, I hate to contradict you, but that is a very ugly dog," the dowager countess said. "Marcus, did you really save it? When?"

Marcus's eyes met Constance's, their expression rueful. She didn't want to have the discussion about how she had fallen in love with him that day, and nor, it seemed, did he. "A long time ago, Mama," he said.

"What's his name?" Constance asked Marcus.

"I believe the stable boys call it Dog."

She snickered. Excited to hear his name, the dog took off on a crazy circuit of the garden.

"Marcus, can't you stop that thing bounding around my roses?" his mother asked.

"That's a much better name for him," Constance approved. "Bounder."

The dog turned its attention to Marcus, nuzzling its head against his boots, then jumping up in excitement when Marcus patted him while grumbling halfheartedly.

"He dotes on you," Constance said.

"He needn't bother," Marcus said. "It's not mutual."

The same thought must have flashed into his mind as hers, for he looked embarrassed. Constance's eyes stung.

"Could we get back to my surprise?" he asked stiffly.

"Oh, yes." She managed a steady voice. "I'm sorry, please continue."

He gave her that impatient look that she knew meant he wasn't dependent on her permission. "I wrote to your father last week."

Apprehension curled through Constance. "Why would you do that?" Did he have a complaint that he wanted to share? Surely he hadn't written about her refusal to— *He said it was good news*.

"I invited your family to visit us in London and to stay for the ball," he announced. "I've just collected the post from the village—your father writes to say they'll arrive at the town house on Friday." If it was possible for the Earl of Spenford to beam, he was beaming now.

Constance sprang to her feet, rattling the tea service as she bumped the table. "Marcus, how could you?"

The beam flickered, vanished. "I beg your pardon?" he said coolly.

His mother murmured, "Oh, dear," which he didn't consider helpful.

"This is the worst thing you could have done," Constance moaned.

His brows drew together. "I fail to see how such consideration of your feelings could be the *worst thing.*"

"Children," his mother interrupted, "it's not easy for me to leave, so might I request you take a stroll to the summerhouse in order to continue your conversation?"

Marcus wheeled around, hands in his pockets, and strode off, leaving Constance to follow. He didn't slow until they were out of his mother's earshot.

"Do you not recall that my *sister* tricked you into marrying me?" Constance panted, as she caught him up.

"I could hardly have forgotten," he snapped. "But nor could I invite the rest of your family and exclude her."

"You shouldn't have invited them at all," she said. "Why didn't you consult me? If you weren't so convinced of your own rightness about everything…"

"I *wanted* to surprise you," he growled. "You give every impression of being devoted to your family. You've mentioned that you miss them. You write to your father, your parents, all the time."

And she'd been thinking about them just ten minutes ago. "I do miss them," she admitted. "But right now, I don't want their scrutiny."

He frowned.

"Having my family attend what's meant to be a celebration will shine a light on—on the travesty of our marriage."

"Our marriage isn't a *travesty.*" He sounded almost hurt.

"It's not a real marriage," she said.

"That is currently by your choice, madam."

It was the first time he'd mentioned that night.

"I realize that," she said. "I—I'm sorry."

She sensed the question on the tip of his tongue was *How sorry?* But he didn't ask it, and he unbent a little at her apology.

"I can't withdraw the invitation," he said. "But, believe me, I meant it for the best."

"In that case, I suppose I thank you." She added ruefully, "That didn't sound very gracious, did it?"

"Quite the opposite. You'll notice my lack of surprise."

Despite her worry about her parents' visit, Constance smiled.

A nudge at her ankles had her looking down.

"Bounder." She stooped to pat the dog, which had obviously followed him. "May I keep him as a pet, Marcus? He could ride around town with me in the curricle."

That disapproving frown was back. "Certainly not. A half-wild mongrel is not a suitable companion for a lady. If you wish for a pet, I'll buy you a poodle."

"Pampered, demanding creatures," she said. "With far too high an opinion of themselves."

His eyes narrowed, sensing comparison.

"I like *this* dog," she said. "He's perfect for me."

"He's dirty."

"I'll have him washed." Constance eyed him steadily.

He let out an exasperated breath. "Very well, if it must be this dog. But he's not to enter the dining room."

"Of course not." Constance wiped the vision she'd had of herself slipping tidbits to the dog beneath the table. "Thank you, Marcus."

"*Now* she thanks me," he muttered.

* * *

The imminent arrival of the countess's family in London meant Miriam had to ready her mistress for a return to town on Wednesday. Pity, she thought, as she placed a carefully folded riding habit in one of the open trunks in the countess's dressing room. She'd been enjoying the quieter life.

Hopefully when they got back to London there'd be a few more evenings spent at home. Miriam couldn't imagine a rector and his wife being ones for late nights. Though with all those daughters…

They were taking one of the maids from Chalmers back with them to help attend to the female guests.

They were also taking the dog. In just twenty-four hours Bounder had become the countess's constant companion—which wasn't the kind of distinctive characteristic Miriam had had in mind when she'd talked about helping the countess to stand out from the crowd.

A knock on the door; Harper stuck his head around. "Miss Bligh, I discovered some items in the attic that might be of interest to you."

"What kind of items?"

He rubbed the back of his head. "It's a, er, surprise."

Intrigued, Miriam followed him up to the top floor, and from there to the attic. The attic stairs were narrower even than the servants' staircase, their entrance concealed behind what looked like a cupboard door.

At the top, the maids' bedrooms were to the left of the stairs, the storage rooms to the right. Miriam sneezed as they stepped into the larger of the two storage attics.

"Over here." Harper led her to a stack of trunks in the corner beneath the dormer window. A brown trunk with brass rivets had been separated from the others.

"The dowager countess wanted some Indian decorations brought back to London for the ball," he said. "There was a load of Indian stuff up here that her brother brought back, years ago. I found these—I thought you might be able to use some of them with the countess."

He unclipped the catches and lifted the lid. A folded piece of muslin covered the trunk's contents. Tom lifted it; Miriam gasped.

"Where did all this come from?" she asked.

"All this" was fabrics, ribbons, jewelry.

"I believe they belong to the dowager, though I don't believe she ever used any of these things," Tom said. "I'm sure if you asked, she wouldn't mind the countess using them."

Miriam began sifting through the jewelry. Some striking pieces, large plain-cut stones that weren't in the usual style but still pretty. Miriam dug deeper into the trunk. "There's no gold in here," she said, disappointed. "It's all silver."

"Maybe they don't do much gold work in India," Tom suggested.

Miriam sat back on her heels. "These are so lovely…but my lady can't wear silver. It's too cheap, not right for a woman in her position. Think about the Spenford diamonds—no silver on those!"

"I see what you mean," Tom said.

"Though I must say," Miriam added, "with her skin color Lady Spenford would probably suit silver better."

Tom rubbed his chin. "Does any other fine lady wear silver?"

Miriam shook her head. "It's not the thing."

"Nor," he said deliberately, "is taking snuff, or driving a bright yellow phaeton."

Miriam caught on. "You're right—no one else in the ton will have pieces like these. And there's enough here for Lady Spenford to wear a different piece every day for a year." She pulled out the lengths of fabric, willy-nilly. "And if I use some of these Indian silks for a trim on her dresses…or to make a reticule…"

"Very distinctive," he agreed.

"Thank you, Tom, that was so thoughtful." To go to all this trouble to help her…why would a man do that if he wasn't interested in her?

He smiled, but appeared to be choosing his words carefully. "I was happy to be able to do something for you."

She had the troubling thought that he sounded as if he was giving her a consolation prize. "Tom, do you think you—"

He crouched next to her and picked up a length of purple organdy. "This color would suit you."

"As if a maid would ever wear such a color," she scoffed. But he was right; the bright tone would work well with her complexion. She thought of that verse in the Bible about the virtuous wife, who wore silk and purple.

More than anything, she wanted the chance to be that wife to Tom. Couldn't he see that? Didn't he think of her that way, not even a little?

She watched his fingers, strong and sure as he refolded the cloth. How would they feel to the touch? Different from all those years ago? Or like a homecoming?

Likely I'll never know.

Unless…

Holding her breath, Miriam reached out and rested her palm on the back of Tom's hand.

He froze. Yet his skin was warm; she fancied she could feel life coursing in his veins.

Slowly, he turned his hand over beneath hers, so they were palm to palm. Miriam's hand trembled; his stayed steady as a rock. Their gazes met, and she saw that his eyes weren't as dark as she'd thought; they held flecks of gold. *Promising,* she thought.

Tom looked down at their joined hands. He sighed. "If only…"

If only did not bode well. Miriam could feel that he was about to withdraw again to that place where she didn't feature in his consciousness.

"Tom," she said quickly, "will you kiss me?"

Shameless!

His head snapped up, his eyes shocked.

"Just once would be enough," she said. Enough to convince him he loved her as much as she loved him, surely.

She hadn't admitted to herself before that she loved him beyond a girlish infatuation, but it didn't surprise her now.

Right there, on her knees next to the trunk, she leaned in to him, her lips puckering for the kiss.

Still on his haunches, he scrambled backward, so fast he fell over on his backside. "I can't do this," he said harshly, righting himself. "Don't ask me to, Miriam, because I can't."

She scrubbed her face with her hands. "You mean you *won't*."

"Can't, won't… You're the one who's good with words."

"Are you saying you don't want to?" she demanded.

"That's right." But a sudden flare in his eyes told her he *did* want to kiss her.

In an instant the glint vanished. He stood, shrinking the attic with his height and bulk. Then he turned on his heel and left.

Chapter Twenty-One

The house in Berkeley Square had been cleaned from attic to cellar, and the air smelled of furniture polish and vinegar, used to shine the windows.

Once she had checked with Matlock that there were no problems with the ball preparations requiring her attention, Constance went to talk to Marcus.

She found him in the study with Mr. Young, whose visits to the dowager were down to three times a week. She greeted the doctor with an inquiry about her mother-in-law's condition.

"As I was explaining to his lordship, it's most important for the dowager countess to continue with the medicine. I cannot speak for any underlying weakness of the heart, but with luck her rapid pulse can be managed."

"Luck has nothing to do with it," Constance said…at the same time as Marcus said, "Luck is not a factor."

He continued, "My wife and I are pleased to thank the Lord for my mother's progress."

After Dallow showed the physician out, Constance said, "I can't believe you would refer so brazenly to that *bargain* you supposedly made with God."

He raised one eyebrow. "I would be interested to hear why your prayers should be more potent than my bargaining."

"I should be interested to tell you, except there aren't that many hours left in the day," she retorted. "Of more urgency, are you aware that my parents arrive tomorrow?"

"Since I was thoughtful enough to invite them, and since your father wrote his acceptance to me, yes, I am."

She ignored that hyperbolic description of his own goodness. "I assume they will arrive late. My mother is a poor traveler, so they will have traveled slowly."

"Naturally, once you told me of your mother's indisposition, I insisted your family travel in Mama's carriage from Palfont," Marcus said. "So they may in fact make good time."

He'd done that? Been so considerate as to— Constance realized he was staring at her, one eyebrow raised.

"Er, thank you," she said. She cleared her throat. "Marcus, I do not wish my family to know the—the true state of our marriage."

"I have no intention of discussing such matters with them or anyone else."

"You won't need to," Constance said. "It'll be quite obvious from the way we speak to each other."

"I am never less than courteous," he said.

Of course he wasn't. Because to be less than courteous would be to indulge in conduct unbecoming of an earl. Heaven forbid that Marcus should commit such a transgression.

She steeled herself. "My father is very perceptive...."

He yawned. So much for his famed courtesy!

"As is my mother," she continued. "We need to agree how we'll behave in the presence of my family."

"This sounds complicated. Why don't you sit down?" He indicated the chair in front of his desk.

Constance sat. Instead of retiring behind the desk, Marcus leaned against the edge nearest her.

Too close. It was hard to concentrate when if she reached out a hand she could touch the thighs encased in biscuit-colored pantaloons.

She swallowed. "I would like you to look into your heart—" she ignored his shudder "—to see if you can find in there any affection for me. Any liking, anything to admire."

The last time he'd stared at her openmouthed was on their wedding day, when she'd accused him of insanity. Was it equally lunatic that he might be in some way fond of her? "Please, forget that I spoke," she said, her voice shaking. "I was only going to ask that if you could find those things, then those should be what my family sees. But if you cannot find any regard for me, then all I ask is that you conceal your lack thereof in the presence of my family."

Chin in the air, she stood, ready to stalk out pretending she still had some dignity.

"Sit down," Marcus ordered. "And tuck that chin away while you're at it."

"I beg your pardon?" she said coldly.

He actually smiled. "Sit," he said again, and this time he planted both hands on her shoulders and pressed her back into the chair.

He resumed his position against the desk. Was it her imagination, or was he a fraction closer?

"I can find regard for you," he said.

Constance's fingers curled around the arms of her chair. "Really?"

He folded his arms across his chest. "You asked if I admire anything. I admire your devotion to my mother."

Oh. That. She nodded stiffly.

"As for liking..." His gaze roamed her face. "I like your eyes." His gaze dropped lower. "I like...to kiss you."

Constance felt her likable eyes widen, as color surged into her cheeks. Why, now, had he mentioned *that?*

"Have I left you speechless?" He smiled wryly. "Will you be more at ease if I say I also like your commitment to doing the right thing, even if your judgment is somewhat misguided?"

Her eyes narrowed. "My judgment is not misguided."

He chuckled. "Now, what else do I like?" he mused.

As he contemplated her, tension rose. Was he taking so long because he couldn't think of anything, or just to tease her?

"My determination?" she suggested, helping him along.

He shook his head. "I do not like that. What else did you ask about? Ah, yes, affection."

Constance's stomach lurched.

His gaze drifted past her, to the fireplace. Above the mantelpiece, she knew, hung a portrait of his father. A man who would surely have despised her as an unfit bride for the Earl of Spenford.

Marcus's voice was clipped as he said, "I have affection for you, Constance."

Constance started. "You do? But…what…"

"You will need to take my word on this," he said haughtily. "I don't wish to discuss the particulars."

She had no idea what he meant. Was it the kind of affection he showed Bounder—Marcus tolerated Bounder when he was in the room, and forgot his existence when he wasn't—or was it something more?

"So this regard, this *affection* will be visible to my family?" she asked.

"I don't believe in showing my feelings in public," he said.

She gritted her teeth. "My family is your family. They are not *public*."

He crossed one leg over the other. "Will your family see

affection from you to me, Constance? Or will they observe nothing other than disapproval and a desire to contradict me?"

"That's not how I behave," she said. *Was* she like that? She knew she could be stubborn and she had expectations of how a husband should be… *Goodness, I'm just like Marcus! Fixed in my views, quick to judge.* "Marcus, I'm sorry," she said. "The last thing I would want is to insult you in front of my family."

"Expedient for you to reach this conclusion now, when you're negotiating my cooperation," he observed.

"You know I wouldn't do anything out of expediency," she retorted. "And I have for you all those things you have for me—admiration, liking, affection—doubtless in far greater degree."

"Doubtless," he said, "since you are so much worthier a person than I."

But he was smiling.

"I admire your care for your mother," she said, though he hadn't asked. "Also, the consideration that prompted you to order a carriage for my parents. I *like* your humor—sometimes just thinking about things you've said makes me smile."

His chin drew back; he eyed her with suspicion, as if she might be jesting.

"I like to have you beside me," she said. "Even when we're arguing, I prefer your company above others." That was a big admission, so she hurried past it. "I like that you took Harper fishing."

To her surprise, he reddened. "You heard about that?"

"Bligh told me." She pleated the muslin of her skirt beneath her fingers, an attention Bligh wouldn't appreciate later when she had to deal with the wrinkles. "As for affection…" She paused.

"There is really no need to elaborate," Marcus said coolly.

But Constance saw the flash of need in his eyes, and once again felt awful that she had shown him so much criticism, and little affection. The very thing his father had done—that her own motive was self-defense didn't excuse her.

"I have affection for your contradictions," she said. "That your worst qualities are also your strengths—your certainty, your authority."

"I see," he said, so slowly it was plain he didn't see.

"But mostly, my affection is because you are you."

His brows knit. "You mean, I'm your husband, so affection is your duty?"

"I mean," she said, "I have affection for Marcus Brookstone, the man. Regardless of whether you are my husband or not, I have affection for you. Regardless of all circumstances."

He seemed to catch his breath. Then he said lightly, "You astound me. Even if I were the husband of another woman?"

"Of course not!" She started to laugh.

"So what you are saying, *wife*," he said, and a shock went through her, "is that you and I have enough regard to put aside our differences when your family is here, and focus on those things that promote unity."

"Yes," she said, though it fell short of what she might have hoped for. "Please."

He took her hand. Shook it. "Then it's agreed. We have a truce."

"Constance, my darling!" Her mother enveloped her in an embrace as welcome as it was stifling.

Constance hugged her back, not caring that they were in the public eye, outside the house on Berkeley Square, her family fresh out of the coach.

"It's wonderful to see you all." In that moment, Constance meant it. "Isabel, how are you?" She embraced Isabel. "I feel as if I haven't seen you for years, not weeks. And you, sweet Charity, I've missed your encouraging words." As she hugged her youngest sister, she was aware of Amanda alongside. The upwelling of anger took her by surprise. No, she had not forgiven Amanda, even though Amanda had sent a letter asking such pardon. Just one letter, which Constance felt didn't indicate true repentance.

Even from the corner of her eye, she could see Amanda was as stunning as ever. Her new, pale blue dress set off her clear skin and laughing eyes. How would Marcus feel to see her? *Please don't let him think Amanda is more beautiful than—* Of course he would think Amanda was more beautiful, it was a simple fact.

Right now, he was talking to her parents about the journey—Constance heard her mother saying it had been almost pleasant in such a comfortable carriage. But he must realize Amanda was there. He hadn't met her after the wedding, as she'd stayed in her room with a headache, so this would be the first time he'd faced the girl who'd deceived him.

But somehow, they ended up moving inside, Constance suspected under Marcus's subtle direction, without either him or her having spoken to Amanda. Marcus took Reverend Somerton to see his mother immediately, while the ladies repaired to the salon to take tea, giving the servants a chance to unpack their trunks.

Constance poured the tea and handed a cup to Charity. "Tell me what's been going on at home," she urged Charity.

"I turned down my first marriage proposal last week," her sister said airily.

"Charity! You're only fifteen!"

"Even if I were twenty-five I should still not want to marry," Charity declared. "I'm going to stay with Mama and Papa forever. Besides—" she screwed up her face "—it was that awful William Foxton. No one would marry him—he was just hoping I was too young to have realized that."

Everyone laughed.

"I know you won't have accepted any proposals, Isabel," Constance said. "You'll have been far too busy caring for your orphans."

Isabel smiled that serene smile that made people catch their breath and fall silent in the presence of beauty. Then she stuck out her tongue and said, "Don't talk such twaddle, Constance—I'll entertain any offers of marriage that come my way, if it'll make things easier for Mama and Papa." Which was the delightful thing about her, she was so pragmatic.

Constance could no longer defer talking to Amanda. Fixing her gaze somewhere on her sister's forehead, she said, "And you, Amanda? You'll be excited to be in London at last."

"Of course," Amanda said, with an irritatingly bright smile.

"She's been all aflutter from the moment Lord Spenford's letter arrived," Margaret confirmed. "She was so excited, she developed a headache the moment we entered London."

Another convenient headache. Constance narrowed her gaze on her sister.

"I feel much better now," Amanda said. Briefly, Constance wondered if her sister's confidence was mere bravado. But she detected no remorse in those blue-violet eyes.

"I've said Amanda may attend the ball for two hours," Margaret said.

"Isn't she a little young?" Constance asked.

"No, I'm not," Amanda said.

"Two hours won't hurt, since the ball is right here," Margaret said comfortably. "Charity won't attend, of course."

"I don't want to," Charity said. "I think dancing is silly, and so is flirting."

"Well, *I* am looking forward to it," Isabel said. "Mama says I can dance even though I haven't been presented at Court, since it's a family occasion."

Their mother talked of her plans to have new dresses made for herself and for Isabel and Amanda. They would need to visit a modiste tomorrow in order to have the dresses in time.

"But most of all," Margaret said, "I'm looking forward to spending time with you, Constance. And, of course, with my son-in-law."

"Wonderful," Constance said gamely.

Chapter Twenty-Two

As far as Marcus could tell, the next few days were bliss for Constance, having her family here…except for Amanda, whom she avoided and whom Marcus had successfully ignored the entire duration of her stay to date. Marcus was keeping his end of his truce with Constance—in the presence of her family, he was attentive, even warm. He had several times been aware of her mother's scrutiny, but was confident her parents wouldn't be worried for her.

He wasn't worried about his wife, but he was about his mother, who'd suffered a minor relapse. Mr. Young pronounced it due to overstimulation, and visited twice a day. Under his care, Marcus's mother seemed to pick up again, and she was more excited about the ball than anyone.

On Wednesday, the day before the ball, they all visited the opening day of the Summer Exhibition at the Royal Academy in the Strand, Reverend Somerton having declared an interest in viewing an acclaimed portrait of St. Francis of Assisi.

Marcus had spent four days with Constance's father—each day his collar had felt tighter, his conversation more stilted. Not that Reverend Somerton said anything negative. It was just, knowing how Constance respected him, Marcus felt under increasing pressure to impress the man.

Ridiculous. He was the Earl of Spenford; he didn't need to impress anyone.

When they reached the Royal Academy, it was a relief to walk with his wife, to tuck her hand in his arm and to pass Reverend Somerton into the care of his own wife.

The Summer Exhibition room was crammed with people. Paintings crowded the walls as high as the ceiling, only inches between them, making it hard to focus on the attractions of individual works.

Marcus suggested to Constance that they escape the squeeze, and view one of the permanent exhibits by the increasingly popular artist, Mr. J. M. W. Turner.

The room dedicated to Mr. Turner's work was far quieter. Marcus could see why—he found the paintings murky.

"This is extraordinary." Constance stopped in front of a watercolor titled *Hannibal Crossing the Alps.*

Marcus squinted, but couldn't distinguish either Hannibal or the Alps amidst what seemed to be mostly gray and black swirls. "It's very indistinct."

"But so romantic," Constance said. "One can feel the grit, the imminent triumph."

"Can one?"

"They say Mr. Turner has the ability to elevate landscapes to the same art as portraits."

"Really?" Marcus said doubtfully.

Constance swatted his forearm. "There are so many beautiful paintings at Chalmers. Perhaps you would like to add Mr. Turner to your collection."

"This more interpretative style would be out of place," he said. "One can immediately see the talent in every work in the gallery at Chalmers. With the exception of the portrait of my great-great-grandfather," he added. "Leonardo himself couldn't have made him look good."

But Constance didn't appreciate his little joke. Her face

stony, she said, "I prefer Mr. Turner's style. I'm willing to look beneath the surface to discern beauty."

Marcus realized that somehow he had offended her. She was prickly because of Amanda's presence, he decided. The troublemaker was on her way over now, arm in arm with Charity.

"Can you believe these paintings?" Amanda's eyes widened fetchingly. "I've never seen such a drab mess of colors in my life—all but a blur. Who could possibly like them?"

Not for the first time, Marcus understood his wife's irritation with the girl. But the way she was babbling, he guessed she was nervous, that she'd steeled herself to address him and had dragged her younger sister along as unwitting moral support. She was bent on making herself sound smart and sophisticated, and was failing dismally.

Beside him, Constance had stiffened. Instinctively, he put a hand to her shoulder. Beneath the brim of her bonnet, his thumb slid over the knot of muscle at the nape of her neck. He heard the catch of her breath.

"On the contrary, your sister and I were just admiring Mr. Turner's work," he told Amanda, undergoing an instant conversion to admiration of the murkier style of painting. "He is extremely talented—anyone who knows the least amount about art will tell you so."

Constance turned a surprised face toward him.

"Oh," Amanda said. "Well, Charity agrees with me."

Marcus smiled at the younger girl, who was blushing.

"It's natural that a schoolgirl will look to someone older and wiser for guidance in such matters. But though you may be older, Amanda, you are far from wiser."

He half expected Constance to protest, but she didn't. Charity's mouth had dropped open in astonishment.

Amanda paled. "You shouldn't—"

"No," he said, "*you* shouldn't. You would do well to speak only when you have understanding."

He was aware of Constance, standing stock-still. He was aware of the skin of her nape beneath his thumb, aware he did not wish the caress to end.

So he kept talking, addressing himself now to Charity and ignoring Amanda. He recalled details of Mr. Turner's biography, which he had read in the newspaper, and influences on the man's talent. By the time he finished, his audience had expanded to include Constance's entire family, not least the dreaded Reverend Somerton.

Under that man's scrutiny, Marcus cleared his throat. "I wouldn't be surprised if one day he's more highly regarded than our greatest portraitists," he concluded. "What do you think, my dear?" he asked Constance.

She blinked up at him, as if mesmerized. It was, Marcus discovered, a pleasing sensation to have mesmerized—and silenced!—his wife.

Then she smiled, and the curve of her lips possessed a beauty he hadn't previously noticed. "I think you're absolutely right," she said.

"Then it's true what they say, there is a first time for everything," Marcus teased.

"There must be," she agreed simply.

Amanda sighed, indicating boredom. Marcus gritted his teeth. The girl deserved some discipline.

If Marcus and Constance were ever to have a daughter...

He froze. He had just thought of having children. With his wife. Indeed, with whom else, he mocked himself.

Still, for the first time, he could envisage Constance holding a babe in her arms. Could envisage her besottedness with the infant. And he wanted to see that. Wanted to be a part of that tableau.

Could he be starting to care for his wife? To...love her?

No, that was not in his nature. He certainly wanted to kiss her again…. That was natural between man and wife. Equally natural was this odd mix of possessiveness and protectiveness—not so different from the way he felt about his favorite horse, he assured himself.

Then there was his bizarre desire to rate higher in Constance's regard than his father-in-law—that was harder to explain. But not so very odd, given his natural competitiveness.

"Spenford—" his father-in-law stepped forward "—I'd like you to show me the portrait of St. Francis. If you know as much about that as you do about Mr. Turner…"

"I'm afraid not, sir," he said. "But I'll certainly accompany you."

He and the reverend left the women behind, which was quite a relief. It was all very well spending time with his wife in the presence of her family, and doing all a gentleman should to support and protect her. But he wouldn't want anyone to think his heart was involved.

The Dowager Countess of Spenford passed a restful night before the ball, and was deemed by Mr. Young fit to attend the celebration as late as midnight.

The invitations had stated a starting time of 9:00 p.m. The family was to dine first, at half past seven.

By quarter past, Miriam had finished dressing Constance.

Constance surveyed herself in the mirror. "The dress is beautiful. I owe much to you, Bligh." Miriam had produced a gorgeous piece of purple silk, shot with silver thread—"silk and purple," just like the virtuous wife of Proverbs!—from the attic at Chalmers. Madame Louvier had used it to make in inset panel in her amethyst silk dress, and to trim the sleeves.

"Your hair looks lovely, too, my lady, if I say so myself,"

Miriam said. Her maid had taken some lessons from Powell, and her work had grown much finer.

"Lord Spenford has sent up the Spenford diamonds from his safe," Constance told her. "They will provide an impressive finish."

"My lady, may I suggest an alternative to the diamonds that might suit you better?" Miriam opened the bottom drawer of the dressing table and pulled out a carved ivory box. She opened it to reveal a necklace of large square-cut amethysts set in silver.

Constance lifted the necklace from its box. "Where did this come from?"

"In the attic at Chalmers," Miriam said. "The dowager countess gave me permission to bring some items back with me for your use. This would go beautifully with your dress."

Constance allowed her to fasten it around her neck.

Perfect. Much more her style than the ostentatious Spenford jewelry collection.

"His lordship will expect me to wear the diamonds," she murmured.

"There'll be a lot of diamonds here tonight, but not another set like this—there are earrings to match."

A knock sounded on her door. Miriam went to open it.

"My lady," she said, "Miss Amanda Somerton wishes to see you."

"Not now," Constance said. However pleased she might be with her own appearance, the moment Amanda stepped alongside her she would feel a dowd.

She closed her eyes as she listened to Bligh relay the message. Then opened them in a hurry as an indignant huff and a swish of skirts revealed that Amanda had barged past the maid.

"Amanda, you need to leave," Constance said.

"Not before we talk." Twin spots of color high in her sister's cheeks made Amanda more beautiful than ever.

"I have nothing to say to you." Constance made a pretense of adjusting the amethyst necklace.

"*I* have something to say to *you*." In the mirror, behind Constance, Amanda paused, head high, one hand pressed to her breast like the heroine in a Greek tragedy. "Constance, dearest," she said dramatically, "I'm sorry."

She didn't *look* sorry.

Aware of Bligh pausing, then resuming her work, Constance said, "I have heard you. Now you may leave."

"Not before you say you forgive me," Amanda declared.

They should be the easiest words in the world to say, when Constance knew her heavenly Father had forgiven every sin of hers, big or small, without hesitation. But they stuck in her throat.

Amanda blinked. "Constance?"

"Now isn't the time, Amanda." Though of course, it was always time to forgive.

"You *are* going to forgive me, aren't you?" Now Amanda sounded genuinely worried.

"Are you afraid that if I don't, you won't be able to think of yourself as a good person?" Constance asked.

Amanda flushed. "I *am* a good person. Maybe not as good as you and the others, but compared to—to lots of people. I did a bad thing, I admit—"

"You did a terrible thing," Constance snapped. "And if you must know, I *don't* forgive you. I can't imagine ever forgiving you."

There, she'd said it. She'd shocked herself, as well as Amanda. Shocked Bligh, too, judging by the maid's bowed head.

But she couldn't lie, could she? Couldn't claim to have forgiven when anger still seethed inside her?

Lord, take away the anger, please, she prayed halfheartedly. And was unsurprised when nothing happened.

"Very well," Amanda said, with unaccustomed dignity. "I shall leave." Tears shone in her eyes; Constance hardened her heart. "But before I do—what is your name?" she asked Miriam.

"Bligh, miss." The maid bobbed a startled curtsy.

"Bligh, do you have any more jewelry in the amethyst set?"

"A pendant, miss, but I prefer the necklace."

"Might I suggest you use the pendant in my sister's hair, so the stone sits just here." Amanda touched the center of her forehead. "It will add to the exotic look of the purple sari fabric."

"Lord Spenford wishes her ladyship to wear the Spenford diamonds," Bligh said.

Constance gave a gasp of outrage at her perfidy.

"The amethysts are much more distinctive," Amanda said. "Besides, the diamonds will be set in gold, which isn't nearly as good with Constance's complexion."

With that, she swept out of the room.

Belatedly, Constance thought how stunning she looked in her simple white muslin.

Miriam began to rummage through the ivory box.

"What are you doing?" Constance asked sharply.

"Beg pardon, my lady, but the young miss was dead right. That pendant will cause a real stir. Ah, here we go." Triumphant, she pulled out a silver chain, with a teardrop-shaped amethyst stone hanging from it.

"I have no interest in following my sister's advice—and expect you to say nothing to anyone of the argument you witnessed."

"I wouldn't," Miriam said, hurt. "But, my lady, there's no point cutting off your nose to spite your face. You're the lady everyone will be watching tonight, and you need to look your very best."

Constance shuddered at the prospect of all that attention. She wanted only the attention of one person.

What would it take for Marcus to find her beautiful? What dress, what accessory, what cosmetic artifice?

Not, she suspected, spurning the Spenford diamonds in favor of cheaper stones set in silver.

But diamonds wouldn't transform her into the kind of wife he wished for, either.

"Very well," she said. "Do whatever you choose."

Chapter Twenty-Three

When Constance started downstairs for dinner, Marcus was in the hallway below, talking to her father. He must have heard her step, for he glanced up, then away.

Then back again.

His gaze stayed fixed on Constance as she descended, one hand firmly on the banister. He came forward to greet her, held out a hand for her as she took the last two steps.

"Good evening, my lord. Good evening, Papa," Constance said.

"Good evening, my lady." Marcus's voice was rich, its timbre warm. He took her other hand in his. "Constance, you look…" He paused, as if searching for the right word.

Beautiful, she completed in her head. *Say I look beautiful.*

Not to the world, she didn't need that, but to him.

"Charming," he said.

She felt her smile slip the tiniest degree.

"Delightful," he added. He kissed her hand.

Silly to be so attached to one word. Especially when God cared more about the heart.

"I'm not wearing the diamonds," she confessed.

"I suspected you wouldn't," he said.

"How on earth…?"

"Harper dropped a hint. He suggested you would look unique, which he assures me every countess or duchess aspires to be these days." To Constance's father he said, "Harper recited a long list of quirks adopted by the females of the peerage. By the time he'd finished I felt I'd be quite glad if Constance's only foible was to refuse my diamonds."

"You won't find me complaining about her lack of fine jewelry," her father said. "Mind you, Constance, I wouldn't object to seeing you in diamonds, if that's what you wish."

"That's because you're the best father in the land." She kissed his cheek. "Marcus, why are we standing in the entry hall, and not sitting down to dinner?"

"Ah." Marcus looked a bit sheepish. "That's because I have another surprise planned for you."

"Oh, no!"

"Constance," her father protested.

"She has reason to fear my surprises." Marcus winked at her—actually winked one eye!—and didn't reveal that the reverend's presence was a former unwanted surprise.

From outside, she heard the rumble of a carriage over cobbles.

"Our surprise dinner guest," Marcus said.

Dallow crossed the hallway and opened the front door. Constance saw a carriage bearing a crest she didn't recognize. A groom was letting down the steps.

"Marcus, who—"

A fair-haired young woman, dressed in white silk with a gold overlay, disembarked from the carriage.

"Serena!" Constance squealed. She darted forward and caught her older sister in a hug. "I can't believe it!"

"Lord Spenford told me in a letter that he wished to surprise you." Serena laughed as she squeezed Constance back.

Drawn by the noise, Margaret Somerton came downstairs,

and managed to outsqueal Constance. As she embraced her oldest daughter, Constance turned to Marcus.

"Thank you, this is the best possible surprise." She laid a hand on his arm.

His eyes settled on her lips, but when he leaned in it was for a respectable kiss on the cheek. "I'm glad you're pleased."

Dallow managed to herd them all—including the dowager countess, wearing a fetching silver turban and helped downstairs by two footmen—into the dining room by warning Constance that Cook was about to sink into depression because her dinner would be ruined.

"I cannot believe we're all here." Constance raised her punch glass in a toast. Next to Serena, Amanda's face was a trifle pale—Constance refused to feel guilty. "How did you get leave from your position?" she asked Serena.

"Ah." Serena sipped her drink. "Things have changed somewhat with my employment."

"What things?" Margaret asked sharply.

"I was about to write to tell you," Serena apologized. "It seems, now that we have an earl in the family, my role as governess has had to change."

Marcus nodded his understanding.

"I should have thought of that," Margaret said.

Serena's smile was wry. "Having gone unnoticed by Mr. Granville this past year, I've been brought to his attention by Constance's marriage."

Constance sliced into her deviled chicken. "With what result?"

"Suffice to say, when Lord Spenford wrote requesting a leave of absence for me, Mr. Granville was more than willing to grant it."

"And he provided a carriage for you to travel in," Margaret approved.

"Actually—" Serena colored, immediately drawing the

attention of everyone at the table "—Mr. Granville and his sister traveled to town with me. Their aunt has a home in Brook Street, and they plan to stay a few days. Mr. Granville has…business."

Her lips pursed, as though she disapproved of her employer's business. Interesting, Constance thought.

"Lord Spenford was kind enough to invite Mr. Granville and his sister to your ball later," Serena said. "Though I think perhaps Miss Granville has a headache." She sighed.

"You're tired, love, and I'm not surprised with five children to care for," her mother said.

Serena nodded. But there was more to her sister's listless state than mere tiredness, Constance thought.

"I hope you have a lovely evening tonight," she said.

"I hope we all do," the dowager said.

After dinner, they adjourned to the ballroom, where Marcus had ordered a raised dais with chairs for his mother and her friends, so the dowager could see all the activity.

"You will save the first dance for me?" Marcus said to Constance, after they'd settled Helen in her chair.

"Of course, if you wish." She would give him every dance, if he asked. But she guessed he would have three dances with her, at the beginning, middle and end of the evening. Any more, and it would look as if he cared for his wife in an unseemly way.

From the hallway, the door knocker sounded.

"Our guests are here," Helen said, triumphant.

When Miriam had discovered the door to the minstrel's gallery above the ballroom last week, she'd realized it was the perfect place to observe Lord and Lady Spenford at the ball. They seemed to have grown closer since the countess's family had arrived—Miriam had high hopes that waltzing together would cement their bond.

She took her place in the gallery toward ten o'clock, after she'd finished straightening the countess's room. Mingled scents of candle wax and perfume and flowers rose, along with the heat of three hundred people.

She had her head wedged between two banister posts, when the door to the gallery opened behind her. She extricated herself, ready to apologize to a guest looking for a quiet spot.

It was Tom.

Her heart stuttered.

He stopped at the sight of her. They hadn't spoken, just the two of them, since the day at Chalmers when she'd asked him to kiss her.

"What are you doing?" His voice was gruff.

Miriam realized her position, kneeling at the banister, was almost identical to when she'd offered her lips to him. She scrambled to her feet. "Same as you, I expect. Watching my lady, looking at the other ladies."

Tom came over to the rail.

"They might see us." Miriam gestured to the throng below.

He shook his head. "I've come up here many times—I always like to be sure Lord Spenford is the best turned-out gentleman. I used to duck down, but no one ever looks up."

He gazed around the room; Miriam pointed in the direction of the earl, dancing a country dance with his cousin Lucinda.

"He looks very fine," she said. *Keep talking about Lord and Lady Spenford, so there'll be no chance of embarrassing yourself.*

"There's Lady Spenford, dancing with Lord Severn." Tom squinted. "What's that on her ladyship's head?"

"A pendant from the amethyst set you found in the attic."

Tom appraised the countess. "Very fetching. Very original."

Conversation dwindled; they lapsed into silence for a few moments. Down below, the countess's sisters, all but the youngest, came down the line of the dance with their partners.

"Her ladyship is from a fine-looking family," Tom observed.

"Miss Isabel is quite beautiful," Miriam said. "Miss Serena's pretty, too. Miss Amanda *looks* very fine, but…" *Careful*. She had to stop thinking of Tom as a confidant, or a friend.

"Lord Spenford doesn't much like Miss Amanda," Tom said, taking the wind out of her sails. "I was with him when we passed her in the hallway. His lordship looked so cold at her, I'm surprised she didn't freeze to death."

"She and her ladyship had a big argument right before we came down tonight," Miriam said. "About something bad Miss Amanda did."

She didn't like to think what it might have been, for both the earl and the countess to be so enraged.

"Look, Lord Spenford is about to dance the waltz with her ladyship." Tom pointed.

Miriam watched as the countess smiled up at the earl.

"Lady Spenford is very fond of Lord Spenford," she said.

"She never told you that," Tom scoffed.

"I can see it in the way she looks at him. The way her voice goes soft when she talks about him."

Tom grunted.

"Do you think the earl cares for her?" Miriam asked. "I know he's not the type to wear his heart on his sleeve."

Silence. At last, Tom said, "A man shows his feelings in actions."

"How do you mean?"

"If he does things for her without being asked—things that will please her. If he seeks her company."

Miriam thought about how Tom had gone to the trouble of scouring the attic for her for those Indian jewels and fabrics. She wouldn't say he sought her company…but he was the one who said everyone took note when she entered a room. Which they didn't—she'd been checking—so he had to mean that *he* took note.

"What else?" she asked, softly, so as not to scare him. It was like sneaking up on a rabbit, the way she and her sister had done when they were children, just wanting to pet it.

"If…if he does things that go against his nature," Tom said, his face flushed. "Just to be the man she wants."

"Have you ever done that for a woman?" Miriam asked. *Have you ever done that for me?*

He said, very quietly, "I praised her ladyship to his lordship." As he'd promised Miriam he would.

"Was that so against your nature?" Miriam asked, startled.

Tom shoved his hands in his pockets. "I was presuming on the friendship I used to have with his lordship. I knew he wouldn't like it, but…"

"But you did it anyway."

He nodded.

"You did it—" she swallowed "—for me."

A hesitation. Then he nodded again.

Was he saying he *loved* her? If so, he didn't look happy about it.

"I always knew, deep down, he and I wouldn't be friends forever, not the way we were as children," Tom said suddenly.

Miriam realized he was talking about the earl purely to avoid talking about something even more awkward: his feelings for her. He must be desperate.

"But we had fun together," Tom said. "Neither of us is a big talker, but we got along."

"I remember," Miriam said.

"When Master Stephen died…I didn't realize it would

change everything so fast, so completely." Tom scrubbed the back of his head with his hand. "I was fourteen—I didn't think about that kind of thing. But from one day to the next, I lost my best friend."

"I'm sorry," Miriam said.

"My fault for being surprised," he said sardonically. "If I'd remembered my place, and his lordship's place, I'd never have presumed on the friendship."

And if he'd never presumed, Miriam realized, he'd never have been so hurt by the loss.

She wanted desperately to comfort him. She especially wanted to come back to the subject of his feelings for her. And why he wouldn't act on them.

"When you said a man shows his love in his actions…" she began.

Tom's gaze, still filled with regret, sharpened on her. "What about it?"

"You refused to kiss me?"

"I had to," he ground out…and then the next moment his arms were around her, his mouth on hers. Miriam pressed herself to him, responded in a way that could leave him in no doubt of her feelings…just in case fear of her indifference should be holding off his declaration of love.

When he finally broke away, her heart was singing. Tom Harper wouldn't kiss her like that if he didn't want to marry her.

"Oh, Tom." She stroked his cheek with her hand.

"I shouldn't have done that." He twisted his head away. "Miriam, forgive me."

"I know you're an honorable man," she assured him.

"I'm not," he said anguished. "Miriam, I'm not."

She stumbled, until she hit the balustrade. "You mean you were—you were toying with my affections?" It sounded so melodramatic, but what else could she say? *You made me fall in love with you, when you had no intention of marrying me?*

"No," he said miserably. "I love you, Miriam." The words that should have made her heart sing sounded more like a funeral dirge. "It's wrong for a man and a woman to be unequally yoked," Tom said. "It'll only bring us pain."

"You think I'm not good enough for you?"

"What? No!" His fingers circled her wrist; he tugged her away from the balustrade. "It's the other way around. *I'm* not good enough for you. There are things…things you don't know."

"Tell me," she said, all hollow in her stomach.

"Miriam," he said, with such gravity, she thought he was going to confess to being that Clapham Common Killer that had been in all the newspapers, "I can't read."

Chapter Twenty-Four

❧

"Can't read what?" Miriam asked, confused.

Tom stared at her, wild-eyed. "Nothing! At least, almost nothing. I can't write, either."

"But…" None of this made sense. "You're a valet. You must be able to read." She realized immediately she'd said the wrong thing. His face turned red as a radish. "I mean, his lordship must sometimes need you to…" She trailed off, her mind boggling at the idea of Tom Harper, the man she'd idolized forever, not being able to read or write.

"I learned to remember well," he said. "If Lord Spenford tells me a list of items he needs, I memorize it. I can read numbers, and a lot of street names—I know the shape. As for the post—letters from the peerage bear a family crest, so I can tell who they're from."

"I know the old earl didn't bother much with school for his tenants' children," Miriam said, "but couldn't you have learned later?" *Like I did.*

"My dad tried to teach me my letters, but I wasn't any good at it. You see," Tom said bitterly, "you already think differently of me. I knew, when I kissed you back then and you started telling me all your plans for educating yourself…

I knew your view of me would change if you knew I couldn't read."

"It hasn't changed," she protested. Halfheartedly. It wasn't Tom's fault he couldn't read…but it did mean he wasn't quite the man she'd thought he was. She pondered, just a few seconds, but long enough. "It doesn't change my feelings," she said, and meant it.

"Not right now, maybe," Tom said. "But it will one day, when the excitement's worn off, and then——" His voiced hitched. "Then you'll despise me, Miriam Bligh, and I couldn't live with that."

Before she could argue…before she knew what to say… he wheeled around, pushed open the door, and left.

Constance had just finished her second dance of the evening with Marcus. As she'd predicted, it took place in the middle of the evening—which in this case happened to be midnight.

The ballroom was stifling hot, thronging with people. Surely all three hundred invited guests had turned up!

When the music finished, they wended their way through the crowd to the dowager.

"Mama, how do you feel?" Marcus asked.

"Never better." Helen smiled at her own exaggeration as she fanned herself with a fan of palest gray kid. "This is quite the most successful ball I've given, and it's you who makes it so, Constance."

"That's kind of you, Mama, but an outright lie."

Helen chortled. "I mean it! Sally Jersey tells me you said that the blue of her dress doesn't suit her."

Constance winced. She sensed Marcus's shocked gaze on her. "Lady Jersey said it first." Goodness, it sounded like one of the frequent squabbles she'd had with Amanda, which they'd run to their mother to resolve. "I tried to demur, but

Lady Jersey practically ordered me to agree. Besides, she was right. Even I, who know little of fashion, could see the color was insipid."

"Sally said she wishes her friends had been as honest," Helen said. "She'll likely tell everyone the new countess is a very good sort of woman. Which in the ton's book is a triumph."

"Were you as honest with Lady Jersey, Mama?" Marcus asked.

"Of course not." Helen's smile was almost impish. "I told her the blue looks wonderful. She all but rapped my knuckles with her fan, she was so annoyed." She chuckled.

Marcus shook his head, clearly mystified by the rules of female friendship.

"Now, you must excuse me," Helen said. "I promised Mr. Young I would retire by midnight, and I see it is past that hour." She stifled a yawn, and suddenly looked exhausted.

"I'll help you upstairs," Marcus offered. He glanced at Constance. "*We'll* help you."

"That will only draw attention. I'd rather leave quietly." Helen did let him help her stand. "Wave to that footman, darling. He can help me."

Marcus did so. When the footman and one of his colleagues had the dowager literally in hand, he kissed his mother's cheek. "Good night, Mama."

She touched his shoulder, then Constance's, with her fan. "Promise me the two of you will waltz together again before the night ends."

"I promise," Marcus said.

When she was gone, Constance said, "Do you think I should apologize to Lady Jersey about her blue dress?" The woman had unrivaled power in the ton. If she gave Constance the cut, her social life would be over, countess or no. At least, her social life among the people who mattered to Marcus.

"It sounds as if she liked your bluntness," he said.

"She said she did," Constance admitted.

"How odd, to like such a thing," he said lightly.

Something passed between them, a connection so fleeting, but so powerful, Constance wanted to grasp it, to clutch it to her chest and not let go.

Then a voice said, "Ah, a chance to dance with my daughter."

"Papa." She turned to her father with a smile. "I haven't seen you all evening."

"I've been in the salon with the older gentlemen. Card playing is vastly preferable to dancing when you reach my age. However, never let it be said I shirk my duty." He sketched a bow to Marcus. "I've come to give your mother a twirl or two, Constance, but she's busy talking about dresses, and has told me I must wait for her attention."

Constance laughed at his feigned outrage.

"Such a blow to my pride," her father joked to Marcus.

"I'm reliably informed, sir, that such blows are good for a man." Marcus smiled down at Constance with such warmth that it took her breath away.

Then her father extended his hand to her, and she was forced to leave Marcus.

For the first part of the quadrille, Constance focused on getting the steps right. It was a minute or two before she could relax.

"We miss you in Piper's Mead, my dear," her father said as they began the second figure, *L'été*—Summer.

"And I miss you."

Her father sighed. "When I considered that the Lord might provide husbands for my daughters, I did not consider the painful loss your mother and I would suffer."

Constance squeezed his hand. "It seems you will always have Charity."

Her father harrumphed. "I'm not pinning my hopes on the fact she's determined upon spinsterhood at age fifteen."

Constance laughed. "She's going to be very pretty, so I suspect you're wise not to rely on her company."

The next figure—*La Poule,* the hen—commenced.

"I must admit to some trepidation when we embarked on this visit to London," her father said.

Constance quailed under his scrutiny. "You mean, because of Mama's travel sickness?"

The shake of his head was gentle reproof. "Your letters haven't said much."

The truth was too difficult, and I could not lie. "I'm sorry," she managed.

"After your wedding, you looked unhappy," her father said. "Marcus the same. I hoped it was mere jitters. I'm very conscious neither of you knew the other well before you married. Also, you were fonder of your husband than he was of you, and that can be difficult."

Constance's face burned. "Papa, you mustn't worry about me."

"Oh, I don't." His reply surprised her, and she missed a step.

It took her a few seconds to catch up.

"Seeing you with Spenford on this visit, it's plain to see things have worked out beautifully," her father said. "As they invariably do when God's hand is upon us, of course."

"In what way is your conclusion *plain to see?*" Constance asked.

"I see your feelings for the earl are as strong as ever," he said. "And I see he returns those feelings."

Constance stumbled over her own feet again—and there were still two figures to go! "Papa, Marcus isn't a man to wear his heart on his sleeve." He wasn't a man to return her feelings at all. Was he?

"Certainly not," her father agreed. "Your mother was right, in that he has a degree of pride that is perhaps not desirable. But when your husband looks at you, Connie—" he hadn't called her that since she was a little girl, and now it brought tears to her eyes "—I see love."

"Perhaps you overstate," she murmured.

Her father eyed her curiously. "As you know, overstatement is a habit I deplore in a preacher. Your husband has showed me in his actions that he loves you. And actions, as you know…"

"…are more important than words," Constance completed.

Marcus's actions… He'd invited her family here in a misguided attempt to please her. He'd invited Serena, which was going beyond any call of duty. He hadn't displayed any haughtiness toward her family. He'd taken Harper fishing, and, according to Bligh, had inquired repeatedly after his valet's health. He'd firmly taken her side in Amanda's presence. He'd accepted her refusal to wear the diamond necklace that honored his family. And just now, he'd been unconcerned by her possible insult to the powerful Lady Jersey.

He loves me! Papa is right. The thought took tentative root in her heart. Could it be true? She had to assume he didn't know he loved her. He wouldn't *want* to love her. That could be a problem.

But I love him, too. And this time, it wasn't a girlish infatuation. This time, she loved the man who had shown himself to be the best husband for her.

If I love him and he loves me, then we can make this work. The sooner the better.

It was nearly three o'clock, and the revelers were thinning out; Marcus was eager to find Constance for their last dance. The evening had been an unqualified success—a last waltz with his wife would crown it.

Besides, he'd seen her dance at least twice with Severn, and had been forced to warn his friend to be more moderate in his attentions. Severn had had a good laugh at that. But now, it was Marcus's turn to dance with Constance, and he would enjoy it to the full.

He found her talking to elderly Lady Gage, who wielded her ear trumpet as a lethal weapon. When Constance caught sight of him, her face lit up. Marcus had the strangest sensation in his chest, a warmth that swelled and lingered.

"My dance," he said. It was far from gracious, but due to that chest contraction and the ensuing lack of air in his lungs, those were all the words he could muster.

She didn't seem to mind. She slipped into his arms as if God had made her for that very purpose.

Maybe He had.

Marcus turned the thought over in his mind and found he rather liked it. The music swelled, and they began to move.

It took a few moments for him to realize Constance wasn't her usual, talkative self. "Is everything all right?" he asked.

She nodded. Then she moved closer to him, convincing him of her reply.

They waltzed the length of the room, Marcus enjoying the sensation of her body pressed to his, the clasp of her fingers. It dawned on him the top of her head was precisely the right height for him to drop a kiss there—how could he not have noticed before? As they executed a turn that put his back to the rest of the room, he experimented. Yes, indeed, the perfect height.

His kiss had not gone unnoticed. Constance raised her gaze to him. She looked almost shy, which he wasn't accustomed to with her.

"Marcus," she said, "I've been thinking."

His heart sank. Her thinking usually involved some defect in his personality that required rectifying. Or some homily from her father that he would feel compelled to live up to. But her eyes were anxious, so he said, "What is it?" with as much grace as he could dredge up.

"You said..." She paused. "A while ago, you said I must invite you to my bedchamber. If I wanted you there."

This was what she wanted to talk about? Here? Now? Marcus's jaw sagged as her parents—her *parents,* hang it!—whirled past them.

"Do you remember?" Constance asked.

He nodded. How could he forget, when the hope of that invitation was never far from his mind?

She licked her lips, those lips he'd kissed not nearly enough. "I am inviting you," she said.

It took a second for her words to sink in. Then Marcus found himself grinning, out of control. He pulled Constance closer, delighted in the tremor that shook her. "Tonight?" he murmured against her ear.

He felt rather than saw her nod.

Tonight.

Chapter Twenty-Five

Constance dismissed Miriam the moment her nightdress was on and her hair brushed. She'd already heard Harper's heavy tread pass her door. She waited until Miriam had had time to reach the servants' staircase. Then, pulling on her dressing gown, she went to the connecting door and unlocked it.

She felt no nervousness at the prospect of uniting with the husband she loved, and who loved her back. How long would it be before he felt confident enough to admit it to himself, she wondered. How long before he would admit it to her?

It doesn't matter. It is the heart that matters.

When she opened the door, Marcus was waiting, still in his evening clothes. He took a step toward her, then another. Then she was in his arms and he was kissing her with a ferocity that startled, but did not shock her.

"My sweet Constance," he murmured against her lips. "My wife. How I have longed for this."

"I, too." She kissed him back, until his mouth grew more tender, his pace adjusting to her inexperience.

A loud pounding on the door of his chamber broke them apart. Marcus sprang back. "Who is it?" he barked.

"My lord, it's Dallow." The butler sounded agitated. "Your mother…my lord, please come."

Even before Constance had drawn in a breath of alarm, Marcus had reached his bedroom doorway. He wrenched open the door. From where she stood, Constance could see Dallow's face, ashen. He was saying something about the dowager, about her ringing for help, then falling….

Lord, no, please.

She hurried into Marcus's room, her dressing gown more than proper enough to be seen by the butler. "I'm coming with you," she told Marcus.

He didn't look at her as he strode to his mother's rooms, the other side of the landing. The door stood ajar, sobbing came from the bedroom. They found Powell, kneeling on the floor, cradling the dowager's head in her lap.

"I've sent the carriage for Mr. Young," Dallow said quickly.

Marcus scooped his mother up from the floor and gently set her on the bed. He motioned Powell to silence as his fingers felt for a pulse in the dowager's wrist.

The eyes he raised to Constance were filled with anguish.

"Sometimes," she said urgently, "it's easier to feel a pulse in the neck." She reached across the bed, pressed two fingers to the left side of the duchess's throat, as she had seen the doctor in Piper's Mead do. *Please, Lord, let me find something. A flutter. Anything.*

Nothing.

She adjusted her fingers, to no avail. Dallow proffered a small mirror, which Marcus held in front of his mother's mouth. No fog of breath blurred the reflection of her lips, which Constance now saw bore a blue tinge.

Hopeless, yet still hoping, she chafed the dowager's warm left hand. Marcus did the same to her right. They were still pressing and rubbing when Mr. Young hurried in.

He stopped short of the bed.

"I can see she is gone," he said. "My lord, my lady, I am sorry."

"No!" Marcus rounded on him. "I want you to make sure."

"Naturally I will do that." Mr. Young already had his stethoscope out.

It took less than a minute to verify his initial conclusion.

"Indeed, my lord, your mother has passed."

"What happened?" Marcus demanded harshly.

"Did she hit her head when she fell?" Constance asked. "She was on the floor when Powell found her."

"I'm told her ladyship rang for a servant," the doctor said. "Probably she felt some chest pain, so summoned assistance. I suspect her heart suffered a major spasm as she got out of bed, causing her to fall. Quite possibly she was already dead when she fell."

Marcus groaned, with a wretchedness that made Constance want to weep. He crossed the room to stand at the window, his back to them, his shoulders shaking.

Discreetly, somberly, the physician packed away his stethoscope. He pulled the sheet up over the dowager's face. Constance made an instinctive move to check him, but stopped herself.

"I will communicate with your butler," he said to Constance. "So he can begin arrangements."

Constance nodded.

When the doctor left, she moved toward her husband.

"I'm so sorry," she said, fighting tears.

"How?" he asked. "How did this happen?"

Had he been too distraught to listen?

"The doctor thinks your mama's heart must have failed as she got out of bed. He—"

"I had a bargain with God," Marcus snapped.

Constance froze.

"I married *you*. He knew I married you for my mother's sake."

Every word stabbed like a knife to her heart. She couldn't speak.

"We—you and I—were about to—" He pounded his fist into his palm. "Confound it, I was doing the right thing! I was willing to be the kind of husband you tell me God requires me to be."

Did that mean he was no longer willing? Constance tried not to think of herself, to focus on the tragedy of her mother-in-law's death.

"And this is how He rewards me?" Marcus demanded. "By taking the life of a good woman?"

"She was ill," Constance said. "God didn't make her ill."

"She'd been getting better. He could have saved her," Marcus charged. "Or don't you believe that?"

"Of course I believe that. I wish He *had* saved her."

Marcus closed his eyes. "All this, to no avail."

All what? Their marriage?

"Your mother was pleased we were wed," Constance said through frozen lips. "It made her happy. You said yourself her improvement was near miraculous." Even she found little comfort in the words.

"I should never have trusted Him," Marcus said. "Nor that doctor of yours. What's it worth now, that brief happiness? If she cannot be here, if she's not with the ones she loves?"

"We'll be reunited with her one day," Constance said.

He snorted. "What use is 'one day'?"

She gasped at the sacrilege.

Marcus pressed his hands to his face.

Beyond the window, the sky was starting to lighten. Soon it would be dawn.

Marcus tracked her gaze. "I'm going to bed. I have much

to do today," he said. Only the barest flicker in his eyes acknowledged that the plan had been for him to be in *her* bed.

"My dear, I hate to leave you." Margaret Somerton kissed Constance's cheek, then pulled her close. Behind her, on the street, the horses shifted, rattling their harness.

"I know." Constance's voice was muffled. "But Papa is needed in Piper's Mead and your place is with him."

Isabel, Amanda and Charity were already in the carriage. Serena had left immediately after the funeral yesterday with Mr. Granville and his sister.

"Besides," Constance said, "Marcus needs some time to mourn in private."

Marcus wasn't even here to say farewell to her family.

In stark contrast with the festive mood of their arrival her family now wore black armbands in tribute to the dowager. Constance wore a black dress made especially for her by Madame Louvier—the color drained her of what little vibrancy she had left.

Marcus's rejection had been total. Absolute.

It was hard to know whom he blamed most for his mother's death: God, or Constance. Either way, he felt he had been cheated, just as when he'd married her.

He seemed to have forgotten the happy times they shared. Forgotten that just a few days ago he had been as anxious as she for their marriage to become real.

Papa was wrong to think Marcus in love with me. True love does not vanish in a puff of smoke, like a conjuring trick. The proof of that lay in her own love for Marcus, a flame that shone as steadily as ever, despite his coldness.

In which case, she assured herself, it was for the best that they had not shared a bed.

"Daughter, will you be all right?" Her father's kind inquiry was almost her undoing.

"Please don't worry about me," she said. "I am in God's hands."

Her father smiled. "That's my Constance. Constant in faith, in hope and in love. You shall receive your reward, my dear, never fear."

Her fear was that this virtue, her constancy, was intended to be its own reward. While she approved of the virtue-is-its-own-reward sentiment in principle, it did not feel like enough to sustain her through years of Marcus's disinterest.

Her parents climbed into the carriage. But before the coachman could close the door, a voice called, "Wait a moment!"

Amanda practically tumbled out—only the fast intervention of the coachman saved her from falling face-first onto the road.

"Amanda!" Concern overrode Constance's hostility. "What are you thinking of?"

"I heard what Papa said to you," Amanda said urgently. "Constant in faith and—and everything."

"What of it?" Constance asked.

"I have always thought of you as befitting your name. I think of you as constant in *grace,* too."

"This isn't the time…." But Constance's defense was half-hearted.

Eagerly, Amanda followed up. "Please don't hold on to your anger, Constance. I know I deserve it, but—but is not grace a matter of undeserved favor?"

Constance blinked rapidly. "I didn't know you paid such attention to Papa's sermons."

"I don't," Amanda said. "I asked Charity what the Bible and Papa say about forgiveness."

Constance half laughed. "You could read the Word yourself, you know."

"If I promise to read it more, will you forgive me?"

Amanda's beautiful eyes widened in a plea that surely no mortal could deny.

Constance gave an exasperated sigh.

Amanda translated it correctly. "Thank you, Constance, darling, thank you!" She flung her arms around Constance's neck.

Unable to resist, in her lonely state, Constance hugged her back. "I must tell you, Amanda," she warned her, "that although I have just now decided to forgive you, my heart may be slow to follow my head."

"And I always thought you were perfect!" Amanda said, in genuine surprise.

"No, that's Isabel," Constance said.

And suddenly, they were both laughing. Shakily, but laughing nonetheless.

By the time Amanda was reinstalled in her seat and the carriage pulled away, Constance felt a glimmer of hope in her heart.

With God's help, all difficulties could be overcome. If she and Amanda could get beyond their rift, then there was hope even for the seemingly insurmountable problem of Marcus's grief and anger.

He will get over this. He must.

Chapter Twenty-Six

Marcus eyed the two men in the boxing ring with grim satisfaction.

Just maybe, this would satisfy the desire he had to take out his anger on everything and everyone about him.

He wasn't used to this kind of rage. Though his father had been easy to anger, his wrath had been icy, focused. The previous earl knew how to target his ire to cause maximum misery, and then to get what he wanted.

What was Marcus supposed to do with the swirling anger that fogged his brain, as invisible yet insidious as the God he'd asked to protect his mother?

"Tom Cribb looks as if he's put on the beef since I last saw him, must be five years ago now," Harper observed.

The crowd at the boxing match was mixed as always. Gentlemen and their personal servants lined one side of the ring. On the other side, workers from the local farms, along with servants from the big houses, cheered and shouted. There were even a few women in their ranks.

Marcus shouldn't be here at all when he was in mourning. But the entertainment was irregular enough that it was difficult to apply a set of social rules, and if he hadn't escaped the house he would have sat in his room and howled.

He couldn't think of anyone who wanted to witness that, least of all himself.

Marcus grunted agreement with Harper's assessment of Cribb, afraid if he spoke he'd bite his valet's head off.

Beneath his brave talk, Harper seemed as little interested in the technicalities of the fight as Marcus was.

It was dashed inconvenient. For the first time in years, Marcus would have liked to vent his ire to someone who knew him well—and now that his mother was dead, his servants had the longest acquaintance. But Harper was somber with his own depression.

The thought of confiding in Constance momentarily seduced Marcus. But she was a part of his troubles, not the solution.

When he thought of all he'd done—the lengths he'd gone to to save his mother's life. And despite the fiasco of marrying the wrong woman, his plan had seemed to be working. Seemed, even, as if the outcome might be happy all around.

Now Marcus cursed himself for the weakness to which he'd succumbed. Before the ball, he'd caught himself entertaining idiotic ideas like canceling his appointments with his steward and his bankers, and spending time with Constance. Insanity!

With the clarity of hindsight, he could see he might have been falling in love with her—and he felt like a man who'd had a narrow reprieve from total loss. Marcus had spent years building himself into the perfect earl; to weaken now, to succumb to infatuation, would be disaster.

Momentarily, the memory of his wife's soft mouth tempted him. He shook off the temptation. The fact was, his wife had found him lacking from the day of their wedding and had never allowed him to forget it. She'd said outright she required him to change in order to be the man she wanted. In her own way, she was as demanding as his father.

So the fact that she now was grief-stricken, that she needed him… *Irrelevant.*

The roar of the crowd told Marcus the fight had started. In the ring, Tom Cribb planted an early facer on his opponent. The crowd roared approval. "He'll have a black eye tomorrow," Harper said with grim satisfaction.

As the fight ebbed and flowed, punches thrown on both sides, crowd crowing and groaning, Marcus had never felt so alone. So bereft.

He hated it.

How had the Earl of Spenford been reduced to this—this sniveling wreck of his former self?

Ever since he married Constance he'd been gradually losing control of his carefully guarded emotions, he realized. All those feelings he'd instinctively known could derail his stability and that of the earldom had somehow been given free rein in her presence, and now they'd taken over his life. It felt as if his mother had died—had been *able* to die—because Marcus had lost control.

I've been a fool. His head had been turned by a pair of brown eyes and soft lips. It wasn't without precedent. Years ago, weak blood had allowed Marcus's grandfather to behave like a lunatic for love. The same blood coursed through Marcus's veins.

He knew what he had to do. Undo the damage of the past few months. Revert to his true self, take rightful pride in his position, demand the best of everyone. Rely on himself, and no one else—mortal or divine. His life worked best that way.

And if that life left no room for a wife like Constance, then so be it.

In the ring, the hapless loser finally found his mettle and lunged at his opponent. The punch connected; the match was over.

* * *

"My lady, there's a black silk dress here. The style's old, but the fabric is in excellent condition." Miriam held up the dress for Constance to see.

They were in the dowager's rooms, sorting out her belongings. The job rightfully belonged to Powell, but the maid had been distraught at the mere prospect, so Constance had given her the day off.

"Quality fabric, indeed. Do you think Powell could make use of it?" Constance would wear black for six months, then the lighter colors of half-mourning for likely another six. She suspected Powell, who'd been left a generous bequest in the dowager's will, would like to do the same.

"I'll ask her, my lady." Miriam set aside the black dress.

Constance returned to the box of trinkets she was perusing. The dowager's will had specified small bequests to various servants, both money and paste jewelry. Constance was seeking out the pieces specified.

She'd told Marcus her intention; he hadn't quibbled. Probably because he wasn't speaking to her.

If only they'd never held that ball! The dowager wouldn't have stayed up so late, and might never have died. Constance wouldn't have allowed her father to convince her of Marcus's love, a conviction now proven wrong. She would never have lifted the lid off her own feelings and allowed her own love to spill over.

Because now, she was deeply, truly in love with Marcus. Just as there seemed less chance than ever he would return her feelings. What hope was there for them if they couldn't talk about anything that mattered?

Constance clicked her tongue. "Why must men be so thickheaded?"

"Stupid," Miriam agreed.

For a moment, Constance thought she meant Marcus, and

was about to reprimand her. "You're referring to Harper," she realized.

"Stupid as the day he was born," Miriam said grimly. "Blind, too. Can't see what's right in front of him."

"It's so hard to know what to do with them," Constance said. "Does one wait until they get over it? Or does one confront them?"

"A girl could be waiting a mighty long time," Miriam observed.

"Confrontation, then?" Constance asked.

Miriam snorted. "If you can catch them. I've been trying to talk to Harper for days. He makes sure he's never alone with me."

"Did you two argue?"

"Not exactly." Miriam hesitated. Then she told Constance what she'd recently discovered: Tom Harper was illiterate. She explained how Tom had managed to conceal his problem. Constance was shocked.

"So how did he come to tell you of this?" she asked her maid. The blush in Miriam's cheeks was all the answer she needed.

"I assume it's an issue of pride for him, as far as you're concerned," Constance said.

Miriam nodded. "Made worse by my habit of reading anything and everything, and telling him my thoughts on it. I admit, my lady, I was shocked when he told me, and perhaps my shock was hurtful to him. But I love him, and I don't care if he can't read. I'll teach him myself."

She looked as if she wanted to rush from the room right now to offer the valet lessons.

"Be careful," Constance cautioned her. "Rushing in where angels fear to tread will not help."

"I'll be careful," Miriam promised. "You won't tell Lord Spenford, will you, my lady?"

"Of course not." Marcus would be too proud to accept an illiterate valet, would consider it beneath him.

How burdened Tom must be, Constance realized, knowing his position would be lost if Marcus discovered the truth—their old friendship would count for nothing. Tom must feel there was no way he could live up to the standard Marcus required; concealment of failure was the only solution.

Marcus labored under the same burden, she realized. He believed he hadn't attained his father's exacting standard before his father died. That he'd somehow fallen irrevocably short.

"My poor darling," she murmured, eliciting a curious glance from Miriam.

If only Marcus—and Tom, for that matter—could understand that the Heavenly Father accepts us with all our shortcomings, that none of us can measure up except by God's grace....

Did Marcus know that she accepted him with all his shortcomings? The same way she wanted him to accept her? Because how could they be happy, unless they were both willing to extend grace and forgiveness to the other?

I will tell him.

I will tell him, Miriam resolved yet again. This time, she wouldn't let Tom fob her off.

She found him polishing the earl's riding boots, almost a sacred duty, the amount of care that went into it. She slipped into the boot room, and closed the door behind her—Mrs. Matlock would definitely disapprove.

He looked up, then glowered. "I don't want to talk about it."

"Well, I do." She sat down on the step in front of the door. "Your...thing..."

"You mean, the fact I can't read?"

She should have prepared better. She weighed words, found none of them ideal. "It's nothing to be ashamed of," she assured him. "I mean, everyone can't read at some time or other. I can help you. I'll teach you.…"

One precious, expensive boot hit the floor with a crash that didn't speak well for its future appearance.

"Stop," Tom ordered. "You think you're so clever, that everything's so easy."

"I'm offering to help you."

"What if I can't do it?" The words were wrenched from him. "What if I can never read?"

"Of course you can." She prayed she was right. "You're clever, I've always thought that."

He stuffed newspaper into the left boot, to help hold its shape. "What if I don't *want* to learn?"

The question stopped her in her tracks. "Why wouldn't you?"

"Maybe I have no interest." His defiance reminded her of her younger brothers.

"That's stupid," Miriam said, just as she would have to one of her brothers.

"You see," he said bitterly. "You think I'm stupid, now you know I can't read."

"Well, you *are* stupid, if you think I think you're stupid," she flashed.

She'd confused both herself and him. They stared at each other, both breathing heavily.

"I don't want a wife who's above me," Tom said, with a finality that brought tears to her eyes.

Still, she tried again. "You think you have to be superior to your wife in every way?"

"I don't mind if she's a better cook and housekeeper."

"You've been with Lord Spenford too long," she said. "This is pride, pure and simple."

He shook his head. "It's about knowing where I belong. A man shouldn't get above himself. It's not right and it only brings trouble."

By trouble, he meant pain, she guessed. He was thinking of how he'd considered Lord Spenford a friend, only to have their differences separate them. But that wouldn't happen with her and Tom. She suspected she could repeat that until she turned blue in the face, but he would never believe her.

Frustration mounted, which meant any second now she would burst into tears. She couldn't bear him to see that.

"That's it, Tom Harper, I wash my hands of you," she said. "Give me a humble man who appreciates being loved, rather than a proud...*blockhead!*"

Chapter Twenty-Seven

In her own way, she was as proud as her husband, Constance realized. She hadn't seen him in two days, but she'd been reluctant to reveal that state to the servants. Now she humbled herself and told Dallow to ask her husband to see her in the salon on his return home.

Unfortunately, that necessitated her staying up until midnight.

"Where have you been?" she asked, the moment he set foot in the salon. She sounded like a nagging Nellie. She tried to soften the words with a smile.

He didn't smile back. "At my club." His tone said, *my whereabouts are not your concern.*

"In mourning?" But the practices of mourning were far more relaxed for men; she shouldn't imply criticism. Constance set down her embroidery. "Marcus, there's something I need to say to you. It's important. Please, sit." She let out a breath of relief when he sank onto the chair opposite. "I owe you an apology."

One eyebrow lifted.

"It has occurred to me that I've judged you too harshly." He froze.

"It wasn't my intention," she continued. "I wished only

to share with you what I saw as the essential attributes of a strong marriage. I shouldn't have implied that you're in any way not good enough. I imagine that must have been distressing after the way your father did the same."

A frown gathered between his eyes. "My father?"

Oh, dear, she was making a mess of this.

"What could you be implying I'm not good enough for?" His voice was clipped. "To be the Earl of Spenford? To save my mother from an untimely death? Or to marry a humble parson's daughter?"

"All—I mean, none of those— It's not about how good we are. Marcus, please, I'm trying to tell you…"

"That you have finally decided I am acceptable as a husband?" he said coldly.

"That I love you!" She clapped a hand to her mouth. She had wanted to gently confess the depths of her feelings. Instead, she had shrieked them like a banshee.

"We have had this conversation before," he said coldly. "It did not please me the first time."

"That was before I knew you," she said. "I loved an image of you that was, in some ways, wrong. But in other ways very right. As I've come to know you, I have come to love your good points and your bad—that is, your not-so-good ones."

"I might have known this would come around to my defects," he said.

"You're the kind man I always thought you, even if you don't want to be," she said. "I love you for your sense of humor, and your intelligence and your instinct for goodness."

He shook his head. "I thought I was too proud for you."

"You are! But I love that, too. I love that you disdain caring about others, and yet you do it anyway. I love when you get that prickly overreaction to an impertinence, and you look down your nose and you sound so haughty."

"You're mad." He moved, as if about to stand.

She grasped his arm. "It would only be mad to love you if you're still sure you can never love me back," she said.

She *was* mad, to have issued such a challenge.

His face was white, his mouth taut. "I wanted you, as a husband should want his wife."

She did not fail to notice his use of the past tense.

"I protected you, I provided for you," he said. "I have been faithful to you. I did my best, and it wasn't good enough for you, or for God. My mother is dead. So, no, I have no thought of loving you."

The words were a stab, calculated to wound. But she saw the pain in his eyes and her heart broke for him. "Tell me what I can do for you."

He stared at her for a long time, as if he couldn't quite believe she was offering him anything of herself after his rejection. Then, he said, "If you truly love me…"

"I do."

He stood. "If you truly want what is best for me, you will leave London and return to Chalmers."

"Marcus, no!" She wanted to help him, not to leave him!

He turned toward the window. "I don't want the burden of your love. I want my life as it was…though of course it won't include my mother. I want to be busy with the earldom, to walk among people who value what I value."

They were back here, back where they'd been moments after their wedding, despite all that had happened in the meantime. To steady the shaking of her hands, Constance picked up her embroidery—and promptly jabbed herself with the needle.

"Ah!" Tears, so close to the surface already, flooded her eyes as she sucked the tip of her finger.

"You're hurt." Marcus took a step toward her, then stopped.

He'd made it plain they owed each other no duty of care.

"Yes, I am hurt," she said. His wince said he realized she didn't refer to the needle prick. "But that—" she drew a shuddery breath "—that is not your concern. Tomorrow I will have Bligh pack my things. On Thursday I will leave for Chalmers."

If she'd hoped he would change his mind, she was disappointed.

Marcus bowed, and left the room.

Had any woman been ejected from her marriage in such sumptuous style as Constance was?

The coach had been freshly painted, the cushions upholstered in new royal-blue velvet.

"My lady, this looks very nice." All morning, Miriam had been trying to raise Constance's spirits. Quite a challenge when her own eyes were red-rimmed. The words rang hollow.

"Very fine," Constance agreed, equally hollow.

"This is for the best, my lady," Miriam said. "Distance and time can be marvelous healers. And we'll sleep better in the country," she added forlornly.

Dallow had informed her they would travel as far as Chertsey today, and would stop at the Lion & Unicorn for the night. Marcus had bespoken a private parlor for her there.

Her trunks and Miriam's valise were strapped on the back, the liveried coachmen ready. Dallow stood at attention, ready to farewell her.

Where was Marcus?

Surely he wouldn't let her leave without saying goodbye.

Just when Constance had dallied as long as she reasonably could, adjusting her bonnet, checking the contents of her reticule, the front door opened and Marcus appeared.

"You are ready?" he asked.

Constance nodded, her eyes full of mute appeal that he ignored. In her black dress and bonnet, she doubtless looked as colorless as when she had arrived here.

He descended the steps. "I wish you a pleasant trip, my lady."

Anxiety crossed his features. Was that because she'd once threatened to go kicking and screaming? Was he worried she would make good on that threat now?

She would not.

She didn't understand God's plan, nor His timing. But she understood her husband didn't love her and intended never to do so. Perhaps it was her fault, marrying him out of a stubborn adherence to her youthful infatuation, rather than seeking divine guidance and leaving her feelings out of it.

It made no difference now.

She held out a hand to him. "Goodbye, Marcus."

He took her gloved fingers, stared down at them, then lifted her hand to his lips, an old-fashioned courtesy.

"Constance..." he said, before he met the hurt in her eyes, and flinched.

"Let us acknowledge this is the end," she said. "You made your choice. I accept it." She'd rehearsed this speech, but it came out stilted. She discarded her learned lines and said desperately, "Perhaps it's even for the best—I have no stomach for further pain, Marcus. Nor, I imagine, do you."

He nodded.

"We won't need to see each other," she said. "An annulment...hopefully there will be a way." For the first time, she was wholeheartedly glad they had never spent a night together.

"Hopefully," he echoed thinly, his voice devoid of hope.

He stepped aside to allow her into the coach alongside Miriam.

"Goodbye, Constance," he said.

He stood back, gave the word to the coachman, and they were off.

As the coach reached the corner of the square, a rush of regret had Constance leaning out the window, undignified, looking back. If Marcus was watching her depart, if he showed any regret...

The road was empty, the front door shut.

"Dash it, Harper, what does a man have to do to get a decent cravat around here?" Three hours after Constance left, Marcus flung the crumpled white linen to the floor of his chamber. He was late for his game of snooker with Severn.

"I'm sorry, sir, try this one." The valet handed over another cravat.

In fewer than five seconds, Marcus had made a hash of that one, too. He muttered an imprecation. "How am I supposed to concentrate on this thing when my agent is bothering me about the need to increase rents? I wish I'd never agreed to meet the man."

Which was not something he'd ever felt before. His responsibility to his estates was paramount.

Harper handed over another cravat. Judging by his closed eyes, he was praying it would take the shape Marcus's fingers required.

And that was another thing. His blasted valet was more morose than ever—it was depressing having him around. Marcus was hanged if he was going to take Harper fishing again; he'd sooner wash his hands of him.

He pulled his concentration back to the task at hand. It shouldn't be so difficult....

Confound it! The third cravat joined the others on the floor.

"What have you done to these cravats?" Marcus snarled. "What you haven't done is supervised the starching properly. You know I like them starched to just so. You know—"

"My lord!" Outrageously, Harper interrupted him. "Perhaps your inability to tie your cravat is not the fault of the starching."

Marcus narrowed his eyes. "Indeed? And what would you consider to be the cause?"

He didn't expect his valet to answer; he merely posed the rhetorical question so Harper would see how insubordinate he was. If he was lucky, Marcus would accept his apology and they would say no more about it.

To his shock, Harper said, "If I may presume on our past friendship, my lord…"

"You may not," Marcus warned.

"Well, I'm going to," Harper said, to Marcus's outrage. "I've made myself miserable as sin—"

"I noticed," Marcus said.

"And I'm blowed if I'm going to let you do the same, when it's obvious what your problem is."

"Oh, is it?" Marcus said, with an attempt at sounding dangerous. As he heard it, he came across as merely peevish. He hated peevish people.

"You have misjudged matters, my lord." Harper firmed his jaw. "Quite badly."

"You insolent…"

"It seems to me, my lord, that if someone loves someone, then the differences between them should not be insurmountable," Harper hurried on. "A man must decide what matters, and there's every chance it's not his pride or his consequence, or his sense of how things have always been. There's every chance his happiness doesn't lie in those things. And a man who ignores the true source of his happiness is—" he hesitated "—a blockhead."

A valet had just called the Earl of Spenford a blockhead.

Marcus was fairly sure this had never occurred in the past five centuries of Spenford history. There was only one thing to do.

"You're dismissed," he said. "Immediately. Be out of the house within the hour." It sounded harsh…but that was by Constance's standards, which were all wrong. Still, he added, "If you pack your bags fast enough, I'll permit you to look at the positions advertised in this morning's newspaper."

More than generous of him, no matter what Constance might say.

Harper bowed his head. He knew, of course, he had done wrong. Marcus stifled a twinge of sympathy. Presume on their friendship, indeed!

"I'll give you a reference," he said gruffly. It was more than the man deserved. But Constance would want— *Constance is gone.*

Harper lifted his head. "My lord, I won't read the newspaper."

"That's your choice," Marcus said. "It makes no difference to me."

Harper took a deep breath—he appeared to have trouble formulating his words. "My lord, I couldn't read the newspaper if I tried."

Marcus made an impatient gesture. "What are you saying, man?"

"I can't read, my lord. Nor write. Not more than a few words."

"Can't read?" Marcus stared. "How can that be?"

"The earl—the old earl—didn't believe servant children needed an education," Harper said. "Nor the earl before him."

"My grandfather built the village school," Marcus contradicted him.

"A school that's too small to allow more than two or three years of schooling for the number of children in the village," Tom said. "For them that don't learn fast, it's pretty soon too late."

"Two or three years? Surely that's not all?" When Harper opened his mouth to protest, Marcus waved a hand. "I mean, I believe you, of course, but it surprises me." He paced to the mirror, and without really looking saw how his own face held traces of his father's. He turned away. "You're telling me many servants on my estates haven't learned to read and write?"

"Not unless their parents had the money and the inclination to buy them an education. A few, like Miriam, buy their own tuition," Harper said proudly.

Marcus's father had believed firmly that each man should know his place and live up to it. Or, it seemed, *down* to it.

Marcus felt the same. Except…to deem servants unworthy of much learning seemed *too* proud. Unworthy of a man of justice and honor.

He paused. Had he just judged his own father as too proud?

Yes. Too proud when measured against the standard of a God who opposed the proud but gave grace to the humble.

"I…regret my father's view," he told Harper. "It is not my view."

"It's not all the late earl's fault. I didn't learn well in school, then my father taught me a little, but I didn't pick it up," Harper said, embarrassed.

"Your father is a gamekeeper, as I recall," Marcus said drily. "Not a schoolmaster."

Harper half smiled. "I could have learned when I was

older. But I suppose by then I was too set in my ways. Too proud to admit I couldn't read."

Proud. Would Marcus never hear the end of that word?

"How have you managed?" he asked. "I know I have dictated lists to you over the years. And passed you notes with details of social engagements."

His valet explained how he'd trained his memory, developed little tricks that fooled everyone. Marcus couldn't imagine the fear of discovery Harper must have lived with.

"This will change immediately," he vowed. "I'll expand the school, hire another teacher, two more if need be...." His mind raced ahead. It would be a major undertaking. But Constance would know exactly what was needed.

Oh.

Ironic that just as he chose a course of action that would thrill her heart, she was gone.

Sent away.

By me.

"And you," he said roughly to Harper. "You'll need to swallow your pride and learn to read and write."

"Yes, my lord." Harper straightened the brushes on Marcus's dressing table in a perfunctory manner. "I should have done it a long time ago. A man must swallow his pride rather than risk losing the love of a good woman."

Marcus's head snapped up. "What?"

Harper's face was a study in regret. "Miriam Bligh, my lord. Lady Spenford's maid. She and I..."

"Really?" Marcus said. Did Constance know about this?

"Miriam reads anything. She's better than a schoolteacher," Harper said. "I was afraid she'd think I was stupid. But now she's gone..."

"She's only gone to Chalmers," Marcus said.

"Yes, my lord. But I told her I couldn't marry her."

"That was stupid."

Oh, yes, it was.

He'd done the same thing. Sent Constance away out of pride and fear. Told her he couldn't be the husband she needed. Deserved.

He'd been so determined to regain his vaunted self-reliance…. But the past few days since he'd made up his mind had not felt gloriously independent. They had felt *lonely*.

He'd made a terrible mistake.

I must fix it. Now.

But how? He thought of Constance saying, "Yes, I am hurt," in that small, strong voice. Could she ever forgive him? He didn't have much experience of requiring forgiveness, but it seemed to him his offence was on the more severe end of the scale.

Would Harper know?

"So this, er, Miriam of yours, Harper," he said. "How forgiving would you say she is?"

Harper grimaced. "She's powerfully strong-minded. When she takes a thought into her head…"

Marcus thought of Constance's chin and his heart sank.

"You don't think an apology would do it?" he asked.

Harper snorted. "Maybe if I crawled across broken glass at the same time."

"Goodness, man, these women are Christians. Aren't Christians supposed to forgive readily?"

"*Supposed* to," Tom agreed.

Whatever Harper had done to Miriam, it could not equal the disservice Marcus had done Constance. His *wife*.

He thought of all the things that had come between them… and they came back to pride. Mostly his, occasionally hers… because say what she might—and here he smiled—his Constance had plenty of pride of her own.

But she had already apologized for any disservice she'd

done him—and it had been tiny. She'd offered him her love. Could she offer it still, after his cruel response?

How could he have behaved like that to the woman he loved?

I don't love her. I'm fond of Constance, that's all. No need to overreact.

All he needed to do was get back to where they'd been a few weeks ago, before his mother died.

"I think, Harper—" he tried his idea out on the valet "—I will send word to Lady Spenford to return immediately to London. You'd like that, eh? To have another chance at your Miriam?"

"Yes, my lord." Harper laid out a pair of gloves. "Ah, do you think her ladyship would agree to return?"

Marcus bristled. "Of course she—" But this was Constance he was talking about. A badly hurt Constance.

He quashed the memory of Constance saying this was the end. She would do as she was told, for once in her life! Even if Marcus had to enlist her father's help in showing her what was proper.

"She's my wife," he said, mostly to himself. "She's been raised to be obedient."

"Yes, my lord," Harper said blandly.

"I'm fond of her. She's excellent company," Marcus rationalized. "The cook and the housekeeper like taking their orders from her."

"Yes, my lord."

"She may not be the most countesslike countess, but she's kind, takes the deuce of an interest in those around her. Servants and the like."

"I'm aware, my lord."

"A woman of faith—she knows what God expects of a wife," Marcus tried. Surely her faith would require her to come back.

"Indeed, my lord," Harper said, suspiciously soothing.

Marcus said briskly. "Have Dallow send to Chalmers for Lady Spenford, will you, Harper?"

His valet's look was of frank disbelief.

Marcus groaned. He was fooling no one, least of all himself. It was time to admit to the truth to himself and to God.

He couldn't constrain his love for Constance to mere affection. He didn't just need a wife, he needed *her*. Constance, who loved him with all his faults. Just as God did.

At least, she *had* loved him. By now, she must hate him. He deserved it. But grace…grace was all about undeserved favor. Marcus had never needed grace more.

Father, please… He wasn't sure what he was praying for, only that it involved him getting it right, and Constance coming back. *Forgive me, Father. Let her forgive me, too.*

Show me how to be a good husband. He wanted her never to know a moment's doubt about his feelings for her, for the rest of her life.

"So, my lord," Harper said casually, "your commentary about Lady Spenford has taken up thirty minutes of the hour you gave me to leave this house. May I be excused now to pack my things?"

Marcus snapped his head around. "Of course not, you fool. And I mean that in the nicest possible way."

Harper bowed. "Yes, my lord. Should I assume I am no longer dismissed?"

"Yes, you dashed well should. Now, get my driving coat."

"My lord?"

"I can hardly ride to Hampshire without it," Marcus growled.

"No, my lord." Harper started to smile.

Marcus groaned. "I always swore the world would never see the Earl of Spenford chasing after a woman, mad with love for her."

"I should think not, my lord," his valet approved.

"Unfortunately, Harper, that is exactly what the world is about to see."

Chapter Twenty-Eight

Constance felt far better than she thought she would by the time they pulled up at the inn at Chertsey.

In part, her state of wellness was due to Marcus. Not only because the carriage had apparently been resprung since she'd last felt ill in it. As they quit London, Miriam had produced a tin, containing of all things a ginger cake. Cook had baked it on the orders of Lord Spenford, Miriam said. Ginger was a remedy for travel sickness.

Whether it was the ginger, or the sustaining power of Marcus's thoughtfulness, Constance didn't feel near as ill as she had last time.

Just angry that a man so kind should be so reluctant to admit to his finer qualities. So reluctant to love and be loved.

Constance allowed the innkeeper to help her down from the carriage. Miriam went to the servants' quarters, while the man showed Constance into a pleasant parlor. "My best, your ladyship," he assured her. With the fire leaping in the grate it was warm and welcoming.

Constance set her bonnet on the table, peeled off her gloves, then sank onto the window seat. A nice dinner, and an early night—that was the sum of her ambitions.

A tap sounded on the door. She smiled at the maid who entered.

"A restoring cordial, my lady?" the girl offered a tray.

"Yes, please." She took a sip of the drink and closed her eyes.

When the girl opened the door to leave, a hubbub of noise leaked in. Constance could hear a male voice, raised. A female voice, pleading. Possibly crying.

"What's going on?" she asked the maid.

"It's a family from down south," the maid said. "They traveled to London because their son was sick there. He died before they arrived—they're on their way home to bury him. It was all unexpected, so they're very upset."

Constance shuddered. "Poor things."

"The missus is near hysterics," the maid confided. "They wanted a private parlor, but…" She shrugged.

"Is it a matter of money?" Constance's hand went to her reticule. There was no denying the Spenford fortune had its uses.

"No, my lady. They seem well-to-do enough. It's just, they're not Quality, and with all three private parlors bespoke…"

Constance understood. If the grieving family had been high enough up the social ladder, the landlord might have forced two lesser persons to share a parlor in order to accommodate the family.

She glanced around the comfortable space she occupied alone. "I insist they have this room," she said.

The maid shook her head. "Oh, no, my lady, Mr. Walker won't hear of it."

"He will hear of it right now. It just depends whether you will tell him, or I will." Constance had no idea she could sound so imperious.

The maid responded instantly to such countesslike behavior, scurrying to convey her orders to the landlord.

How odd, Constance thought, that she should discover a benefit of her position just as she was about to relinquish it.

Marcus pulled up at the Lion & Unicorn Inn toward five o'clock. He handed the curricle's reins to a waiting hostler and jumped down.

He patted the neck of one gray horse, then the other. "Good fellows," he said. "Excellent timing."

Harper descended from the other side of the curricle with considerably more caution, tottering as he hit the ground. He was distinctly green around the gills.

Marcus eyed him with affectionate impatience. "Since when have you been such a poor traveler, Harper?"

"Since three hours ago, my lord." The valet closed his eyes as if waiting for the world to settle. It was several seconds before he opened them again and looked around. "This was no ordinary journey."

Marcus lost interest in his valet's delicate stomach. He should be more concerned, of course; Constance would expect it. But he wasn't, and if she didn't like it, she could tell him so to his face.

Assuming she would speak to him at all. He had hopes—he'd been able to pray during the wild ride down here, and felt better for it. It had been a relief to put his trust in God, Who suddenly seemed much more reliable than himself.

Now, though, confidence leached out of him. Constance had every right to disbelieve his love. To refuse a man who had treated her so callously.

"Shall I ask the landlord where her ladyship is, my lord?" Harper asked faintly.

Marcus shook his head. "I'll find her. You go to your Miriam."

Both men stood rooted to the spot. Both reluctant to take a step that could seal their fate.

"Afraid, Harper?" Marcus taunted him.

"Are you, my lord?" came the reply.

"Impudence!" Marcus said. Then, "If you must know, I'm terrified."

"Me, too," Harper said glumly.

"But we are men of courage." Marcus rallied him. "We're Englishmen!"

"Englishmen likely to get a box around the ears," Harper said.

Marcus grinned at the thought of Constance boxing his ears. He considered himself fairly safe from that particular punishment. No, if she wished to hurt him, all she had to do was refuse to come home.

His smile faded. "I'm going in."

Tom found Miriam at the big table in the servants' dining room, the remains of the meal being cleared by a scullery maid. He took a moment to scrutinize her from the doorway. Her dear, angular face, her straight brown hair. Her keen eyes, observing the men and women around the table...and now observing him.

She pushed her chair back from the table. "Tom? What are you doing here? Is something wrong?" Her blue eyes were wide with anxiety.

He beckoned to her to join him out in the yard—noisy as it was, it offered more privacy than indoors. But when he had her there, standing so close he could smell starch and lavender soap, he was as tongue-tied as a green boy.

"Tom, what's *happened?*" she urged.

So much, he didn't know where to start. Then, suddenly, he did.

"I told Lord Spenford I can't read nor write," he said.

Miriam gasped. "Tom, you great looby, what did you go doing that for?" But she clutched his hand in a way he found most encouraging. "I suppose he dismissed you? That's downright wicked." Her indignation on his behalf was also, he considered, a positive sign.

"His lordship's keeping me on, and he's hiring a tutor for me," Tom said. The earl had announced that intention in one of the brief periods during their journey where Tom had been capable of listening. "Who knows, I might even be able to read the Bible one day."

"*I* could tutor you," she said, offended. Then she blushed. "Except, you might not want me to."

"That I wouldn't," he said. Her face fell. "You'd be forever nagging me, and you know I don't take well to a woman telling me what's what."

She started to smile. "True, you're right old-fashioned in many ways." She stuffed her hands into the pockets of her dress. "It's not as if I could tutor you anyway, since I'll be at Chalmers and you'll be in London, at least until the Season ends. But maybe, you know, when you can write something, you could practice by writing a letter to me."

He had the idiotic notion of writing her a love letter. Which would be the last thing he needed to do if things went according to plan and she was right beside him as his wife.

"Maybe you won't be at Chalmers," he said. "His lordship came to talk to Lady Spenford." He shuddered at the thought of the journey he'd endured. "I believe he'll ask her to return to London."

Miriam tut-tutted. "He can ask."

"You don't think she'll agree?" Tom said. "She's his wife."

"As his lordship now remembers." Miriam gnawed at her lip. "Lady Spenford is very upset, Tom. She won't settle for less than a complete about-face by Lord Spenford."

Tom tried to imagine his employer abasing himself to such an extent. And failed.

"So if you're in London and I'm at Chalmers…" Miriam said.

"No!" Tom whipped off his hat. "Miriam, I love you. I want to marry you."

Going by her utter shock, by the sag of her jaw, he hadn't conveyed that yet. He took advantage of her unusual silence. "If Lady Spenford won't come to London, then maybe you could leave her and find a position with another lady." Though it was rare, perhaps unheard of, for a lady's maid or a valet to be married.

"Or we can both go to Chalmers and work in the house," he said. "Our positions wouldn't be so important, but I have some money saved. Or—or we can both leave, and open a shop. Be master and mistress of ourselves, raise a handful of children."

She was still staring at him.

"Do you hear me, Miriam?" he asked. "I can't read, and maybe I never will be able to, but I love you and I don't want to live without you. You're above me in just about everything—good sense, good looks—" She laughed. At last he was getting through to her. "So I suppose I can get over you being above me in reading. I'll do whatever it takes for us to be together."

Miriam let out a long, slow sigh. Then she grabbed Tom by his lapels. "That, Tom Harper, you great looby, is the cleverest thing you ever said."

She kissed him. That lasted for all of half a second before Tom took the lead in the embrace. As he wrapped his arms tighter around the woman he loved, he found himself quite taken with his earlier notion.

A love letter to his wife, wouldn't that be a fine thing for a man to do with his new lettering skills?

* * *

Marcus pushed open the door of the front parlor, whose situation suggested it was the best in the house.

"Constance—" He stopped. None of the three people staring at him was his wife. A mother and daughter, both weeping, and a father who looked as if he, too, might be shedding tears.

"Excuse me." Marcus closed the door quickly and went in search of the innkeeper. Who informed him that Lady Spenford had insisted on sharing a smaller parlor with two other travelers, in order to allow a recently bereaved family some privacy as they mourned their son.

Marcus thought of those stricken faces. Thought of how it would feel to lose a child—his and Constance's child—and wanted to howl. Constance had done the best thing; of course she had.

"Could you please conduct me to my wife?" he asked.

The back parlor was still pleasant, but considerably smaller. A maid was setting a table for dinner. The space was almost crowded by its four occupants. An older lady with her companion, a young man in foppishly high shirt collars. And Constance.

She sat in a rustic-style rush-back chair, her head bent over her needlework. The candlelight lent a coppery sheen to her hair, and as he watched her profile, the straight nose, pointed chin, the pale column of her throat, all in harmony in this moment of concentration, he was captivated by her beauty— the beauty of her nature. It shone like a beacon, drawing him to her.

"The Earl of Spenford," the innkeeper announced.

Constance's head snapped up, her sewing slid to the floor.

"Marcus?" she breathed. Wholly inappropriate to use his Christian name in a roomful of strangers, but what would she care about that?

What did *he* care about that? Nothing!

"My lady." His own sense of propriety was far harder to shake off, but he put all the warmth he could muster into his voice and his eyes as he walked toward her.

She rose. "Is something wrong?"

"Very wrong." He took both her hands in his. Behind him, the old lady sucked air between her teeth in a way intended to convey disapproval. The young man had his eyes on Marcus's cravat, tied in the complicated Oriental style, and didn't look away as a gentleman should.

Ah, well, so be it.

Marcus went down on bended knee.

Chapter Twenty-Nine

"Marcus!" Constance squawked. "What are you doing?"

"Come back to London with me, Constance. Come back and be my wife."

She was struggling to make sense of the fact he was here in the first place, let alone begging her to go back with him.

"Why?" she asked. "Marcus, what's going on?"

"I've missed you horribly."

Embarrassed, she glanced around the room. Shouldn't these people at least be pretending not to listen? "I've been gone eight hours," she hissed.

"It feels like eight *years*. If you won't come for my sake, come for my tenants'. I plan to expand the school and I need your help."

He was raving like a lunatic.

Constance turned to the innkeeper, still standing in the doorway, agog at the earl's misconduct. "It seems I will require a private space, after all, landlord. Is there somewhere my husband and I can talk?"

He offered them the last empty bedchamber. As Constance gathered her things, in her fluster taking twice as long as she should have, Marcus picked up the embroidery frame she'd dropped when he walked in. "You finished it?" he asked.

"Almost," she said, distracted. "I'm on the last letter."

He read it aloud: "'He will beautify the humble with salvation.'" He smiled. "You are the most beautiful woman I know, Constance. In every sense of the word."

She gasped.

He took her elbow. As he steered her from the parlor, the old lady said, "Vulgarity!"

The landlord seemed to think much the same, going by his curt manner as he showed them to their room.

"You realize you're ruining your reputation," Constance told Marcus as the man left, still trying to comprehend that he thought her beautiful.

He laughed, almost giddily. "Too late, my darling, my reputation is already in tatters."

His *darling?*

He lifted her hand to his lips, and kissed her knuckles. A thrill coursed through her.

With difficulty she recalled herself to the reality of their history, their situation.

"Marcus—" she extricated her fingers "—you sent me away. We agreed this was the end. Whatever the reason you want me back, it's not enough. There's nothing left to say." *Please, Lord, help me be strong.*

He paled. "Not even, I love you?"

How strange, that his declaration of love should hurt just as much as his declaration that he would never love her.

Constance sank onto the edge of the bed. "When, exactly, did you realize this?" she asked stiffly.

"In my heart, I suspect some time ago," he said. "The first time I kissed you."

"The day you denied all feelings for me? I don't think so!"

"I admit it took longer—much too long—for my head to realize it," he said. "That came this morning, and the moment it did, I came after you." He took her hands. "Do you believe me, Constance?"

She turned her head away from his searching blue eyes. "I believe you're fond of me, and you're lonely. Don't confuse that with love."

"Fond!" He let go of her hands as if she had the plague. "Is it fondness that makes me think all the time of taking you in my arms, of kissing you, and more?"

She blushed. "Maybe not, but that's not love, either."

"Is it fondness that makes a smile from you something to be sought, coaxed, treasured? Is it fondness that makes me defend the worst paintings I've ever seen to your brat of a sister? That makes me laugh to think of you and your determined ways, even when you're setting yourself against me and insulting me in the worst ways you can?"

"I…don't know," she said.

He looked grimly satisfied to have confused her. "Is it fondness that makes me want to be a better man than I've ever been?"

He couldn't have advanced a more powerful argument. And yet…she was wary. "All that means is I'm a good influence on you."

He gave a shout of laughter. "My darling, you're a shocking influence! Before I married you I was a model of propriety."

She started to smile. "And now you're not?"

"Might I remind you that ten minutes ago I knelt before you in the presence of strangers?"

"That was very odd," she admitted.

"If you think that's odd, let me tell you about my journey here."

He went on to explain that he had left London with Harper soon after midday, racing his curricle to Chertsey at insane speeds—Constance shuddered to think of it.

"We passed carriages with inches to spare," Marcus said. "I thought Tom was going to throw up all over me."

Tom? Did he mean Harper?

"I would have been here earlier, if Tom hadn't insisted on food to settle his stomach," he grumbled. "The place where we stopped was packed to the gills—we would have waited an hour if I hadn't stood on my chair and announced where I was going and why."

"You did not," she said, alarmed.

"I told them I'd made a big mistake in sending my wife away, and now I must go after her and beg her to return, implore her to bestow her glorious presence on my wretched life."

"You didn't!" she said laughing.

"I did. You can expect to hear pretty much those words repeated back to you at any number of ton parties, if we're still on any invitation lists—the Mottram boy and Lady Jersey's nephew were among my audience. All of London will know I am crazy with love for my wife." He was smiling at her, tenderly, but anxiety lurked in the back of his eyes. He had deliberately set out to show the world he was, as he said, crazy for love; she believed that.

Which meant...

"Marcus, have you no pride?" she asked wonderingly.

"I have far too much pride," he said cheerfully. "As you have repeatedly informed me."

This time it was she who clutched his hands. "What about your reputation, your bank loans?"

Without breaking the contact, he sat next to her on the edge of the bed.

"They'll have to accept my weakened mind—they'll soon see proof that my finances aren't suffering." Then, more seriously, he said, "I know I have too much pride, Constance, but I promise, my love for you exceeds it. From now on, it always will."

She couldn't speak, for emotion welling in her throat.

"Constance, beloved?" He drew her into his arms. "Tell me it's not too late, set my heart at ease and say you forgive me."

"I forgive you," she said.

He laughed, and his breath fanned her forehead. "That felt too easy. You could make me suffer a lot more, you know."

"I don't want you to suffer," she said. "I want to be with you every day for the rest of my life. I want to share every sorrow, every joy."

"That can most definitely be arranged." He kissed her lips, but it was constrained, almost chaste. "Constance…are you speaking out of your Christian compassion, which I know to be great…or something more?" He hesitated. "Though I know I may suffer for it, I must ask you to *speak the truth or say nothing at all.*"

"Marcus, you idiot." She pulled one arm free of his embrace so she could smack his shoulder. "I love you, of course."

"Of course," he said, laughing. "The clue was in the smack."

She chuckled…but he cut it off with a kiss. This one was deep and reverent.

When it ended, Marcus was trembling.

"Since it's so late," he said, "shall we stay here tonight and return to London in the morning?"

Here? In this small room that was far more intimate than their rooms in London?

"Yes, please," Constance said shyly.

"Are you hungry?" His gaze roved her face. "For dinner?"

She shook her head, wrapped her arms around his neck.

Marcus dropped a kiss on her nose. "I'd better tell Harper

our plans. He'll be pleased not to travel farther today—if he hadn't been too ill to talk on the journey, he'd have resigned his post."

"Poor Harper," she said. "I believe there's still some of that ginger cake, if it would help him."

"Why don't I just go and wait on the servants," he said drily. Seeing her about to agree, he held up a hand. "I'll ask the landlord's wife to do her best for him. Besides, he probably won't even need her ministrations. If all has gone to plan, your maid is about to marry my valet—we may need new servants." On his way to the door, he said over his shoulder, "Dashed inconvenient."

When he returned from issuing his instructions, Constance said, "Marcus, I remember, when you were raving on your arrival here, you said something about expanding a school?"

"The Earl of Spenford never raves, my love." He sat next to her again, and told her his plan to offer much more schooling to the children of his tenants, boys and girls. And how he intended to hire a tutor for Harper.

"That's wonderful." Constance planted a kiss on his chin. "No wonder I love you."

"In the interest of complete honesty, an honesty that was lacking on our wedding day," he said, "I should tell you I've made another bargain with God."

"Marcus, no," she said, dismayed.

He touched a finger to her lips. "The bargain is this—from now on, I will leave everything in the Father's hands."

Constance waited for more. Then: "That's it? That's the bargain?"

"That's the bargain," he confirmed.

"It seems one-sided."

"It has to be. I'll be too busy making you happy to take charge of everything else."

"What an excellent plan," she murmured.

His eyes darkened. "I adore you, my beautiful wife. I adore everything about you, but most of all, I adore your chin."

It was so unexpected, she laughed out loud.

"I knew that chin meant trouble from the day I married you," he said with satisfaction. "And I was right." One finger caressed the chin in question. "This chin has the power to bring a man to his knees. To make him resolve to change his character, to be the kind of husband he should be."

"You're already the only husband I could want," she said. "I love you dearly, my proud earl."

"And I love you, my constant countess. For always."

* * * * *

INSPIRATIONAL

Wholesome romances that touch the heart and soul.

Love Inspired HISTORICAL

COMING NEXT MONTH
AVAILABLE JANUARY 10, 2012

THE COWBOY TUTOR
Three Brides for Three Cowboys
Linda Ford

AN INCONVENIENT MATCH
Janet Dean

ALL ROADS LEAD HOME
Christine Johnson

THE UNLIKELY WIFE
Debra Ullrick

REQUEST YOUR FREE BOOKS!

2 FREE INSPIRATIONAL NOVELS
PLUS 2
FREE
MYSTERY GIFTS

Love Inspired.

HISTORICAL

INSPIRATIONAL HISTORICAL ROMANCE

In the exciting new FITZGERALD BAY *series
from Love Inspired Suspense, law enforcement siblings
fight for justice and family when one of their own
is accused of murder.*

Read on for a sneak preview of the first book,
THE LAWMAN'S LEGACY *by Shirlee McCoy.*

Police captain Douglas Fitzgerald stepped into his father's
house. The entire Fitzgerald clan had gathered, and he was
the last to arrive. Not a problem. He had a foolproof excuse.
Duty first. That's the way his father had raised him. It was
the only way he knew how to be.

Voices carried from the dining room. With his boisterous
family around, his life could never be empty.

But there *were* moments when he felt that something
was missing.

Some*one* was missing.

Before he could dwell on his thoughts, his radio crackled
and the dispatcher came on.

"Captain? We have a situation on our hands. A body has
been found near the lighthouse."

"Where?"

"At the base of the cliffs. The caller believes the deceased
may be Olivia Henry."

"It can't be Olivia." Douglas's brother Charles spoke.
The custodial parent to his twin toddlers, he employed
Olivia as their nanny.

"I'll be there in ten minutes." He jogged back outside
and jumped into his vehicle.

Douglas flew down Main Street and out onto the rural
road that led to the bluff. Two police cars followed. His
brothers and his father. Douglas was sure of it. Together,

they'd piece together what had happened.

The lighthouse loomed in the distance, growing closer with every passing mile. A beat-up station wagon sat in the driveway.

Douglas got out and made his way along the path to the cliff.

Up ahead, a woman stood near the edge.

Meredith O'Leary.

There was no mistaking her strawberry-blond hair, her feminine curves, or the way his stomach clenched, his senses springing to life when he saw her.

"Merry!"

"Captain Fitzgerald! Olivia is…"

"Stay here. I'll take a look."

He approached the cliff's edge. Even from a distance, Douglas recognized the small frame.

His father stepped up beside him. "It's her."

"I'm afraid so."

"We need to be the first to examine the body. If she fell, fine. If she didn't, we need to know what happened."

If she fell.

The words seemed to hang in the air, the other possibilities hovering with them.

Can Merry work together with Douglas to find justice for
Olivia…without giving up her own deadly secrets?
To find out, pick up
THE LAWMAN'S LEGACY by Shirlee McCoy,
on sale January 10, 2012.

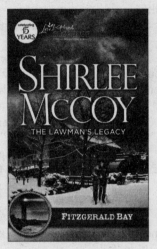